CHRISTMAS *in Canada*

A CELEBRATION OF STORIES FROM PAST TO PRESENT

CHRISTMAS *in Canada*

A CELEBRATION OF STORIES FROM PAST TO PRESENT

Rick Book

Red Deer PRESS

Publisher
Red Deer Press
813 MacKimmie Library Tower
2500 University Drive N.W.
Calgary Alberta Canada T2N 1N4
www.reddeerpress.com

Credits
Edited for the Press by Peter Carver
Cover and text design by Erin Woodward
Cover illustration by Heather Collins
Printed and bound in Canada by Transcontinental Imaging for Red Deer Press

Acknowledgments
Financial support provided by the Canada Council, the Department of Canadian Heritage, the Alberta Foundation for the Arts, a beneficiary of the Lottery Fund of the Government of Alberta, and the University of Calgary.

National Library of Canada Cataloguing in Publication Data
Book, Rick
Christmas in Canada : a celebration of stories from past to present / Rick Book.
ISBN 0-88995-286-8
1. Christmas stories, Canadian (English) I. Title.
PS8553.O636C47 2003 C813'.54 C2003-905077-7

5 4 3 2 1

To

Dad and Mom, Betty-Lynn and Bob, Cathy and Dwayne.

Thank you for your support in every way.

Contents

Introduction

I don't know if this happens to you but whenever I'm driving the Trans-Canada Highway, Gordon Lightfoot is with me. He's singing Canadian Railroad Trilogy. I like to think of it as our second national anthem, a loving tribute to this sprawling, magnificent land, and the tough, big-hearted men and women who learned not only to survive here, but to thrive. I think of the First Nations people, the explorers and railway surveyors who paddled and walked across the continent, the war- and famine-ravaged refugees of today who find sanctuary in this vast country.

What a privilege it was to meet some of these unknown but extraordinary Canadians in researching this book about how individual Canadians across time and over cultures have, or in some instances may have, celebrated Christmas. A Cree elder on James Bay told me stories across the table that I'll never forget. I listened one day on the telephone as a western rancher wept at the pain of losing some of his cattle in a killer storm almost forty years ago. I was told about a middle-aged dog walker in Toronto whom we would call mentally challenged and who is probably blessed with more holy spirit than entire churches full of people. I met a World War II vet who was a nineteen-year-old kid in a Sherman tank when the Allies landed at Normandy and helped liberate Holland. A retired railway porter and his wife invited me into their home and described what it was like to be black and work on the trains that rattled virtually empty across the country during Christmases in the fifties and sixties. Their stories were gifts, and it was humbling to be entrusted with them. I hope the fictional versions written here do honour to their experiences.

There are other stories about people I would love to have met. Cartier was the first known Christian to spend a winter in New France. In a rough log fort, surrounded by suspicious Iroquois, suffering from a mysterious disease (scurvy), Cartier's men experienced a miserable and dangerous time. A few decades later, Champlain tried to ward off scurvy with great food, French wine and high spirits. For the most part, his Order of Good Cheer worked, and it was a pleasure to visualize their Christmas feast. Then there was Frederick Schumacher, founder of a gold mine and the Ontario town near Timmins that bears his name. The children of Schumacher continue to enjoy the man's generosity to this day. You'll find Cornelius

Krieghoff in here, too, the painter who left such a rich record of early life in Quebec. And Lord Stanley, the man whose greatest legacy is our national game's championship trophy—the Stanley Cup.

Several of these stories are simply works of the imagination. One story appeared in my mind in the instant I awoke one morning, the entire plot, the tiniest details fully formed and understood within a second or two. I quickly made notes and wrote the story in three days. Others were more reticent about presenting themselves. That's when it's called work. Most of them (with only a couple of exceptions) are rooted in the probable or are based on snippets of real stories or real people. In other words, they might have happened.

Every one of these stories revolves around the celebration of Christmas throughout our history. Not the frenzied, consumption-driven Christmas we have come to know, but often a simpler, certainly more pious and low-key celebration. Our ancestors and recent immigrants brought the notion of Christmas to this country with them. During the early European part of our short history, Christmas day itself was often a workday much like any other, with prayers, perhaps a church service if there was a church, and a good meal to mark the occasion. In several of these stories, the religious celebration or family gathering took a backseat to a more urgent demand—survival.

Finally, I want to make it clear that I'm not an historian; I'm a writer of stories. So this is not a history book. It's a collection of stories that reflect the redemptive power of a rich, varied season in this extraordinary country. I hope you'll find in these stories very real people living compelling lives, and that they'll prompt you to tell your family's Christmas stories, the ones from the past and the ones you are creating today.

WHEN the Mummers Came

There was a shuffled scraping on the back stoop.

"They're here," someone whispered. Giggles. A sharp rap. The door flew open.

In stormed a five-man rogue wave of tomfoolery, cloaked, hatted, be-wigged, arms waving wildly, blackened or masked faces leering at their hosts, peering under lids of pots on the coal-wood stove, poking into cupboards, teapot, sugar bowl, stomping snow over the canvas stretched across the kitchen floor. No one minded a bit.

"Room, room!" the Roomer called, motioning for we O'Haras to push our kitchen table over to the wall. He pretended to yank the oilcloth off the top, spilling the cups of evening tea, the few cookies left on the plate. *"Room required here tonight, for some of my bold champions are coming forth to fight."*

Declan O'Hara, my father, shoved the table, then his chair to the wall, his pipe clenched in his teeth, smiling. Seated again, he struck a match on the stove, lit his finger-tamped tobacco, crossed his heavy-booted legs, and leaned back to enjoy the show. Maeve, our sprig of a mother, jumped up to fetch more Christmas cookies from a tin in the hutch, set them on a Dublin Castle plate, got down an almost-full bottle of dark Jamaican rum.

There were others in the room. Grandma Siobhan rocked in her chair, a merry glint in her eye, thumbs twiddling excitedly on her lap, long, brown stockings hanging limply under her dress, arthritic knees akimbo—hence our behind-her-back name, "Knickerknees." Cousin Tom was there, too. All the way from Saint John. Had himself a job working for a ship's chandler and, after many years away, seemed suddenly grown-up. Then there was my sister, Margaret May, whom everyone called Pegs, looking all of her sixteen years, with long, crinkled brown hair, wearing one of father's old fisherman sweaters—elbows holed and frayed like a whale-wrecked net—over her brown dress, wool socks slumped down on her man's black boots. And finally me—Seamus—scrawny, freckle-faced, barely nine. "The watcher," they called me. "He could outstare a cat," Grandma Siobhan had said one day. And that was the assembled audience in attendance that night in Joe Batt's Arm, a day after Christmas, stuffed to the gills with leftover roast, seated, the evening's entertainment about to begin.

The Roomer straightened his wig under his rumpled hat, stepped towards one of his accomplices. *"For I am the very champion that brings old Father Christmas and boldly declare thy way."* He swept a tall, white-bearded man into the centre of the cramped floor area with a stately bow.

The man stepped forth, pushing up the pillow that slipped down under his shirt. *"Here comes I, old Father Christmas; welcome or welcome not, I hope old Father Christmas never will be forgot."*

"I know that voice," Pegs whispered to Tom. "It's Peter Hoy, sure as shootin'!"

"Shhhh!" Grandma Siobhan waved her hand. "It's bad luck to be guessin'. You'll be breaking the Mummers' spell."

"Right you are, good woman," Father Christmas continued. *"And if you don't believe these words, I say: step in, King George, and boldly declare thy way."*

Father Christmas stepped back from centre stage as King George stepped in, his tinfoil crown slipping down the thick, grey strings of hair that only recently had been a mop. *"Here comes I, King George, from old England did I spring. Some of my victorious works I am going to bring. I fought the fiery dragon, I brought him to the slaughter. And by those very means I'll win fair Zebra, King of Egypt's daughter . . ."*

Dad's pipe was going full blast now, the smoke rising up to the kerosene lamp as he puffed. Mom's eyes were merry, too, and Grandma rocked busily in her chair. Pegs, on the wooden bench against the wall, threw back her head and laughed at their antics. Cousin Tom, beside her, was laughing, too. He put his arm around her then, in the sheer unthinking joy of the moment, in the heart's content of being back home in the outport for Christmas. I do believe that's when the play started to unravel.

King George stopped abruptly, leaned over the kitchen table, his mop-hair dangling across his blackened face, his hand on the wooden sword on his belt. *"Whist, whist, bold man,"* he hissed at Tom, *"what art thou doing?"*

"What?" asked Tom, sitting up, perplexed at suddenly being *in* the play instead of watching it.

"Stand where thou art!" King George shouted at him, then straightened. *"I call in Brother Turk to act thy part."*

Another rascal-in-disguise stepped forward. This one had a black mask over his eyes, blue towel of a headdress, a short piece of rope around his forehead to hold it on, flowing crimson bathrobe with white shirt, black pants tucked into rubber boots. Standing there, wood sword drawn, he was some picture, though not of villainy. *"Here comes I, the Turkish Knight, come from the Turkish land to fight; I'll fight King George with courage bold; if his blood is hot I'll make it cold."*

"Who art thou that speaks so bold?" shouted King George, drawing his own sword, glancing over again at Tom and Pegs, both of them laughing. Something was happening, something that wasn't in the play. I didn't know what, but I was beginning to worry for Tom. I'd begun to think of him as the older brother that I always wished I'd had.

"Haul out thy purse and pay for satisfaction I will have before I go away," the Turk continued. But his King George was too distracted now.

"No satisfaction thou shan't get, while I have the strength to stand; for I don't care for no Turk stands of this English land." He paused, glaring at Tom. "I don't care for no Come-From-Aways either, come to think of it. Get your hands off that wench!" King George pointed his sword at Tom.

"What the devil!" Tom quickly lifted his arm off Peg's shoulder.

"Billy?" Pegs cried. "Billy, is that you? What are you up to?"

But Billy/King George ignored her then, turned to face the Turkish Knight. They raised their swords, wood struck wood as they came together. *"You and I the battle try; if you conquer I will die,"* they cried, more or less in unison. Then King George struck down the Turk with a fatal blow, sent him sprawling onto the kitchen floor. No sooner had he hit the hand-painted canvas, than King George—or Billy—went around and grabbed cousin Tom, pulled him out from behind the table, pushed him down onto the floor beside the Turk. "Keep your bloody hands off my girl!" the King/Billy hissed.

Pegs opened her mouth, but no words came out. It was as though she didn't know whether to laugh or yell. She did neither. Father, a bemused look on his face, was moved enough to take the pipe out of his mouth. Granny's chair stopped rocking. Mom, alone, seemed to be enjoying this little play within a play. "That's Billy Hennessey, all right," she said to no one in particular. There was a strange glint in her eye.

The Turkish Knight raised himself up slightly. *"I am cut down, but not quite dead,"* he said. *"It is only the pain lies in my head; if I once on my two legs stood, I'd fight King George to my knees in blood."*

King George circled the wounded knight, his sword waving menacingly at his throat, ignoring Tom for the moment. *"On the ground thou dost lie, and the truth I'll tell to thee, that if thou dost but rise again thy butcher I will be."* Then he pointed his sword at Tom. "That goes for you, too, city boy."

Dutifully, Tom stayed put, but his narrowed eyes and furrowed forehead suggested it wouldn't be for long. The Turkish Knight struggled to his feet, tearing his robe in the process. *"Come, Valiant Soldier, be quick and smart, and with my sword I will pierce King George's heart."* He grabbed Tom by the arm, helped him up, then turned to his adversary. *"I do not care for thee, King George, although thou art a champion bold; I never saw an Englishman that could make my blood run cold."*

Tom looked over at Peg, clearly wanting to return to the bench and to his role of spectator. But the Turk had hold of his shirt. Then King George stepped in his way. *"You Turkish dog.* You mangy cur," an aside directed at Tom, *"King George is here, happy for another hour to come; I'll cut thee and I'll hew thee, I am bound to let thee know, I am bold King George from England before I let thee go."*

"What have I done to you, brave king?" asked Tom, tentatively, trying his best to play along with this strange twist in the performance. But I could see the fear in his eyes. Billy had gone too far.

King George and the Turk both stopped, their comrades, my family—all eyes on Tom and King Billy. "That's my girl. Keep your mitts off of her. Or you'll get more than slivers from this." He brandished his sword.

"Oh, Billy!" Peg threw back her head and laughed.

"Your girl?" Tom held up his hands in front of him. "Look," he said, shaking his head, "I'm her—" His explanation was cut off, but the rest of us understood.

"You're a gutted mackerel is what you are, if you don't shut up and stay away from this house."

"Hrummph." My father cleared his throat then. "So, Billy," he said quite slowly, "it is you, I'm guessing?" King/Billy nodded his head. "You say this is your girl here, boy," he nodded at Pegs. "Just how do we know that for sure?"

King/Billy seemed stumped by the question, the corners of his blackened mouth turned down, his sword drooped. "Well, sir, I . . . I . . . we've been together . . . sort of . . . since . . . well . . . for years now. . . ." His words just petered out until there was nothing left, like the bitter end of an anchor line disappearing over the gunwale. He looked at Pegs for help, but there was none coming from that direction. Frantic, Billy looked at mother, Grandma, even me. No one came to the rescue.

"So," said Father, tapping his pipe out on the tin lid of an ashtray. "Just what are you proposing to do about this, Billy?"

"Huh? Well . . . I . . . I don't—"

"I see," said Father, fetching his pouch of tobacco out of his pocket, opening it. "So if a young man doesn't have any intentions or plans, then perhaps she's fair game for any CFA that comes along from the mainland, say, and sweeps her off her feet. Is that what you're saying, Billy?"

It was a new play now, the old one totally forgotten. Its costumed characters had become part of the audience, standing awkwardly in their elaborate disguises, unsure of what to do or say, so they did and said nothing. "Well, yes . . . I mean no, sir." No one moved a muscle. We sat and watched the cod squirm on the firmly planted hook. "I guess I mean . . . I'll come back later tonight for a talk, sir . . . with you, if I may."

My father, busy loading up his pipe, raised his eyebrows and looked up at the former hero and king, now an uncertain, almost tragic figure. "No need to come back later, Billy," he said matter-of-factly as he fumbled for a match, then lit it. His attention went to the bowl of his pipe as he sucked the flame down into it. "We can talk right now," he said, releasing a great white puff of a smoke signal.

"Here? Now?" said Billy, looking less and less kingly with every passing moment.

"And why not, my boy? You're among friends." My father, his pipe now well lit, leaned back, enjoying Act Two of this play, which he, himself, was directing.

Billy turned around, a desperate, pleading look in his eyes. But his former thespian colleagues seemed to have deserted their king and were now enjoying new and certainly less supporting roles. Billy glanced at Pegs, then at my mother, and my grinning grandmother, but there was no refuge there for a soul at sea. Finally, he cleared his throat, his Adam's apple bobbing like a storm-tossed buoy.

"Well, sir," he began, looking furtively at my father, "me and Pegs—" He stopped then, changed his tack. "Well," he started again, "I've been saving me money from the good catches an' all, and I'll soon have me own boat—" He stopped abruptly as if grounding on a shoal. "I'd like to marry your daughter, sir!" There it was, blurted out like a cork from a bottle of homebrew.

Pegs was all smiles. So was Grandma Siobhan. Mother was crying and smiling at the same time. Tom was looking this way and that, a part of it, yet not. Father's face was a mask of serious consternation. Billy tore off his crown, his mop hair, the former king now completely dethroned. "I loves her, sir, ma'am. I do."

Father slapped his knee then, and leapt to his feet so suddenly that Billy stumbled back, had to be restrained by the Turkish Knight, now his ally.

"That's what I was waiting for, Billy. Of course you can marry the girl." And he extended a rough fisherman's hand to shake on it.

"Yippeee!" Pegs yelled in a most unladylike way, jumped up herself, and ran to give Billy, then our father, a hug and a kiss. Grandma's chair rocked furiously once again. Mom swiped at her tears as she poured dark rum into glasses.

"Th-th-thank you, sir," stammered Billy. "I'll take good care of her. I promise I will."

"I'm sure you will, my boy."

"What about the play?" asked the Turkish Knight, stepping forward finally, his sword safely back in his rope of a belt.

"She's on the rocks," said mother. "I don't think she'll sail again in this house tonight." She set the bottle down. "Here you go, boys. It was a good play though while it lasted."

"To Billy and Pegs," said the Roomer, finding his everyday voice once again. Father Christmas pulled his white beard down and raised his glass with the rest of us.

"Pegs and Billy," we all replied, for mother had no objection to my having a bit of the spirits on this occasion.

"I'm so glad cousin Tom could be here for this," sighed Pegs, leaning against her future husband.

"Cousin!" Billy cried. The room went silent. He looked at her strangely. "Did you say 'cousin?'"

"Indeed, she did," my father replied. "Sure, you remember young Tom, my brother Sean's son? Left here maybe six years ago for the mainland. Of course, Tommy was no higher than a lobster pot then—"

"Tommy O'Hara?" Billy blurted, his face contorted as he tried to untangle the line of logic that had brought him to this point.

"One and the same," said Tom, reaching out to shake his hand. "Congratulations—you got yourself a great catch of a girl here."

Billy looked at us all in wonderment, then rocked back on the heels of his boots and laughed. A good, belly-deep laugh that echoed down through the years and from outport to outport.

We never got tired of telling the story of how Pegs and Billy got engaged. And although the mummers visited every Christmas holiday, whenever it was mentioned in our family, there was only one night when the mummers came.

STARRY Night

It is night. In the great, dark vastness of the north, the muskeg lies frozen and asleep. Snow-covered rivers and ponds lace through shadowy swaths of brush and low trees. On the lip of a long river, four wooden shapes hunker against the winter: a mission, trading post, storage depot, and house. The house is empty now. Yet, in this stillness, one senses movement.

Three figures dressed in furs shuffle in the cold, their breath falling like feathers. Dogs bark and tug impatiently at the moosehide harness. A sleigh is packed for the journey ahead. After closing the door one last time, a woman climbs into the sleigh. She is young, in her early twenties. A boy of five nestles against her under the fur robes. The young father lifts the anchor out of the snow and calls to the team.

"Whhaite! Whhaite!"

The sleigh lurches ahead as the half-wild dogs race for the river. They careen down the snowy bank and out onto the ice. Another word to the dogs—"Olay!"—and they veer left, following the hard-packed snow on the river. The man lopes in knee-high moccasins alongside his home-built sleigh. They head east, pass a small oblong island on the right, and wind down the curving, widening river until soon they are out on the frozen ice of James Bay. Ahead in the darkness, twenty miles away, is the island they call home. But they left there three days ago, left their bark and moss wigwam cold and empty. Left the graves of three children.

"Ack!" The sleigh swings right and to the south. That is the direction in which hope lies now.

They speed through the night. There is no barking, only panting and the fast, sharp whisper of padded feet as the dogs run for the joy of running. To their left, disappearing into the black, lies a flat, deserted sheet of ice that reaches to Québec. To their right, the low, undulating line of Ontario shore. And above—an infinite, ice-cold ocean of twinkling stars, more stars than most people see in a lifetime, enough to light their way this Christmas Eve.

The boy's muskrat hat rises out of the fur robes. He sits up, tilts his head, and listens to the runners humming on the snow, on bare ice. He loves the bumps as they jump the cracks of pressure ridges. He loves the long, swishing song of snow, feels every thrumming note in his body, stores every feeling in his soul.

His mother loves it, too. She begins to sing an old French carol translated into Cree by the Jesuits. A fur-muffled hymn to the Creator offered from the glittering ice to the glittering sky.

The father smiles. He rides on the runners for a while and listens. He is happy to hear his wife singing again. It cools the burning sadness and regret. He is happy to have a boy still alive, stronger than the killing cold and hunger that haunted their wigwam. In three days' time, they will be in Moosonee and on a steaming black train that will take them to Cochrane—a town they've never seen—and to a paying job. There'll be work in the forest with a lumber company and later, laying bricks for a new school in the boom of '52.

There will be money, a warm place to live, and food to eat. The boy will grow up, become educated in the south, return home to be a respected leader in his community. He will hunt and trap on his parents' and his grandparents' island. He will honour their memory. But all that is a story yet unwritten.

Now it is time to rest. The team veers right and heads to shore. They poke along the frozen marshes, among shaggy cattails where snow geese feed in spring and fall. They find a willow thicket and dry wood. They stop, build a fire, melt snow to make bush tea. There is bannock and smoked fish to eat. Not many words are spoken, no gifts exchanged or even thought of. The night itself, clear and crisp, is its own gift, its own rich blessing.

Of all the journeys large and small, it is this night the boy will remember throughout his life, this Christmas night when his father guided his family over the ice serenaded with a mother's song.

Come, all you shepherds, leave your
flocks where they graze,
A new king is born amongst you,
bring him your highest praise.
Do not forget your torches
or your accordions sweet,
To ring out the joyous music of this great retreat.

Ah! What brilliance illuminates this dark night?
It can only be the King of Heaven
whose birth brings this light.
Already in my soul I feel the grace
that lights the way for me,
Its light is enough for such a magnificent mystery.

Come then shepherds, do not delay to
show him your zeal
For we cannot hasten our steps enough
when God makes His appeal
Hurry to awaken the people so that all may race
To see in the cradle the Saviour full of grace.

Divine child, accept these tributes
to a Heavenly King,
Mere tokens of our ardent faith these
meager gifts we bring.
At the foot of your sacred cradle, we're embraced
by a tender love. Arouse in us a newheart, a per-
fect flame from above.

THE *Visitors*

Bang . . . bang . . . bang.

There it is again. Mag opened her eyes this time. It was still dark as a coal bin. She listened to Angus's breathing, deep and sonorous beside her. She listened to the storm outside, whistling under the eaves, turning the lighthouse dwelling into a shrieking, scraping fiddle. *Good Lord, Angus, didn't you hear that?*

She listened for the children. Perhaps Katy or Andrew had got up to use the chamber pot, or throw on another blanket. But there was nothing except the mad, howling wind, its icy fingers trying to pry every shingle off the roof. She waited, not wanting to stir from her feathery cocoon. Perhaps a storm shutter had come loose. *We should have closed them last night. We knew the weather glass was dropping.* But they had both been tired. Angus had finished knotting the twine mane on a broomstick horse for Andrew. She had sewn a new rag doll for Katy, one with black button eyes. It was after midnight when they'd finally put them under the tree. Angus stirred. She felt the stub of his right arm against her back. Felt it still red and angry against her flannel nightgown.

Bang . . . bang . . . bang.

Am I the only one with ears in this wind-blasted place? Mag folded back the covers, sat up, searched the cold floor in the dark with her bare feet, found the seal fur, and slipped her feet inside.

Bang . . . bang . . . bang.

It sounds like—but it can't be. She wanted to say "door," but the thought was too unlikely to be uttered, even to herself in the dark, here on this island. Quickly now, she threw on her housecoat, felt for the matchbox, and struck a match. Its flaring phosphorus light found the oil lamp, and the warm yellow glow pushed the darkness back to the sloping corners of their room. Angus stirred, muttered something in his beard. The parlour clock showed half past two. The chill air reeked of kerosene and oil from Angus's clothes, and there was just a whiff of brandy.

Bang . . . bang . . . bang.

Down the stairs she floated, half asleep, more than half mad at Angus for not closing the shutters, for not hearing them now. But he had had a drink or two, and who could blame him? He had fumbled with the presents until he threw the scissors across the room. With his one good arm, he could wind the weights that kept the beacon turning or polish the glass. But the little things often defeated him, left him frustrated. He hardly touched her anymore. There was a chill between them, like two icebergs drifting.

She descended to the wide-planked floor of the living room. Tin ornaments, candies, and white paper angels on the tree caught the lamplight and shot it back into her sleepy eyes. An ember lay dying in a sea of ashes in the hearth. She stopped in front of the door, fear closing like a cold hand around her throat. She waited, listened.

Nothing. Nothing but wind and sleet lashing the windows. She reached for the iron bolt, slid it back, then pulled. Pulled. The door was stuck. She pulled again, and finally it opened.

"Mercy sakes, woman, you're an angel, sure as we're standing here. We'd just about given you up for dead or at least deaf if we weren't half dead ourselves." The faltering light fell like a net over a wretched huddle of humanity. Mag's hand went to her mouth.

"Oh, my Lord, how—?"

"Beggin' your pardon, ma'am. Do you think we might come in before we tell you our woeful tale?" It was the captain who spoke. At least, she took him for a ship's captain. There were three men with him—sailors, for sure—and a woman clutching a dripping bundle.

"Oh, I'm sorry." She pulled the door open wide. A horizontal blast of sleet and rain slapped her. "P-p-lease forgive me," she said glancing first at them, then behind her towards the empty stairs. "Come . . . come in." A deep shiver shook her as they slogged into the room.

She slammed the door behind them, slammed the bolt home, then turned, clutching her lamp with one hand, her wet, frayed robe with the other. The strangers stood in the dim light dripping. "We were shipwrecked, ma'am," the captain said. "Forty-six poor Irish souls on board, and we're all that's left. Her husband," he nodded at the woman, "gone." At that, the woman coughed and coughed until she bent over in convulsions.

Mag reached out to her, put an arm around her sopping shoulder. A colder human being she had not touched. "Quickly now, come over here and sit, you poor thing." She guided her to Angus's chair beside the fireplace. The woman collapsed into the cracked brown leather. She gave off an air fragrant with seawater and kelp, and a mustiness that Mag only thought about later. She motioned to the fire. "Please, gentlemen, can someone get this going again? There's kindling in the box. I'll get some blankets. I've got some chowder in the kitchen."

One of the sailors, a short, thin man with a dripping wool cap and soggy beard, lifted a finger. "And a wee bit of brandy might help if you could spare some, ma'am."

Brandy. Do we have any left? Has Angus . . . ? She did not finish the thought. She glanced again at the stairs. *Why does he not hear them?* She hurried to the cedar trunk by the window where the children sat and looked out to sea on rainy days. There were blankets here for cold evenings by the fire and impossible nights like this.

Mag wrapped a grey wool blanket around the woman. She did not move, only stared at the black hearth. The captain bent over the ashes, fussing with the kindling. Mag grabbed the bellows. "Here, sir, sit yourself in that chair. You're half frozen, too, and still in shock no doubt. I'll get this going for you." The captain gratefully backed himself up and sat down. She threw on some larger pieces of cut driftwood and pumped the bellows. The coals grew bright, then tiny wisps of flame appeared. At the first snap, she rose and smiled. "There, it'll be roaring soon enough."

She handed out more blankets and a heavy sweater of Angus's she'd knit him for Christmas a year ago. Two of the crewmen pulled wooden chairs up before the fire. Another sat on the floor beside the woman's chair. "Just make yourselves at home," she said, her eyes checking each of the visitors. "I'll get that soup on the stove." She turned to go into the kitchen, then stopped, looked up the dark staircase.

"Angus," she called up. "Angus, wake up. I need you."

She sensed five pairs of eyes on her and turned. They all averted their gaze. She rushed into the kitchen.

Angus had filled the scuttle. She was grateful for that. She cranked down the ashes, lifted a black lid on the stove, and shovelled in three heaping scoops of coal. She pulled the chowder pot over, uncovered it. The sweet, thick smell of onion, lobster, and scallops gave her no comfort. *There's not as much as I thought.* With the enamel dipper in the water pail, she ladled more water in and gave it a stir. *It'll have to do.* The wind howled in the stovepipe, a mournful death rattle of a sound. A tremor rippled through Mag. It wasn't just the cold. *Don't be silly, girl.* She shook her head, went to the high cupboard where Angus kept his spirits, reached back until she felt it. Brandy. *Good, it's half full.* She grabbed five glasses and put them and the bottle on a wooden tray that Angus had made before the accident.

The fire was well up, throwing monstrous shadows across the ceiling and walls. Five backs were to her as she entered the room. They turned as one. Mag let out a gasp, almost dropped the tray. *They're pale as sheets.*

"There," she said, forcing a smile. "That's a proper fire you've got." She walked past the Christmas tree, set the tray down on the table behind the captain's chair. "I've found some brandy and the chowder's on. We'll have you warmed up soon enough."

"Thank you, ma'am," each sailor said as she offered him a glass. But when Mag handed brandy to the woman, she made no move to receive it, and no flame flickered in her pale green eyes. Mag looked at the bundle as if for the first time.

"Oh, Lord forgive me. Your baby," she cried. "We need to get your baby into something warm and—"

"Ahem." The captain cleared his throat. Mag turned. His eyes went to the soggy package, and he shook his head.

"Ohhh . . ." Mag inhaled sharply at the horror in that hopeless look. She turned again to the woman whose red tangled hair still dripped with seawater. "Can I take your baby?" she said gently, reaching for the infant.

A chair scraped beside her. "I wouldn't do that, ma'am." It was the sailor with one eye. "She'll want to be holding her. Just let her be."

Mag backed away. She needed Angus. Now! *Where are you?* She felt her skin go cold. *Why aren't you coming down?* She felt their clammy eyes on her, stepped back again.

"More brandy anyone?" The four men muttered their thanks and offered up their empty glasses. She retrieved the bottle and parceled out the last of it.

Again she went to the bottom of the stairs. *Why don't I just go up and get him?* Yet something as powerful as an anchor held her back.

"Angus," she called again. And again she felt cold, burning eyes on her back.

One of the men, the oldest one with a yellowing beard and missing teeth, motioned to the spindly Christmas tree and the meager pile beneath it. "Can you tell us, ma'am, what day it is today?"

The answer took her by surprise. "Why, it's Christmas Eve," she said, then checked herself. "No, it'll soon be Christmas morning." She might as well have said "Tuesday" for all the reaction. *Andrew and Katy will soon be coming down for their presents. What will we do?*

Bang.

Mag jumped, jerked her head towards the door. But it was a different sound heard above the moaning wind, a small sound, and it only came once. "The soup must be ready." She ran to the kitchen. *Get hold of yourself, Mag. They've just been shipwrecked, that's all. They're harmless.* She cut some bread she'd made for her family's Christmas supper, lathered on fresh butter the children had churned, loaded five steaming mugs of chowder onto the tray, and went out again.

All five turned their heads, watching with hungry eyes.

"I hope this will help," she said. "I made the bread this morning, and the butter's from our cow we keep out here. She just came fresh a few weeks ago. It's so good to have our own milk and cream again."

As they ate, Mag stopped talking and listened to the howling wind. The captain cupped his mug in both hands to warm them, ate his bread slowly. The one-eyed sailor slurped his soup and tore at his bread like a starving dog. The man with the yellowing beard stared at his steaming mug for a long while, then finally took a spoonful. On the floor, the sailor sitting beside the woman whispered to her from time to time. She did not eat. The mug rested untouched on the bundle in her lap. Mag could stand it no longer.

"If you don't mind my asking, Captain, what ship were you on?"

"It was the *Marie Gallant,* ma'am," he replied. "A schooner she was, out of Dublin, bound for Boston." He stopped, shook his head, "but storm after storm delayed us, and this one . . ." He paused again. "We hadn't taken a sight in four days. Sailed right onto the rocks. Ground to match sticks in a trice, we were." Grim-faced, the other men nodded. "It was the five of us clinging to a boom when we saw your beacon through a lull in the storm. We were swept ashore, somehow safely. It was your beacon what kept us going, ma'am."

"It is Angus's beacon," she replied, then flushed at her correction. "We only came out here this autumn past." Mag paused for a moment as the fire cracked. "He was a whaler until last spring, a harpooner. But the whale . . . his hand got caught in a line. . . ." She clasped her own hands tightly. "They had to amputate. So when this position came available . . ." She stopped with a sigh, looked upstairs again, and shrugged. "I don't know why he isn't down here."

"Aye," offered the captain, nodding, "it's a hard enough job with two hands, ma'am, but when a man loses his right hand, he deserves to be left to his dreams."

Mag flinched. *How did he know which hand?*

The one-eyed sailor eyed her closely. "You're lookin' a bit peaked yourself, ma'am. Perhaps you'd like a restorative tot of brandy? It's been a harrowing night, to be sure." He rose to retrieve the glass still untouched at the woman's side. "No use lettin' it go to waste." He motioned to his empty chair. "Here. Sit down a spell. You've done a fine job of looking after us since we intruded on your Christmas sleep."

"Oh . . . well, I . . ." Mag stammered as she sat, took the brandy. "I don't take spirits, I don't—"

"It will do your heart some good, ma'am, in a time of crisis," the captain joined in. Then he looked up at his one-eyed mate. "Seamus, I could use a bit more of the nectar myself."

"Oh, I'm sorry," Mag broke in, "I'm afraid it's all gone."

"Ahh, I believe there's a finger or two at the bottom here still," said Seamus, picking up the bottle and holding it to the light of the fire. "Perhaps enough to fortify a skipper and maybe a mate or two."

Startled, Mag looked closely at the bottle in his hand. *I emptied it. I know I did.*

"Then I'll have a ration more myself," said the other sailor, holding up his empty glass. Mag watched as Seamus filled his glass to almost overflowing.

The sailor on the floor held up his glass, too. "If you'd be so kind," he said, and his own glass was filled to the brim. Mag paused for a moment as they drank, then took a sip herself, felt the warmth of it drizzling down inside her. *Where are you Angus? Wake up! I'm afraid!*

They sat that way for a while with their brandies, in a half-moon around the fire, lost in the hypnotizing flames while the storm railed against the unyielding building.

"Well, my friends," said the captain, finally breaking the spell. "This is not such a merry Yule night outside nor in. Perhaps we need a tune to lift our spirits. Liam, would you care to give us a reel or two?"

Mag looked to see which one was Liam. The sailor on the floor struggled to his feet. "Surely, Captain," he said. "I'd be happy to oblige." And as he said it, he withdrew from somewhere in his clothing a fiddle. Mag's mouth fell open as he flicked a few drops of seawater off the instrument and onto the hearth where they sizzled and danced on the hot stones. Jamming the fiddle under his chin, the sailor plucked the strings and adjusted the tuning pegs. From under his right arm—and it might as well have been thin air—he produced a bow, held it hovering above the strings, stopped momentarily as the firelight glanced off the nicked and varnished wood. "This is for you, Deirdre O'Sullivan," he said softly to the red-headed woman, "and for your poor wee colleen."

Then he began to play.

He played an ancient lament. The sorrowful sound that rose from those strings told of lives of hardship and toil on stony ground and rough seas, of hunger and starvation, of love lost and found and lost again, of shipwrecks and troubled, restless souls. Liam closed his eyes as he played. A salty tear ran down and mingled with the rainwater dripping still from his beard. The rivulets ran across the swaying fiddle and dribbled here and there on the floor. Mag herself finally closed her eyes and was swept away by the enormous, haunting sadness of this wordless tune that contained every Irish tear that was ever shed.

When he was done, the six souls were still as stones. Even the storm outside abated for a moment. Mag wiped the tears from her own eyes, took another sip of brandy, glanced again over her shoulder at the stairs. She had almost given up hope that Angus would hear the music and come down. Surprisingly, she was no longer worried.

Finally, the captain spoke. "That was a fine and fitting keen, my man." And he raised his glass to Liam, and he drained it.

"Thank you, sir," said Liam with a slight bow. "Now I believe I'm ready to answer your request." With a sharp strike of the bow to the strings, he launched into a fierce and rousing jig.

The captain slapped his knee and said, "That's more like it." He threw off his blanket, got up, and began to dance. For the first time that night, there were smiles in the lighthouse keeper's cottage as Mag and the sailors watched. The captain was a fine dancer. His feet became a blur, and his eyes crinkled merrily as Liam sawed faster and faster.

"I can stand it no longer myself," Seamus exclaimed as he jumped up, dropping his blanket to the floor. He joined the captain, who grinned even wider when he saw him.

Surely Angus will hear this. Mag found herself tapping her toes. She felt a warm glow inside that she had not felt all night, nor throughout the evening before for that matter. She glanced over at the woman called Deirdre, who had turned to watch, still holding her ragged bundle. Even she had a hint of a smile on her face.

The other sailor, whose name she did not know, leaped up, extending his rough sailor's hand to Mag. "Would you do me the honour?"

"Oh no, I couldn't." She half laughed, waving a hand. *What would Angus think?*

"I'm sure he wouldn't mind at all. It's just a harmless Christmas frolic we're havin'."

Mag no longer cared that these strangers could read her mind. The brandy and the music had reassured her somehow, loosened her up. She smiled and cinched the belt on her housecoat tighter as she rose. Liam saw her rising, grinned, and began to play even faster.

The soggy boots of the sailors pounded the wooden floor while the frantic notes of the fiddle chased their shadows across the whitewashed walls. Mag, surprised herself that she was dancing, kicked her slippered feet, flashed her flannel nightdress, threw back her head and laughed.

"Give us 'Cooley's Reel' then," the captain shouted.

"'Cherish the Ladies,'" cried Seamus before that was done.

"'The Duck's Leg,'" the other man called out. And at each request, Liam would swing seamlessly from one tune into the other without so much as a breath.

The captain went over to Deirdre now, whispered something in her ear. Gently, he took the tiny parcel as the woman rose. He set it carefully on her chair. "It will do you some good," the captain said. Deirdre drifted slowly onto the floor—as if she, too, were waking from a dream—and began to dance, tentatively at first, then in a minute not.

How can this be possible? Mag wondered, astonished at herself as much as at the grieving mother, now with red hair flying and a flashing smile. Mag twirled around, nodding happily at Seamus, then the captain. *It's as if I've been in mourning, too. But for what?*

And then it struck her. *Angus!* Ever since he'd lost his hand, there'd been a pall over their lives. It was a shocking revelation to her. Angus was managing well enough now, getting better every day. Sure, there were frustrations, but she had hated his whaling job: the danger, the uncertainty, the long weeks away at sea. Now they were here together as a family on this island. Katy and Andrew loved it. Even though she missed her family, she, too, was warming to this windy, craggy place. *And yet I've been acting as if this tragedy continued every day. Oh, Angus, I'm so very sorry. I've been no support to you at all. You lost your hand, but we've gained so much.* A sudden rush of elation flooded through her, swept her along on a crest of music. *I feel as though I've been in a bad dream, and now I'm awake.*

Mag danced and danced. She was only vaguely aware of the captain, Deirdre, and the others now, of Liam's enchanting, flying fiddle, the swirling music, and leaping shadows. And some time later, she was only dimly aware that, one by one, the visitors drifted back to the fire, and fell asleep under damp blankets to the soft notes of a lullaby. Mag, too, then floated up the staircase just as the eastern sky turned a muddy grey. She stole in to check her sleeping children, then into her own bedroom. Blowing out the lamp, she carefully slipped under the rough, cool covers so as to not to wake her husband, her fine good man.

"Mother! Father! Get up. It's Christmas." Mag started awake as Katy and Andrew jumped on the bed.

"Ooohh," groaned Mag, forcing her eyes open, flinching at Katy's weight on her leg.

"Merry Christmas, young tiger." A smiling Angus grabbed his son with his left hand to keep him from crushing his chest.

Still very groggy, Mag turned to Angus. "You missed the Christmas party."

His smile disappeared. "What do ya mean?"

"What party?" Andrew asked.

"Didn't any of you hear them? There was a wreck. Four sailors and a woman came in last night—"

"Last night?" Angus exclaimed, sitting up. The kids stopped bouncing. "But I didn't hear a thing. How did they get here? Why didn't ya call me?"

"Shhh." She hushed them with a finger to her lips. "They're downstairs, probably still sleeping. They've had a terrible—"

Angus jumped out of bed. "Downstairs!" He reached for his trousers, pulled them over his nightshirt. "Mag, how could you not ha' wakened me?" There was injury in his voice.

"I tried, Angus." Mag quickly got out of bed, too, put on her housecoat. "I called and called, but you didn't come down." Her voice rose, but Angus wasn't listening.

"Oh, Mag," he said, turning and racing downstairs. The children and Mag hurried behind.

Angus stood in the middle of the room, his brow furrowed. "Where are they, Mother?" asked Katy. "Where are the shipwrecked sailors?"

Mag stopped on the last stair, looked around the empty room—at the cold hearth, then at Angus and her children staring at her, waiting. "They were here." She pointed to the two chairs by the fire. "They slept right there. I gave them blankets. We danced. We—"

"You danced?" Angus looked incredulous. "You danced with people who'd just been shipwrecked? Mag!" Angus laughed.

Katy laughed, too. "Mother, you were dreaming."

Mag stepped onto the floor, looked at Angus. "It was storming. I . . . I fed them chowder and some brandy—"

"Let's see," Angus said as he turned to go into the kitchen. They filed past the Christmas tree without giving it a thought. Angus uncovered the pot on the stove, looked inside, then motioned to Mag. "Isn't this as much as there was yesterday?"

She looked in, shook her head. "I don't understand. It appears about the same." Angus put the lid back on.

"Let's check the brandy." He reached up into the back of the high cupboard, pulled out the bottle.

"Oh," Mag gasped. It was half full.

Angus smiled, cheerfully putting his good left arm around his wife. "I see you did the dishes, too." His voice softened then. "I'm afraid it was just a wee dream, my dear, but I'm sorry to ha' missed it." He turned to the children. "Now I believe there are one or two packages under that tree in there."

Later, after Katy had exclaimed over her beautiful new doll and the most wonderful orange she'd found in her shoe, and after Andrew had terrorized them all by galloping around on his new horse, Mag found herself alone with a cup of tea by the fire. She absentmindedly picked up the grey blanket lying on Angus's chair. It's damp! She sat down suddenly.

Later that morning, Old Mick, the former lighthouse keeper, sailed over with their Christmas packages and mail. They had a merry lunch catching up on the news from shore. Then they adjourned to the fire for tea. Mick, they knew, took his with a little something special. Angus had the brandy ready and poured. Mag noticed happily that he did not add any to his own cup.

"So," Mick began, straightening out his bad leg, "what do ya think of yer first Christmas here?"

"Oh, it's a bonny place," answered Angus. "We're all getting used ta living—"

"I was askin' 'bout yer Christmas Eve." His blue eyes went from one to the other. Mag blushed.

"Well, I . . . I . . ." she stammered.

Angus laughed. "Oh yes, Mag had a dream. She swore there'd been a wreck and that survivors came here in the middle of the night." Mag dropped her head in embarrassment. Angus reached over and touched her hand with the stump of his right arm, chuckling. "She fed them. Even danced with them, she says."

Mick didn't say anything for a moment, just looked from one to the other as he stroked his grey beard. Mag could hear Andrew and Katy playing at the kitchen table. "That's quite the dream," he said at last.

Mag looked up at him. She had heard something in his voice.

"And was there a woman and wee bairn with them, too?"

Mag felt a cold rush go through her. She glanced at Angus. His eyes were on her, his mouth half open. "Yes."

Mick's eyes crinkled kindly. "And what was the colour of her hair?"

The house seemed to go quiet. Mag looked at Mick hard, with gratitude and fear. "Red," she whispered.

Old Mick nodded, leaned back in the chair, took a long sip of tea. "I wondered if they would come," he said finally. "I had the same dream then myself every Christmas for eighteen years."

Then he told them the story, but not before he'd stoked his pipe, lit it with a stick from the fire, and had a puff or two. "They figure the *Marie Gallant* went down on Christmas Eve in '39. They found the bodies of four sailors, a red-headed woman, and her baby here on the island the following spring. They had starved ta death, likely froze, too. They buried them up there on the hill. That's when the decision was made ta build the lighthouse. I got the job as keeper, so the wife and I ha' been here from the start."

"And they came every Christmas?" Mag asked.

"It was just something I got used to," he said nodding. "They were almost like family. Strange. I always felt better after their visit. Can't tell you why." He paused again, took another suck of his pipe. The pungent smoke enveloped them like fog. "When my poor Nellie was taken with consumption, I buried her up there beside them. I hoped she'd be with them when they came next time. But she wasn't."

Angus and Mag stood on the small, icy dock as Old Mick cast off his freezing lines, hoisted the faded, gaff-rigged sail, and turned his skiff for home. Mag felt Angus's right arm over her shoulders as he waved with his left. It didn't feel angry anymore. Her own sadness was gone. Vanished. She sighed a deep sigh and realized what it was—contentment. They watched until the skiff was a black speck on the darkening sea as it made for the faint line of shore in the distance.

Angus looked down at her. "Well, ma'am, seeing as how I missed the party," he said, his eyes crinkling with mischief, "perhaps you would care for a dance?"

"Sir, I would love to." Mag gave him a hug before they turned and walked back up the stone path to the cottage.

CHICKEN NOODLE *Soup*

The taxi slowed to let a car rush by, then swung over to the curb. There, an elderly man in a beret and blazer lowered his arm and nodded his gratitude. As he bent over and squinted into the open passenger window, a row of military medals on his chest swung slightly.

"Do you speak English?" he asked.

"Yes, of course," said the driver, a small, thin man in his mid-fifties.

"Good," said the war veteran. "Can you take me to Balgoy, near Grave? It's right on the Maas River."

"Balgoy? Yes, sure, I can take you there. Hop in."

The old soldier bent lower now, the regimental crest on his black beret level with the top of the car door. He was seventy perhaps, stocky, with short white hair. Tiny red and blue veins mapped his tanned, wind-burned cheeks. His eyes narrowed at the driver, brown eyes that had seen a thing or two and didn't want to be fooled with.

"How much will that be?"

"Oh, maybe fifteen guilders, no more," the driver answered cheerfully. "It's only about fifteen kilometres." He paused, smiled wryly. "Don't worry, I won't cheat you. We don't do that here."

The veteran nodded again, straightened as he opened the front door, then bent down again. "Do you mind?" he asked, motioning to the seat.

"No, not at all." The driver smiled, grabbing the morning paper lying there, a picture of a military parade on the front. He stuffed it down beside his seat and waited while the man put a leather satchel in the back seat, then settled into the front, seatbelt fastened across his ample belly. "Have you been in Nijmegen long?" the driver asked, flicking on the meter and nosing the car back onto the street.

The old man turned his head, shoulder-checked, too, as they eased into the noon-day traffic. "No, I just landed in Amsterdam yesterday. I was in Apeldoorn this morning."

"You are here for the VE-Day anniversary, then?"

"Yes." He gazed out the window at the passing buildings, at several modern glass and steel boxes. "City looks a lot better than the last time I saw it." They stopped at a light and watched a group of giggling schoolgirls cross the street. One waved at him. He seemed startled by it, as if remembering something, or someone.

"When was that?"

"Huh?"

"When were you here?"

"Oh . . . 1944."

"With the liberation armies?"

"Yes."

"Which one?"

"Second Canadian Armoured Brigade, Fort Garry Horse. We were in tanks."

"Ahh, Canada," the driver said warmly. He smiled and glanced at his passenger with new interest. "I was just a boy then, running around in short pants. I don't remember much. My parents said it was very hard. Of course, we learned *all* about it in our history."

They drove onto the famous humpbacked iron bridge on the Waal River. Below them, rowing sculls crawled like water spiders across the cloud-specked surface. "I don't imagine you learned all about it," the old man said finally.

"What do you mean?"

"Because it was hell. You can't begin to know what it was like from school books. Or TV."

"Don't you think some of those war movies are pretty realistic?"

The old man turned to his driver. "The movies can't tell you what it's like to smell your best friends roasted alive inside their own tank." His voice was gruff, the anger reduced to irritation after years of experience.

He looked down, fiddled with his folded map. "Did your parents tell you what hunger felt like? How tulip bulbs taste when you're starving? Or about the fear of knowing a Nazi could shoot you any time just because he felt like it?"

The driver shook his head.

They were quiet for a while, as they reached the outskirts of the city, driving on a narrow, freshly paved highway lined with trees. The man's prairie eyes took in the tidy brick farmhouses, the orchards of fruit trees pink in blossom, fields of tulips, yellow, then a splash of purple, a sea of bright red.

"Christmas colours," the old man muttered to himself.

"What?"

"Back in Canada, red and green are Christmas colours."

"And lots of white snow, I guess. It's pretty cold there, yes?"

"Yes, it can be, very." A pause. "We spent Christmas here that year. In '44. It rained a lot. I think I prefer snow to rain." The old man drifted off into his memories, and the driver let him be. Before long, they exited the highway at the Balgoy turn-off, and continued south on a small, paved road. They travelled with their windows down, enjoying the lush fragrance of May. "It's a beautiful country," the passenger said finally.

"Yah. We have a saying: God made the Dutch, but the Dutch made the Netherlands." He smiled as he said it. His companion nodded and smiled, too. In minutes, they were in Balgoy, passing the plain two-storey town hall made of brick. The town wasn't much more than a collection of farms along the small Maas River, winding between grassy banks, the water high and grey with mud.

"There's the bridge," said the man, pointing to the iron structure, then scanning the trees and fields nearby. "The trees, they're all different, but I'd know that bridge anywhere. The farm must be—yes, there it is. Over there."

He pointed to a metal country mailbox with the name *Huffman* painted in neat letters. Two small Canadian flags, crossed, had been taped to the top of it. The driver slowed and turned off the road through a gap in the trees and into the farmyard. As he did, the old soldier leaned forward slightly, gripping the car door with his right hand. His eyes scanned the brown brick farmhouse, the attached brick barn, the farm sheds. A small, red, International Harvester tractor sat in front of one.

"The roofs have changed," he said. "Those tiles weren't there. The roofs were thatched then. Otherwise, it's just about as I remember."

A lace curtain moved at a window as they stopped. "Can you pick me up in a couple of hours?" the man asked, leaning left as he reached for his wallet. "Say, four o'clock?"

"Yes, of course. Don't worry about the fare," he said waving off the man. "We can take care of that later. I have a sister not far away. I think I'll go visit her."

"Thank you." The man got out slowly, retrieved his satchel from the back seat. "See you at four then," he said, closing the door.

A cow mooed from a pasture nearby. The farmhouse door opened, and an older, dark-haired man appeared. The taxi driver waved, called out, "Hallo," then turned his car around and drove out through the opening in the trees.

"Welcome to Holland, John McCracken. It's been a very long time." The Dutchman smiled as he extended his hand, shook the Canadian's, then grabbed him by the shoulders.

"Hello, Rene. It's great to be here." The two men stood clutching each other's arms. "Why is my hair white and half gone, and you've got a full head of it still almost as black as can be?"

"Ahh, well, the Germans left some good boot polish behind." Both men laughed.

"Hallo, John." It was a soft voice, and the Canadian turned to see a handsome Dutch woman in a blue dress smiling broadly at him.

"Helena. It's so good to see y—" He went to shake her hand, but she ignored that and hugged him hard and long, her eyes squeezed shut.

"It's been so long. You look terrific, John." She finally let go and brushed a grey hair off her face.

"No, I don't," he laughed, "but you . . . you look wonderful." They were surrounded now by a crowd, family who'd come out of the farmhouse, all smiling.

"John," said Rene, "now that my sister has released you, let me introduce the rest of our family. This is my wife, Miep, and our son, Harry. He runs the farm now." He shook hands with both. "This is Annie, Harry's wife. She's a nurse. Their son, our grandson, Michael. We call him Misha. He's sixteen. And our granddaughter, Mieke, who's thirteen. She's going to play something on the piano for you later."

Helena grabbed John's arm then. "And this is my dear husband, Pieter. We have a daughter who couldn't get off work today, but this is our granddaughter, Janneke. She's twelve."

Janneke, blonde and skinny in a light blue cotton dress, clutched a small bouquet of yellow tulips. She smiled nervously and handed them to the Canadian. "Thank you for saving our country, Mr. McCracken."

The old man stiffened a bit. His eyes watered up, and his hand shook as he took them. "Thank you, Janneke. Thank you very much."

Helena cut in quickly. "They're from our garden, John. She picked them herself this morning. But come, come inside now. I hear you insisted on bringing lunch. We are very curious, you know, and hungry, too." She guided him by the elbow towards the house. "Children, bring Mr. McCracken's bag, please. Watch your head, John," she said as they approached the door.

"I remember banging myself silly on this more than a few times," laughed John as he ducked through and into the house.

In the small foyer, the Canadian stopped and turned as he took off his beret. "If you'll bear with me, Rene, I wonder if the children would make lunch. It isn't hard, and it won't take long."

"Yes, of course," Rene said, a bemused looked on his face. "We are not used to this, of course. It was all I could do to keep the women from cooking a feast in your honour."

"Yes, I'm sure of that. But as I said on the phone, I thought we might have a different kind of meal to celebrate our reunion, if you don't mind."

"No, not at all. We don't mind," Helena answered, smiling. "This is very exciting, and it's such an event to have you here."

"Is the kitchen still this way?" John asked, motioning ahead down the hallway towards the back of the house.

"Yes, yes, go ahead."

John looked at the three young people. "Janneke, Michael . . . ahh . . . I'm sorry, what is your name again?"

"Mieke."

"Yes, Mieke . . . would you like to make the lunch for us that I've brought along?"

"Yes." They all nodded their heads.

"Good. Then let's go. I'll follow you." And turning to Miep and Helena he said, "Now, please don't come in the kitchen. But I can tell you we will be having soup."

"Ahh, then, I will get the Delft for this very special mystery soup," Helena said.

The old man disappeared into the kitchen with the three young people and his leather satchel. A minute later he was back and found the adults in the dining room. They were putting chairs around the wooden table. It was a cramped room with dusky rose wallpaper, a dark wood plate rail holding blue and white Delft china plates with pictures of windmills and dykes and skaters on frozen canals.

"Pieter, would you get the piano bench, please? We don't have enough chairs," said Annie, as she set the table.

"John, can I get you a drink?" asked Harry. He was in his late thirties, looking almost supplanted as host in his own house. "How about a jenever, our excellent Dutch gin? Or beer, perhaps"

"No, thank you, but I could use a drink of water."

"Water it is," he said cheerfully, easing himself past the buffet and out to the kitchen. "Anyone else?"

"Milk or water will be fine," Helena answered, taking the cue from their guest. Turning to him she said, "Ingrid sends you her best, John. You do remember her?"

"Yes, of course. How is she?"

"She's very frail, but her mind is good. She just turned ninety. She lives in a seniors home in the north, near her husband's family. He was killed at the very end of the war, you know. She never remarried."

"No, I didn't know. I remember she spoke five languages. Yes, please say hello for me. In fact, can you give me her address? I'll drop her a line." Helena's brow furrowed. John laughed. "I'll write her a note."

"She would love that. She often talks of those days when the 'Canadian boys' were here—that's what she called you."

"Well, we were boys then," he replied lowering his eyes. "Young and stupid. We thought we knew everything, but we knew nothing. Nothing at all." The room went silent.

"Your wife, John?" asked Miep, quickly switching the subject. "I'm so sorry she couldn't be here with us."

"Yes, yes, that would have been nice. Mary wanted to come, but she's very involved with her university. She taught history and is giving a paper this week on how the fur trade helped spread music—you know, fiddles and bagpipes and such—throughout North America. She said to say hi."

"Well, that sounds fascinating," replied Helena. "You two must have some very interesting conversations. . . . I wonder how the children are doing?"

Annie had finished setting the table with plates, soup bowls, and glasses. Pieter returned with glass jugs of milk and water. Mieke, her dark eyes flashing with excitement, stuck her head around the corner. "It's ready, Mr. McCracken."

"Good. Bring it in then, please." As she disappeared, John turned to the group. "Are we ready?"

"Oh yes," replied Helena. "John, please sit there," she said, pointing to the end of the table. "Rene, why don't you sit here beside me," she said, pointing to the end closest to the kitchen. "I know it's Annie's place, but she won't mind just this once."

"Ta-da!" sang Janneke as she, Mieke, and Misha entered. The girls carried plates of black bread and butter. Misha, with great concentration, carried the large blue and white soup tureen, steam rising around the lid. Annie set it in front of her on the table.

"Thank you, children. Let's all sit now."

There was much scraping of chairs and shuffling as the family crowded into seats around the table. When everyone had settled, Rene cleared his throat, pushed his chair back and stood. He looked at John and then at each member of his family.

"It is still hard to believe that fifty-one years have passed since Holland found itself in the darkest days of its history. Our beautiful country occupied, our people starving, almost without hope, squashed by the jackboots of fascism and hatred. Then came D-Day—June 6, 1944—and the flame of hope flickered a little. In August, Paris was liberated and in September, Belgium. In November, the Allies fought their way road by road, bridge by bridge into Holland, and finally we were free. Even though the German armies were close by, I can tell you we got drunk just breathing the fresh air of freedom again. Even if there still wasn't much to eat." He paused and looked at the young people. "And fighting alongside the British and American armies were the Canadians, whom everyone says were the best and toughest fighters of them all."

John laughed in embarrassment at the extravagant compliment.

"It's true, John. You know it. Anyway, children, into our lives came five strangers, five wonderful young Canadian boys driving tanks. Our guest of honour here, John, was nineteen at the time, the same age as me—and we lived together for six weeks and formed a bond—"

"It was four weeks, Rene," John interrupted, a twinkle in his eyes. Everyone laughed.

"Well, it seemed much longer at the time," replied Rene, laughing along with everyone else.

Then he grew serious again. "John, we thank you and your Canadian comrades who gave us more than we can ever repay—that is our freedom. We are so honoured that you are here, and we Dutch thank you, as Janneke has already done, for helping to save Holland in war and for remaining our true Canadian friends in the peaceful years that have followed." He reached for his glass of milk. "I ask my family to please rise with me as we toast you, John McCracken, and your fellow soldiers.

"To the Canadians!"

"Mr. McCracken and the Canadians," the young people said, clinking their glasses of milk.

"To John and the Canadians," repeated the adults.

The old soldier waited, his mouth a thin, grim line, until everyone sat down. He stood up slowly, looking intently at the red and white tulips in middle of the table.

"War is a terrible thing," he began, raising his eyes to look directly at the children. "I hope you never know what it's like because it is impossible to explain the fear, the taste and smell of terror, the utter senseless waste." He stopped and his face brightened a little. "I know you're hungry, and we don't want the soup to get cold, but I want to tell you why I brought this particular soup and bread. Then, I hope, you will forgive me for not accepting your offer of hospitality.

"As Rene said, we landed on D-Day, at St. Aubin-sur-Mer in Normandy, the first armour to come ashore. We were in Sherman tanks and saw heavy fighting through the north of France and into Belgium. In November, with the German army retreating, we crossed into the Netherlands. We arrived in Balgoy on November 25. Our job—"

"Forgive me, John," interrupted Helena, "but I will never forget that day as long as I live. The squeaking of the tracks on those tanks was the most beautiful sound. . . ." She paused. A tear rolled down her cheek, and she wiped it away with the back of her hand.

Rene nodded his head. "Still sometimes, when I smell diesel, I don't think of tractors; I think of you in your tanks, John. It's remarkable what sticks in your mind."

John nodded, smiling. "Yes, it is. At our age, it's what we have." He looked at the young people. "Have you young people seen the movie *A Bridge Too Far?*"

Misha looked to his parents, questioning, then shrugged his shoulders. "I don't think so." Mieke and Janneke shook their heads.

John looked at the adults. "Well, I recommend you see it. It's about how the Allies tried to take the bridge at Arnhem. You see, we needed your bridges—here, at Grave, Nijmegen, and Arnhem—to get our troops and supplies across the rivers as we headed for the German line. Once we took these bridges, our job was to guard them, keep the Germans from blowing them up or from coming back across them, for that matter." He chuckled at the thought.

"I remember we camped near the river the first couple of nights, pitched our tent beside the tank. It was pouring rain, and our old army tent leaked like a sieve. On the third day, a farmer came over and introduced himself. It was Hans Huffmann, your great-grandfather," he said to the children. "He invited us to sleep in the loft of your barn, above the cows. I'll tell you, we were so happy to get out of that rain. Some of us were farm boys. We sure didn't mind sleeping with a half dozen milk cows. Every tank crew was taken in by a family here.

"We stayed here thirty days. Rene, Helena—you remember we ate many meals together at this table." He touched the wood with his fingertips. "There wasn't much to eat, but there was milk, and you had chickens. What your great-grandmother, Anneke, could do with an egg! To this day, I've never tasted better omelettes in my life.

"We brought our army rations, although they sure weren't much to write home about. We had this hairy oxtail soup—"

"Ohh, I remember that," groaned Helena. Rene laughed and shook his head.

"Yes, it was just about the worst soup in the world. But of course we ate it anyway. Oh, and we had some tins of bully beef from Brazil. Remember? That was excellent. And hardtack biscuits you just about had to jump on to break."

The children laughed as John continued.

"Your grandmother made this wonderful black bread," he continued, pointing to the sliced bread on the table. "Very wholesome and without a doubt much better than what I was able to get in Nijmegen." He stopped, grinned. "I'm sorry, I am going on a bit here—"

"No, John," cried Helena, "we love hearing this. Please."

"Soldiers and food, you know. So the morning of December 24, Christmas Eve day, we got new orders: we were to pull out that night and go to the barracks at Grave. We were very sad to leave, especially because it was Christmas. And being so far from home. You were like our family. We'd just received a parcel from home with socks and cigarettes and packages of soup. Do you, by any chance, remember what kind of soup it was?" He paused and looked at Rene and Helena.

They both looked at each other and shook their heads.

"Chicken noodle soup," John said.

Rene's face lit up in recognition. Helena's hand went to her mouth. "Yes, yes, now I remember."

"We brought that soup over here and had it together, ten of us squeezed in around this table—as we are today. I forget, but maybe we had it in this very dish. That's why I thought it would a good way to celebrate our reunion today, with a simple meal of chicken noodle soup and some bread—as we had fifty-one years ago."

"What a wonderful idea, John," said Helena, her eyes full of tears. Annie's shoulders shook, and a tear rolled down her cheek.

John continued. "It was Hans and Anneke, you, Rene, and Helena, Ingrid, of course, and the five of us." John McCracken stopped and looked around at the still faces. "I'm the only one of us five still alive. I want to tell you the others' names."

He looked up at the brass lamp that hung over the table as he spoke, reciting their names in a roll call, his voice quavering. "Gord Middlemiss, crew commander; Clayton Simpson, gunner; Alex Boychuck, radio; Gunther Lichtenberger, driver." He stopped and bowed his head. The names hung in the air like ghosts over the silent table. "In war, when you face death together with someone, you become like family. Those who sat here and had this Christmas meal, you—they—were my family."

He cleared his throat. "If you would please stand, I'd like to toast them before we eat." The family stood again and somberly raised their glasses of milk. The old Canadian raised his glass. "To family and friends who were here with us."

Everyone drank, then sat. "They are still with us, John," said Helena. "I feel them here. Don't you, Rene?"

Her older brother looked surprised by the question. "Yes . . . yes, I do." He turned to his guest. "Thank you, John, for your story and these memories and for making this such a special occasion." John nodded his head slightly.

"Now, everyone," he continued, brightening, "shall we eat?"

"Yes," came the unanimous response. Immediately, the happy clatter of lunch and conversation lifted the mood around the table. Annie stood and ladled the soup from the tureen into everyone's bowl.

"This is good," said Pieter, who'd been very quiet.

"It's actually a very ordinary soup, something every Canadian kid grows up eating, especially after a day of skating or hockey or playing in the snow," John explained. He seeming relieved now, more relaxed, his duty done.

"Mr. McCracken, I have a question about your friends, if you don't mind?" asked Misha, a thoughtful look on his face.

"Of course," John answered.

"One of your tank crew had a German name. That Gunther you mentioned? How was that possible?"

"Yes, Gunther Lichtenberger." He put down his spoon. "I'm glad you asked me about him. As you can imagine, being at war was very hard for German people living in Canada, and for Italians and Japanese. In fact, in Canada and the States, we rounded up the Japanese and put them in internment camps. It was a terrible thing to do, not exactly our finest hour. That happened less so to Germans, perhaps because they are white, I don't know. But Gunther was a third generation Canadian, and he was just as upset about the Nazis as anyone. He wanted to beat Hitler, too. So our crew never called the enemy 'Germans,' out of respect for Gunther. We called them 'Bosch' or 'Nazis' instead. That's the way it was with us."

Miep shook her head. "War is so strange. Such civility in the midst of incivility and madness."

"What happened to Gunther and your friends, Mr. McCracken?" Janneke asked shyly. Then a frown of doubt creased her face, and she looked at her grandfather. Pieter nodded and smiled back his encouragement.

"We were lucky. Every one of us made it. But we did run into trouble in Kleve, just across the border in Germany, not far from here. It was February. There was a tremendous firefight, and our tank took a hit. We all scrambled out and left the motor running. Then we got back in and were hit three more times, bad, so we all bailed out again. Three of us were injured. Gunther was missing half his leg. That was one o'clock in the afternoon, and we lay in a shell hole until seven that night, when it got dark. They were sniping at us because they knew we were hiding there. It was probably the longest six hours of our lives. Finally, the Red Cross stretcher bearers came to get us, and the Germans stopped shooting while they pulled us out. We really respected them for that.

"Gunther lost his leg . . . later got an artificial one. Didn't slow him down much. He became a tool and die maker, worked for General Motors after the war. As for the others, Gord opened a hardware store in a small town in western Canada. Clayton became a dentist. Allen didn't do much of anything. Couldn't seem to settle down. Drifted from job to job. I think the bottle finally killed him. That happened to a lot of guys. Nobody knew anything about post-traumatic stress then. You came home, didn't talk about the war or the nightmares, not even to your wife. You just tried to get on with life.

"They sent me back to Belgium to recover. I sat staring at the English Channel for a while, then went back to Germany to help disarm the Nazis. We took their guns and sent them on their way. We weren't set up to look after them. When Germany finally surrendered, I'll never forget it. I just sat down against the bogie wheels of the tank and slept for twelve straight hours. It was peace. At last."

There was silence for a moment. "And after the war?" Pieter prompted.

"The Canadian government had a land program for veterans who wanted to farm, so that's what I did. Grew wheat mainly, not far from Saskatoon in Saskatchewan. That's in western Canada. I went to university in the winter, and that's where I met Mary. She became a professor after we got married and commuted three days a week. We have a son, Danny, who's very interested in music. He travelled as part of the road crew for a big Canadian rock and roll band. Did that for years. Finally settled down and got married. They have a young family. Our daughter, Linda, is a doctor, a pediatrician. She married a doctor, and they have a clinic in a small city a couple hours away. They've got young kids, too, so we have seven grandchildren—"

The sound of tires on the gravel driveway distracted him. John glanced at his watch. "Oh no. Is it that time already?" A look of dismay crossed his face. "I'm sorry, I've done nothing but talk since I got here." Misha jumped up from the table to look out the window. A car door closed.

"No, no, John," Helena cried. "It's been wonderful. Our children needed to meet you and hear all these things you've been saying."

"It's the taxi." Misha confirmed. There was a knock at the door.

"Misha, please tell the driver to come in," said Rene. Then he turned to their guest. "Before you go, John, Mieke has been practising something for you." He nodded to her. Smiling shyly, Mieke got up from the table and disappeared into the living room, just as Misha and the driver appeared in the foyer doorway.

"Hello," Rene greeted him. "We're just ending a very special anniversary celebration with our Canadian friend here. Please, will you join us for a moment?"

"Yes, thank you," he replied as he took up a spot in the doorway.

"Ready, *schott?*" Rene called around the corner to his granddaughter.

"Ready, *Opa,*" came the reply.

Rene smiled. "Perhaps we can all stand one last time."

John McCracken had a puzzled look on his face as he rose. Then Mieke struck the first chord, and the Huffmann family of Balgoy began to sing.

O Ca-na-da.
Our home and native land.

The old soldier automatically stiffened and stood at attention. But he could not sing. His mouth was clamped shut. The taxi driver straightened, too, and tried to mouth the words as the family sang them.

True patriot love in all thy sons command.
With glowing hearts, we see thee rise,
The true north strong and free.

Perhaps it was the sight of young, sweet Janneke, singing her heart out beside her grandparents, who had seen and survived so much. Perhaps it was a delayed response to the moving parade and ceremony at Appledorn in the morning. Perhaps it was jet lag and the fatigue of being so far from his Mary and their family. But at that moment, tears slid down the old soldier's face, splashing on his Legion tie, his white shirt, his blazer. And when he bowed his head to wipe his eyes, they fell on his row of war medals. Images of the Dutch family and his crew flashed through his mind. Scenes of blasted mud, of laughing young men, of bombed-out towns, of pretty nurses covered in blood and bodies rotting on the roadside.

O Ca-na-da
We stand on guard for theeee!

As the singing ended, John looked up and saw that he had not been alone. Everyone in the room had tears in their eyes. Mieke dashed around the corner and stopped, as if she'd run into a wall. John nodded to her. "Thank you very much, Mieke." He looked around the room. "The words to that anthem have never meant so much to me as they do right now."

The goodbyes were said. There were hugs and handshakes, promises to write and visit. Then John climbed into the taxi with his bunch of tulips, and they left.

"Can you do me a favour?" John asked as they turned onto the road.

"Yes, what is it?" asked his driver.

"Can you slow down while you drive past the bridge. I want to get one last look at it."

"Sure," the man answered.

And he did.

A LONG String of Lights

"Merry Christmas. See you in a few days."

"You, too, fella. Have a good run." The bus driver opened the door. A gust of polar wind and snow reached in and right-hooked them both in the face. The passenger pulled the hood of his parka over his toque and stepped down into the wind tunnel that was Main Street. Whirling snow dimmed the street lights, made them pale as dying flashlights. Trees were mere suggestions of trees. The red tail lights of cars drifted down Broadway on a running sea of snow. They and the swinging traffic light were the only spots of colour in the storm.

The man half crouched, then dashed across the street towards the massive grey shape that squatted there. He slipped between the idling taxis, disappeared into the snowy cocktails of their exhausts, then burst through the wood and glass doors into a cavernous calm.

"Good grief," he said out loud to himself, yanking off his toque. He shook it, stomped the snow from his boots, brushed snow off the arms of his parka, and laughed out loud at the ritual dance of a Winnipeg winter.

The station was almost empty. A couple of redcaps were having a smoke on a wooden bench. He waved to them. Only one of the ticket wickets was open. A pale, thin-faced girl sat behind the brass bars reading a book. He didn't know her.

He looked up, as he always did, to the domed ceiling of the rotunda a hundred feet above. The vastness of the building never ceased to amaze him, its huge arching windows and acres of gleaming marble floors. The extravagance of it all made him smile. The same architects had designed Grand Central Station in New York.

The smile vanished as he checked the station clock. 5:13. "Gotta shake a leg," he muttered. Striding quickly across the floor and down the stairs, he remembered the one time he was five minutes late. They'd sent him home.

Had to sit there until my run came back in again. "No work. No pay. You know the rule," they said. Man, you can't feed a wife and kids on that.

He went through a door marked Canadian National Railway Offices and into the reporting room.

"Hiya, Jack," boomed a large man with merry eyes and heavy jowls. "What'd you do to displease the good Lord so much he sent you out on a Christmas Eve like this?"

"Hey, Sam. Must have been up to some awful good sinning, same as you," replied Jack, grinning. A loud guffaw rolled out of Sam like thunder.

"Merry Christmas, Madge." Jack nodded to the grey-haired woman at one of the wooden desks. She glanced at the clock, stubbed out a red-rimmed cigarette.

"Evening, Jack," she said, the words addressed mainly to the ceiling tiles and transported on a plume of smoke. She wrote his name and the time in a book.

"Sure is blowing something awful. Guess we'll have the plough on tonight." Jack said, to neither of them in particular.

"Uh-huh," Madge grunted, fishing in her purse, finding another pack of smokes.

Sam winked and smiled broadly. He opened the door to the locker room, and Jack followed him in.

"Sure be nice if Santa'd bring that woman a personality," Jack said quietly as he stood in front of his locker, turning the combination lock.

"I don't think any man ever brought her nothing that she liked," grunted Sam as he yanked his door open. They both laughed.

Jack opened his locker, hung up his parka, and stowed his winter boots. He pulled out his porter's cap, picked off a few pieces of lint, and put it on over his short black hair.

"Them folks in rainy old Vancouver is going to be sitting on their hands for a while waiting for this train," Sam said, struggling with his jacket.

"I never remember the weather being this bad in Africville." Jack retrieved his red jacket, freshly cleaned. It slid easily onto his slim frame. "Surely it wasn't this nasty?"

"Worse!" said Sam, grunting at a troublesome sleeve. "Don't you remember those darn nor'easters come howling along the coast? They'd blow the feathers off a puffin's bottom."

Jack put one black shoe up on the wood bench, buffed it quickly with a scrap of sheepskin. "Who's conductor this trip?"

"Our old friend, Lyndon Pollard." Sam was now trying to fasten his jacket buttons. It seemed an impossible task.

"No!" Jack looked up, a frown creasing his face. He was in his early thirties, not a young man anymore, at least not in his eyes.

"Afraid so. You hear they're going to fight us over this group business?"

Jack shook his head. "What are we going to do?" There was a weariness in the question, like a man used to being sanded down a little each day until the shoulders were rounded, the sharp edges of youth gone.

"Lee wants to have a little meeting sometime on board. That's what I heard. Good!" The last button held. Sam slammed his locker door shut. "Well, time to rock 'n' roll."

Both shoes shined, Jack stood and started walking with Sam. They exited the locker room, went down a long corridor, through a door that said Platforms 1 & 2, and up a flight of stairs. They stepped out into the covered train shed. The air was cold as a butcher's meat locker. The train was right there—big, burgundy cars with Canadian National Railway in gold letters, clouds of steam boiling up from the heater hoses.

"Hey, Jimmy!" Jack called as a redcap trotted by pulling a baggage cart with five suitcases on it. "Light load tonight, eh?"

"Just three lonesome souls on board so far. Gonna be a quiet run."

"That's good," muttered Jack as Jimmy pulled away. Sam went off in the same direction, giving his usual two-handed wave without looking back.

"See ya later."

Away to the right, almost out of sight, was the engine, where the engineer and brakeman would be in the cab, waiting. Pollard was up there, too, in the day coach. *Wonder what kind of mood he's in tonight.* At the dining car, boxes of groceries were being handed up to Olie Svenson, the chef, and a couple of stewards. In front of him was the lounge car, where Jack could see waiters already tidying the tables and cleaning ashtrays. He waved at J.D., another porter named Jack. This one liked his Jack Daniels Kentucky bourbon, so the initials had stuck.

Hurrying to the first sleeping car to his left, Jack grabbed the ice-cold handrail and swung up onto the train. The door closed behind him with a solid metal *clunk.* He stopped to feel the comforting warmth, the train smell of polished wood, diesel fumes, and freshly washed linens. His watch said 5:45.

Anna'd be at her folks' place by now. Her dad would be wearing a sweater, sitting on the couch, visiting with Devon and Tyrone. Her mom would be fussing over Carla, maybe in her high chair in the kitchen while the women were getting supper ready. It never got easier, leaving them at Christmas. He'd given each of them a big hug, trying to hold onto the feeling of their soft flannel kisses. He always got choked up after closing the door to their apartment, after one long, final hug from Anna, with Carla balanced on one hip. He didn't want her to know how much it hurt. But she probably knew anyway. *She knows everything, that woman.*

A familiar shudder went through the car. Then a slow tug and roll as the train began to move. *Six o'clock. Right on the nose.* Jack automatically started into his routine. He checked each seat for litter. The Toronto crew had left the car in good shape. The linen man's bag was sitting on a seat. Jack stowed the clean towels, sheets, blankets, and pillowcases in the linen cupboard. There were only two passengers on the manifest who'd be sleeping in his car tonight. *Good, no need to pull down a bunch of berths.*

He had never expected to end up living in Winnipeg. He'd heard the CNR needed porters up here, so he'd left Halifax and headed west along with a couple hundred other guys. That was in '51. *Eleven years ago already!* Some of them were still here. The rest scattered with the wind. Jack had only intended to stay for about six months, but then he'd met Anna. He warmed at the thought of her, that make-your-knees-melt smile, smooth chocolate skin, her wonderful singing in church and at home when she was cooking supper. They'd been married in '53. *Man, it rained hard that day!* And now they had two boys and a girl—so far anyway.

"I'm late," Anna told him the other day. "Over two weeks." She was going to the doctor right after the holidays. That would mean six mouths to feed on a porter's wages—a buck and a quarter an hour.

The door at the far end of the sleeping car opened. Sam sidled in, reached inside his breast pocket and pulled out a silver flask.

"Want a little Christmas cheer, Jack? Take the chill outta your bones."

Jack shook his head. "Thanks, maybe later." Sam nodded, took a swig himself and sighed.

"Anna thinks she's pregnant."

"A-ha!" Sam's face broke into a big grin as he slapped his friend hard on the back. "That's my man. Let's see." He held up his pudgy fingers and, with a wink, began counting. "One, two, three, four. Man, that woman's going to be calling the CNR one of these days, asking them to keep you away on longer runs." Sam roared at his own joke, took another swig, then handed the flask again to Jack. "Come on. We got something to celebrate now."

Jack reached for it tentatively. "Well, we don't know for sure yet—"

"Chill out, my man. You're going to be a daddy again, and it's Christmas." Jack took a quick drink, grimaced, and shook his head. Vodka, straight.

Sam laughed. But Jack was not smiling. "We need a bigger place. It's too crowded above the store as it is." He handed the flask back to Sam, feeling the liquid fire trickle down. "Know of anyone who might rent to us?"

Sam shook his head. "Did you ask old Mrs. Rotman?"

"No, not yet. We tried a couple of places—white. When we called, they got a place, but when we show up, it's taken." Sam nodded, knowing.

"Better stick to the Jews. They're the best bet. Ask Mrs. Rotman if she knows of anything. She's been a good landlord, right?" Jack nodded. "Then ask her. I'll keep my eyes open, let ya know." Sam turned to head back into the next car.

"Thanks, Sam."

Sam turned around. "Been through the galley yet?"

Jack shook his head.

"Saw a couple a mighty fine looking birds come aboard. And they're not getting off in one piece, I can tell you that." Sam patted his belly, laughed, then slipped away like a dancer leaving the stage. Jack shook his head. Guys like Sam made the job easier.

He went to a cupboard marked *Employees Only* and took out a bucket and mop. He filled the bucket from a water spigot in the closet, poured in some clear industrial soap, then began to mop the floor. The train was picking up speed as it headed towards the Fort Rouge Yards. Jack didn't even hear the clicking of the wheels on the tracks anymore. The train's motion and all its various clacks, rumbles, and rattles were background sounds, heard only in the unconscious or when they stopped. Christmas lights in the city streaked by the windows in a snowy blur.

It wasn't that Winnipeg was a bad place to be, Jack thought as he swabbed the floor. In fact, it was a real nice place. Both he and Anna found it friendly, interesting, too. Gateway to the west, they say—Canada's breadbasket. They could have lived anywhere, but decided to stay here where they had friends and a job. There was just this one thing . . . this *work* situation.

"Hey, Jack." He started, whirled around. It was an older man with touches of frost in his black, slicked-back hair, pencil-thin moustache, and under it, a grin.

"What the devil, Lee? I'm too young to die of a heart attack!"

The older man laughed. "Merry Christmas, Jack. How come I have to hear from Sam that Anna's pregnant, instead of you telling your poor old uncle to his own face?"

"That Sam." Jack shook his head. "She *might* be, Lee. We don't know. She'd be mad as a wet cat if she finds out I been blabbing to you guys."

Lee held up both his hands, palms out. "I heard nothing." He winked. "But I expect to be among the first to know when it's official." He laughed, then looked around the car. "No one else here?"

Jack shook his head. "Nope."

Lee motioned him to the end of the car, let down the pull-out seat. "I gotta sit. These old legs are killing me." Jack waited while Lee made himself comfortable. "We're going to fight them, Jack," he said.

"Who?" he asked.

"The gol-darned CNR and the Brotherhood. We're going to take them to court. It just can't go on like this." The train car rocked and tilted. Jack reached out and steadied himself as they went around a curve. He knew exactly where they were—on the outskirts of the city, swinging west towards Brandon and the prairie.

"How we going to do that, Lee? Take on both the railway and our own union." Just the thought made his guts churn. He couldn't afford any trouble. The union—the Canadian Brotherhood of Railway Transport—had him. The "Brotherhood" part seemed like a cruel joke.

The door opened behind them. Sam and J.D. came in. "Good, glad you're here. The others coming?" Lee asked.

"They'll be here shortly," said J.D. Just as he said it, the door at the other end of the sleeping car opened. Four more porters came in.

"Men," said Lee with a nod. "I know it's Christmas and all, but we need to have a little meeting here. I had a talk with Mr. Diefenbaker a few days ago and—"

"The prime minister?" a man called Lou asked. He was a new porter, from down east somewhere, Toronto maybe—Jack couldn't remember.

"Yeah, of course," said Lee. "He and the missus—Olive, she's a real sweet lady—they ride all the time, back and forth from Ottawa to Prince Albert. Known him for years."

"I'm surprised he'd actually talk to an old nigger like you," said J.D. Everyone laughed.

Lee waved the joke off. "He's just regular like anyone else, especially here, I think. He's probably just happy to have a normal conversation with ordinary working stiffs instead of those gasbag politicians and professional butt kissers up there in Ottawa." Laughter.

"I told him the whole sorry story: how we all get shunted into Group One and aren't allowed to advance into anything else while the whites go into Group Two and get all the plum jobs: conductor, steward, service manager, and such."

"Like that seventeen-year-old kid they hired last week," said Sam, his voice rising with indignation. "I got eleven years here, and this silly-ass beatnik comes off of the street and he's got seniority over me because he's white. Now that's just plain wrong."

"And what about the rooming houses?" Jimmy asked.

"What about them?" Lee asked.

"Well, how come the white guys get to stay at a hotel in Vancouver, and we have to go off to Mom Mitchum's just because we're coloured? That sure don't seem right, either."

"Same with Mrs. Bowen's in Montréal," added Lou, "and Beckford's in Winnipeg."

"You're right on all accounts," Lee replied. "But I think we have to fight one fight at a time."

"So what'd Mr. Diefenbaker say?" Jack asked.

"He says it's a disgrace. He's a lawyer, you know. He says it's against the labour law they got in parliament down there and the new Bill of Rights. If we go to court, we'll win, he says. Hands down."

"Well, let's go then," said one of the dining car stewards. They called him Dutch.

Lee cleared his throat. "Lawyers cost money, gentlemen." He paused and looked around. "I figure we need about twenty-five dollars per man if we're going to hire this guy and fight."

Someone whistled.

"What guy?" Sam asked.

"Mr. Diefenbaker told me about a friend of his. Young Ukrainian guy, can't remember his name offhand. Said he was real good and that he'd go to bat for us."

There was silence in the group. Just the clicking of wheels. Then the train whistle sounded. Lights from crossing gates flashed red as they streaked by. The clanging of the warning bells fluttered away on the wind like prairie chickens rising. Was the warning for them? Jack wondered.

"Twenty-five bucks is a lot of money," J.D. said finally.

"Especially on our salaries," said Jack, thinking he and Anna'd have to stay above the store another year.

"Well, think it over," said Lee rising. "I don't know about you, but I'd rather be poor and coloured with my head up high, knowing I'd tried my darnedest, instead of shuffling around all miserable under whitey's foot." Lee stood and looked at his watch. "Portage La Prairie's coming up, gentlemen. Gotta go."

The sleeping car emptied out again. Jack stood there for a moment, mop in hand. *What I wouldn't give to be a conductor some day. Man oh man! Collecting tickets, making sure all the porters are doing their jobs right, looking after people. Sure would be nice to be the boss of someone for a change, instead of being low man on the totem pole.*

The stop in Portage La Prairie was short. No one got on. By the time they pulled into Brandon, it was 8:00 p.m., already forty-five minutes late because of the storm. No one got on there either. But there was a delay. A switch was frozen, jammed with ice and snow. A crew was out with picks and crowbars somewhere in the dark in front of the train. *Poor guys,* thought Jack. *Leastways, I'm in here, where it's nice and warm.*

Jack tidied the storage cupboards, folding and refolding bedlinen and blankets. The train started again. He cleaned fingerprints and nose prints off the windows, and damp-wiped the seats. Then he took a cloth and some oil, and polished the wood on every seat in the car, including the private compartments and roomettes. It was strangely quiet. Only a few porters came through. By the time he was finished, it was 11:05. *We should be well into Saskatchewan now.* They were moving slowly. He had no idea how late they'd be. He went to the porter's jump seat at the end of the car, folded the seat down, and sat with a sigh. *Heavens, why am I so tired?* Leaning his head against the bulkhead, he closed his eyes and let the vibrations lull him. They'd all be in bed now. He gave each one a kiss, whispered, "I love you," and said a prayer for them all.

Bang!

A door flew open. Laughter.

Jack jumped, his eyes popped open. "What the dickens?"

A young woman and man had come in at the other end. "Wheee!" the woman cried as the train lurched around a curve. They grabbed at each other for support.

How long did I sleep? Jack looked at his watch—11:30—as he struggled to his feet. *Only twenty-five minutes.*

"Well, hello there, George! Wakey, wakey!" She threw her head back and laughed. The man standing behind her wrapped both hands around her waist.

Couple a drunks. They've been in the lounge car, thought Jack. *Americans.* They're the only ones who called porters "George," after George Pullman and his Pullman railcars, full of coloured porters like himself. Down in the States, they had become known as "George's boys."

Jack frowned as he walked towards them. "Can I help you folks?" he asked, barely able to smile.

"Yes, George," said the man, tall, angular, wrapped in the arrogance of youth and entitlement. He wore a blue suit and thin black tie. The red rose in his lapel was crushed. "We'd like—"

"We're not *folks,"* interrupted the young woman, dark eyes flashing hotly. She was pretty. Her brown hair was long, braided, and tied with leather thongs like the beatniks he'd seen on TV. She wore a denim dress, buckskin vest, a string of brown beads. "We're Mister and Missus Tom O'Rrrrreilly." Her mouth twisted as she navigated around the troublesome consonants. "We just eloped. He's poor an' Catholic, and, well, I'm not. Buddhist maybe. We're on our honeymoon. Daddy's going to be s-o-o m-a-a-a-a-d." She leaned back against her husband. Jack tried to place her accent—New York, New Jersey maybe. "It's a Christmas we'll never forget, isn't it honey? Aren't you going to congratulate us, Georgie?"

Jack's face was hot, his stomach in a sickly knot. "My name's not George, nor Georgie." With great difficulty, he added, "ma'am."

Tom, the poor Catholic, straightened. "How dare you talk to my wife like that. I—"

A hot surge of anger rose up and warmed Jack's face. "Excuse me, sir, but you are welcome to call me Porter or even Jack, but—"

Tom snarled, "Why you uppity—"

"If this was America," the woman chimed in, "things would be diff—"

The door opened behind the couple, and Lyndon Pollard, conductor, appeared in his black suit and hat. He stopped.

"What's going on here, Jack?" The couple clamped their mouths shut.

"Well, sir." Jack paused. *I could get demerit points for this. Gotta be cool.* He looked at the couple, flashed them an apologetic smile. "They insist on calling me George and Georgie, sir. They may have had a bit to drink—"

"Oh, they did, did they?" The conductor took three quick strides to the couple, raised his portly self up within inches of Tom O'Reilly's face.

"You people come up here and think you can get away with that kind of behaviour?" Pollard wagged his finger at the man, the gold watch chain on his vest shaking. His face was florid, eyes glittering hard as diamonds. Jack had been on the receiving end of that look a couple of times. "This is not the States, at least not yet, and that kind of attitude is not tolerated here. This is Canada."

Only later did Jack think about the lie in that statement. Right then, he was so relieved at Pollard's unexpected support that he felt lightheaded.

"Do you understand me?" Pollard continued, looking from one to the other. They both nodded their heads. The conductor turned to Jack. "If I hear of so much as another insolent peep outta these two, we're going to put them off the train in Moose Jaw. I'm sure on Christmas morning they'll find nice luxury accommodations, say on River Street." He winked at Jack. The train didn't go through Moose Jaw.

"Yes, sir," said Jack, smiling his gratitude. "I'll let you know."

"Good," said Pollard. "Carry on then, Jack." Pressing past him, he continued through the car and out the door.

Jack, almost giddy, turned to the young couple, now suddenly sober. "Are you looking for your berth?"

"Yes . . . er . . . we are," Tom answered, fishing in his jacket pocket for their tickets.

"Don't worry about that," Jack said, "I've got your names on my list." The young ticket seller had put them into an upper berth. There was no reason to because the train was empty. *She must've had trouble with them, too.* "You can sleep in here," he said, pointing to 11B, a lower berth he'd made up. There was no way he was going to spend the rest of the night carrying the ladder to these two every time they had to go to the washroom. "Toilets are right behind you," Jack said, pointing them out. "If there's anything else you need, just press the service button right there." He showed them the black button mounted under the window. *But I pray that you never touch that thing.*

Jack retreated to the end of the car, sat down on the jump seat. His heart was still pounding. He smiled. *Lyndon Pollard! Who'd believe it! Man! Maybe the good Lord gave him a dose of Christmas spirit.*

In a while he heard voices and leaned over to look down the corridor between berths. It was the O'Reillys coming back from the washroom. They crawled into the berth and pulled the green velvet curtains shut. Jack looked up at the indicator board filled with numbered metal disks. His eyes rested on IIB, waiting for it to flip down with a buzzing sound. Five minutes went by. Nothing. All was quiet except for the clicking of train wheels counting off the miles.

Later, he leaned out again. Two pairs of shoes sat on the floor outside their berth. Quietly, Jack walked up and retrieved them—hers were brown penny loafers, brand new. His were older, cheap black dress shoes, the heels worn on the inside. Normally, Jack would mark the berth number on the soles with a small piece of soap. That wasn't necessary tonight. Only one other passenger was on board. *Maybe he's sleeping in Sam's car.*

Jack didn't mind shining shoes. It was quiet, gave him time to think. If there were lots of passengers, the porters would often get together, talk, and shine shoes for hours. Just after he'd first started, when the Korean War broke out, the trains were full of soldiers, and they'd shine boots from top to bottom all night long. *That was something else.*

At 3:00 a.m., they still hadn't reached Saskatoon. *An hour and ten minutes late, at least.* Jack flipped a switch on his indicator board and went into the next sleeping car. The other passenger wasn't there, either. No berths were pulled down. *Maybe he's rich and in a compartment.* He found Sam snoring in a seat, shook him slightly.

"Huh!" The big man startled awake.

"Sorry to do this to you, brother. I'm heading down to the smoking car to catch some shut-eye. The board's all yours. Only two young brats in my car, and they're sleeping off their drinks."

"Okay," Sam nodded and waved him off. He was probably back to sleep before the door closed. The porters spelled each other off all night. That's how it worked. The one going to sleep turned control of his indicator board to the porter in the next car, so if a button were pressed, it would buzz there. That way, the passengers were still being looked after.

The smoking car lived up to its name. The lights were low. A pungent fog filled the air—cigars. Three porters were asleep under blankets on the pull-out seats. Four more were playing poker at the back, their jackets and hats off, sleeves of their white shirts rolled up, ties pulled loose. They hunched over a low table covered with cards, heaping ashtrays, and glasses of rye and Coke. "How's it going, Jack? Heard you had a little trouble."

"A little," he replied, trying to sound matter-of-fact. "Couple of kids, drank too much. Pollard straightened them out."

"He did, eh?" They looked at each other. "What's got into him?"

"Maybe the Ghost of Christmas Past," said one. They all laughed.

"Night, boys—I'm going to turn in."

"Wanna play a couple of hands?"

"No, thanks. I'm bushed."

"How about a nightcap?"

He waved them off, flopped down on a sofa, and leaned his head against the window. The cold felt good on his forehead. He cupped his hands around his eyes to cut the reflection and looked out. Nothing. Not a spec of light. Just cold black iron running through cold black air. There was no thought now about Christmas. Jack simply closed his eyes and fell asleep.

The train had stopped. It was four in the morning. The American couple was getting off. They yelled at Jack to get their luggage. Pollard, grim-faced, pulled his pocket watch out of his vest pocket.

"It's way back in the second-last car. Won't you spot it for me, Mr. Pollard?" Jack asked.

Pollard just shook his head. "Against company policy. If we moved every car up to the station just to save you porters a few steps, we'd be late all the time," he said, snapping his watch shut.

Jack ran through the cars, found the two suitcases. They were heavy. He lugged them down the steps and carried them through the snow towards the station. Porters weren't allowed to drag luggage through the cars. The blizzard was still raging. Pollard and the O'Reillys were just grey shapes in the snow ahead, but he could hear the woman yelling, "Hurry. Hurry." He had to stop and set the suitcases down a couple of times to catch his breath. Finally, his heart racing, he reached the couple. "Look," the woman pointed, her face twisted with rage, "you got snow all over them!" She turned to Pollard. "My green bag. Your stupid George forgot my green bag."

Disgusted, Jack turned and ran back through the snow to the end of the train. He found the green bag. It weighed a ton. He dragged it banging down the steel steps. He didn't care anymore. Suddenly, a shape appeared beside him—Whitney Crummel. "Whitney, what are you doing here?" asked Jack. "You died a few weeks ago."

"That looks heavy, Jack. Can I give you a hand?" asked Whitney, hardly visible in the raging snow as he walked beside him.

"No, I can do it."

"That's what I thought, Jack. I thought I could do it, too. They wouldn't help me, Jack. They wouldn't spot the train for me."

Jack tripped, fell face first into the deepening snow. Whitney stood over him as he lay panting, spitting snow out of his mouth. "Same thing happened to me, Jack. My heart just exploded. You gotta talk to Lee. You guys gotta fight. They have to spot the trains for us." Jack rose. Whitney picked up the green bag and walked off with it, not towards the station, but away from the train, out into the white and swirling snow.

"Whitney!" Jack called. "Whit-neee!"

"Hey! Hey, buddy. Wake up." Someone was shaking him. Jack opened his eyes. It was Sam. He was frowning. "You okay?" Jack looked around. He was still in the smoking car. The card game over, a couple of porters had awakened and were staring at him.

He smiled, embarrassed. "Sorry, I—"

"Don't worry," Sam interrupted. "I think about him all the time." He stood up. "Want some coffee?"

Jack nodded. "Thanks." He raised himself, looked out the window. There were stars winking at the dark-white prairie. The storm was over. By the feel of it, the train was moving faster now. It was 6:30. *I must have slept right through Saskatoon!* He thought of the two passengers still in his car. *Got to get back to work.*

With a hot coffee in hand, Jack went back into the sleeping car, happy to see the curtain pulled shut on 11B, the shoes still in the aisle, where he'd put them. He stood, sipping his coffee for a moment. *We're going to be awful late for Edmonton. I hope folks aren't sitting in that station waiting.*

Then he remembered. *It's Christmas morning.* Winnipeg was an hour ahead, so Anna and the kids would already be up. Jack refused to let himself ache the way he used to. He managed a smile, imagining the boys shaking every present. Anna always let them open one each. The rest would wait under the tree until he got home, so they could celebrate together as a family. He thanked God that Anna understood. Her father had been a railway man. And, of course, her uncle, Lee, was a porter, too.

"Good morning, sir." Jack turned, startled out of his reverie. It was the O'Reilly woman, in a pale satin nightgown, the colour of champagne. She'd undone her braids last night. Her hair was loose and tangled.

They are on their honeymoon after all. "Good morning, ma'am." Jack checked himself, then added, "Merry Christmas." He scanned her face, looking to see if more trouble was brewing.

Her brow furrowed as she tilted her head and looked him in the eye. "I am very sorry for last night. Truly I am. We were just awful, and I don't know—"

"No harm done, ma'am. Thank you for saying so." Jack felt his insides loosen. He hadn't realized he'd been so tense. "Looks like it's going to be a beautiful Christmas day on the prairies." He checked his watch. "We're running about two hours late now 'cause of that storm, so take your time and enjoy the beautiful scenery when the sun comes up. I'd say we've just entered the Province of Alberta. Farm country, big ranchers, too. And boy, these people here, they've got oil. Struck it big just outside of Edmonton in 1947. Leduc Number One—that's what they call the well. Made this a very rich province. So when you and your husband are ready, the chef will have a nice breakfast laid out for you up there in the dining car. And lots of fresh coffee."

"Thank you," she said, stifling a yawn and covering her mouth. "Oh, excuse me, maybe I'll just go back to bed for a while."

"Sure thing, ma'am."

Jack busied himself with chores and watched the sun come up—painting the sky of northern Alberta a Christmas red. A couple of hours later, the couple got up, dressed and went off to breakfast. He stripped the sheets from their berth, folded it back into seats and stowed their green carry-on bag. The manifest said they'd be riding through to Vancouver. He had just begun to mop the floor when J.D. came in.

"Had breakfast, Jack?" He reeked of liquor and cigarettes.

You're not going to hang onto your job smelling like that. "No, and I'm starving. Go ahead. I'll be there in a minute." But Jack took his time finishing, then put away the bucket and mop, and headed to the dining car.

Sam and Dutch were drinking coffee, their backs to the "iron curtain" that separated the "help" from the paying passengers. "Morning, Sam . . . Dutch." J.D. was sitting with three other porters.

"Morning, Jack."

He sat down with them. "What's on the menu this morning?" It was a joke they repeated every day. The porters didn't eat from a menu. Railway rules. They got what the dining car staff gave them, often leftovers. Sometimes it was so bad, Svenson would come out and glare at them, daring them to complain.

"You boys better eat that because it's all you're getting," he'd say. Often they wouldn't, just to spite him, or they simply couldn't. Jack's expectations weren't high.

"Waffles," was Dutch's reply.

"Waffles! No kidding?"

"Waffles and sausages," added Sam. "New company policy. If they're going to work us to death, they want us to die fat and happy." He laughed as he drained his cup.

"Morning, gents." It was Peter, a dining car steward. He held a big steaming white pot of coffee with a red maple leaf and CNR written on it. "Coffee?"

"Yes, please."

All three held out their cups. Peter hesitated. The train was on a sharp curve. "Another quiet Christmas run, eh?"

"Nice 'n' quiet," said Sam.

"I dunno." Dutch shook his head. "I'd like it to be busier. The time passes quicker when you're working. Too much time to think about home and what you're missing out on."

Jack held up his cup while Peter poured. "Yeah, isn't that the truth. It's hard enough when you're busy. Thanks," he said as Peter finished. He poured in some milk from a small pitcher, dropped in a couple of sugarlumps, stirred.

"How are the newlyweds doing up there? They treating you all right?" Jack asked.

"Oh, sure. They're so lovey-dovey and kissy-face, they hardly notice I'm around." Peter replied.

"That's good." Jack nodded. "They're on their honeymoon."

"No kidding!" said Peter. "Who'd get married at Christmas, for crying out loud? Are they Jews?"

Jack shook his head. "Catholic—at least he is. They eloped."

"Well, I'll be," said Sam. They all drank their coffees for a moment.

"By the way," said Dutch, "did you know some of the whites are getting a lawyer to stop us from changing the Group One rules? That's what a friend of mine told me."

"Yeah . . . heard that, too," Sam said, frowning.

"Here you go." Peter was back with three heaping plates. Waffles and sausages, just as he'd promised.

"My, oh my," said Sam, bending his head and sniffing in the steam rising off the food. "Doesn't that just warm your poor old homesick heart on a Christmas morning."

It surely does, thought Jack. Instinctively, he checked his watch and thought about Anna and the kids. They might just be having a late breakfast right now, too. Carla'd be making a mess in her high chair, up to her elbows in whatever she was eating. The boys would probably be rushing so they could get back to playing with the gift they opened.

"Mmm, these are something else," mumbled Sam. "Quit hogging the maple syrup there, Dutch, and pass it over, if you please."

"You know that friend of mine? He said if we win this fight, the whites are just going to get all their friends and stack their names on the boards, whether they can speak English or not.

So we still might never have a chance to become a conductor—that's what he said. He says the bosses upstairs are putting the pressure on them, you know, to make sure they keep us in our place."

"That so," said Sam, putting down his fork. He looked at Dutch. "Dutch, don't you know it's Christmas morning, for crying out loud. I don't want to talk about this stuff no more, I don't want to hear about it no more, I don't even want to think about it no more, do you know that? So for the love of God, please drop it, and let's enjoy this fine repast that our good friends in the galley have prepared and have a nice, friendly bit of conversation. You boys okay with that?"

"That would be great," said Jack, relieved that Sam had said what he wanted to.

Dutch shrugged. "Sure. Fine. Sorry, I didn't mean no harm. I—"

"No harm done, my friend." Sam reached across with a big hammy fist and punched him on the shoulder. "I could sure use another splash of that fine CNR coffee. Oh, hi there, Saint Peter. Aren't you just an angel of mercy doling out the java to hardworking men such as us." They all laughed, too hard, as Peter refilled their cups.

They arrived in Edmonton at 10:30, two and a half hours late. The day coach passenger got off—a Jehovah's Witness, Dutch said, who didn't believe in Christmas. No one got on. It was cold in Edmonton—thirty below. The sun sparkled on a skiff of fresh snow. The passenger and a redcap disappeared, leaving only two sets of tracks on the platform.

After breakfast, Jack went back to his car. As they pulled away, he watched the smoke rising up from the city's chimneys, flattening itself out against the cold air hovering above, grey and glum as a rooming-house ceiling. It felt like the people on the train were the only ones in the world alive. *My God, we live in a hard place! Why couldn't we have weather like Jamaica, hot and sunny all the time, beautiful flowers year-round, swim in the ocean any time you want, warm breeze off the turquoise ocean. Ahh, man, that'd be the life.*

Jack had never been to Jamaica. It was just what Canadian winters did to you—made you think about somewhere else. That was one reason Jack loved being on the trains. It gave him time to think about all kinds of things and about places he'd like to go someday and the places he'd been.

"I tell you, I'm getting an education on the railway." That's what he often told Anna when he got home. "Travelling to different places, seeing the mountains. You can read about it, but when you see it, it makes all the difference in the world." The people, too, were fascinating. People from overseas—Europe, Japan. All over the world. Different from the people he'd met here. They told Jack what was happening where they came from, and it gave him new information about how other people live. Information that they sure didn't teach in the threadbare schools of Africville. *Come to think of it, we didn't get much of an education there at all.*

"Penny for your thoughts," said a voice near Jack.

"Huh?" He turned to find the American, Mr. O'Reilly. "Oh, excuse me, I was just daydreaming, I guess. Can I help you, sir? Are you enjoying the trip?"

"Yes, we are. Thank you." He nodded towards the snow-covered fields and swatches of bush. "Doesn't look much like the Wild West out there, does it?"

"No, sir, it doesn't. Nothing like a foot of snow and thirty below to subdue the spirits." Jack was relieved that the husband, too, seemed to be trying to make up for last night. "Course, up here, it never got too wild. We had the Mounties, you know. The Royal Canadian Mounted Police?" Tom nodded as he leaned down, rested his arms on the back of the next seat as he looked out the window. "'Red Coats.' That's what the Indians called them. They pretty much kept the peace out here. Oh, there was trouble from time to time, bootlegging and horse thieving, but not quite the same as down in the States, if you'll pardon me for saying so." Jack checked to make sure he wasn't offending his passenger.

"There was something of a rebellion out here once. Guy called Louis Riel led a group of Métis—they're a French and Cree mix. They wanted their own province and rights to the land they'd been living on. The government in Ottawa called it a rebellion and sent the Mounties out on the train, horses and all, to put it down. They hung Louis Riel back in Regina. Some say he was insane, thought he was a prophet or something. But you know the guys who win always get to say what they want."

"That is a fact," Tom said. "Like our government and the lies they're telling us about the Bay of Pigs invasion in Cuba. We're definitely not getting the straight goods on that one."

"Exactly so," Jack continued. "Funny thing—I read this in a book just the other day—just nine days before they hung Riel, they pounded the last spike, a gold one, to finish this here railway. In fact, they rushed the building of it so they could get troops out here because of Riel and all the troubles. They also wanted to make sure British Columbia way out here on the tail-end of the country didn't up and become another U.S. state." The American smiled at that news.

"Course, they're still threatening to go from time to time," Jack said with a smile as he straightened up. "I'm sorry. I'm bending your ear too much here."

"No, no, it's fascinating." Mr. O'Reilly stood up, too, still looking out the window. "We never hear about this in America. All the news we get, the stuff we take in school, it's all about our own country. No wonder we're so damn myopic."

My-o-pic. I better look that one up. Jack kept a small, well-thumbed dictionary in his bag.

"Well, I should go see what my bride is up to. Nice chatting with you . . . ah, Jack."

"Very nice visiting with you, sir."

Jack watched him walk towards the day coach. *People aren't so bad after all.*

He spent the next half hour cleaning the toilets, washing out the bowls, and wiping the walls and the taps with disinfectant. Then he washed the floor, refilled the tissue dispensers, and added more toilet paper. Just as he finished, he heard the door open. It was Olie Svenson, still in his white chef's apron, going back to the smoking car. Something smelling awfully good trailed along with him.

"Hello, sir. So what's for supper tonight?" Jack was still in high spirits after his conversation with Tom.

Olie stopped, frowned. "Well, for the passengers, ve got some nice fat Christmas turkey in de oven. Mashed potatoes, gravy, and all dat." He paused and with a wicked grin said, "And for you *boys,* I think ve got some hamburger, left over from last week, yah." Jack's face went very serious, and Olie threw back his head and laughed. "But don't worry, I add lots of hot sauce to kill de bugs. You people like that stuff, yah sure, I bet." He hurried away, still laughing.

Jack's insides roiled. *More than ten years in this job, and I still have to put up with this crap.* It was more than anger and frustration; it was grief. For the porters, his brothers, for every coloured couple who tried to rent apartments, for all they had to put up with. *And just when you think things are going good—bang! You get hit between the eyes by some white guy, an immigrant yet! Hey, what about me? I was born here!*

Jack felt very alone. With great effort, he forced himself not to think about Anna and the kids. His work done, he picked a *Saturday Night* magazine from the rack and sat down to read. But he couldn't concentrate. *Damn that bastard! Sorry, God, for cussing on Jesus' birthday and all. I'm so damn—so darn mad—I just can't help myself. Please watch over my family for me and for all the brothers here on the train. Help us get through this Christmas okay. Thank you for all your blessings.* Immediately, he felt better. *Hamburger or not we'll have a little get-together tonight for sure.* He picked up the magazine again and lost himself in a story.

He looked up as the train began to slow. *There they were—the mountains!* Jack loved the Rockies more than any place he'd ever seen. "Someday, I'm going to take us all on a train trip through those mountains," he'd tell Anna. "We'll get a roomette for ourselves and one for the kids and ride in the observation car—and when you see those snowy peaks sticking their heads up into the great blue yonder, you just won't want to go home." That was a trip, Jack realized, they might not take for some time.

The Jasper train station was a grand building made of stone and stucco with cedar shingles on its steep roofs and gables. Jack had dreams of building a house just like it, only smaller, on a mountain somewhere where they could live. *Heck, we could take a jigger into town to get groceries.* He was laughing at his crazy idea when the O'Reillys burst through the door.

"Jack, these mountains are s-o-o-o beautiful!" Mrs. O'Reilly exclaimed. Jack looked out the window. It was 5:00 p.m. now and dark. Christmas lights blazed on the buildings along the main street, many of them made of logs and stone hewn from the mountains.

Tom O'Reilly picked up their carry-on bag. "Bye, Jack. We're getting off here."

Jack jumped up. "But I thought you were going through to Vancouver. Least—"

"We were," his wife chirped. "But this! This is gorgeous! Fantastic! We've got to stay here for a few days and see it."

"Who knows? We may never come this way again. We can always catch another train later." And then he chuckled. "It's not like we have jobs or anything to get back to." They both giggled and waved. "See you, Jack. Take care. Thanks for everything." And they left. The door closed with a bang. He watched them shivering on the platform, watched as Tom counted out five American dollar bills for the redcap who brought their bags.

Jack stepped out onto the rear platform of the car, opened the top half of the metal door, and inhaled deeply. An intoxicating perfume of pine and cold. *Ahh, I'd love to give a bottle of this air to Anna.* He stayed there as the train started with a small jolt, then slowly rolled out of town. They would head west for a bit, climb up through the Yellowhead Pass, then turn south and follow the North Thompson River to Kamloops and west to Vancouver. The door opened behind him. It was Sam.

"Incredible, isn't it?"

"The view?"

"The view, the air. Boy, I sure wish Anna could see this. I'm going to bring her out someday."

"Yes, Betsey and I were here once. It's beautiful, quiet, elk just walking around like they own the place. Man."

They stood there while the train picked up speed. Sam looked at Jack. "Hey, guess what? It's time for Christmas dinner."

"I wouldn't count on too much. Olie said we're having hamburger."

"What!" Sam roared. "You fall for that? He's just joshing you, brother. There's no one on this train anymore except for us. We're rattling on empty most likely all the way to Vancouver. And all I can smell is that turkey 'n' gravy—so are you coming or not? Let's go."

"Be there in a minute, Sam. Just want to soak up a little more of this first."

Snowy peaks still glowed orange from the sun, which had long since set. The train rumbled along the dark floor of the valley, winding beside a shallow river that ran through gravel beds, black water on white, then disappeared beneath the ice and snow. Slowly, they climbed into mountains so rough-hewn they looked like they were made just yesterday. Jack had spent many nights peering out into the darkness. These mountains were so majestic, so mysterious. They tugged at him like magnets. He wanted to be out there—like the original railway surveyors searching for the pass that would take them to the ocean—with nothing more than a good horse, a couple of blankets, and a scrap of canvas for shelter, living all winter in rude log cabins they'd built with sharp axes and a saw. A man riding on a dark train dreaming in the night.

He shook himself a little, shivered, and wondered, as he always did, about how many pairs of eyes were watching him—cougars, grizzlies, and wolves. *Lick your lips all you want; that turkey is mine.*

A wall of noise and warm, fragrant air hit Jack as he opened the door.

"Hey, guy! Where you been?" yelled Dutch. He was standing in the aisle talking with J.D., Sam, and Lee, who nodded to his hello. Jack did a quick count. There were ten of them there, talking and laughing. Olie, the steward, and maybe four waiters would be in the galley sweating over supper. The brakeman, Oscar Jorgenson, would come back from the engine later. The engineer, Art Sawyer, couldn't leave the cab. Someone would bring him supper.

The tables were set with white tablecloths, shining cutlery, and white plates with the red Maple Leaf at the twelve o'clock position. At every table, white candles were lit, their bases trimmed in green pine, red poinsettia leaves, and cranberries. *So this is what it's like on the other side of the curtain.* It took him by surprise every year.

"Hey, Peter," he said as the waiter came to fill the water glasses. "You got this place looking great."

"Thanks, Jack. Yeah, Olie's been driving us hard all day."

"Merry Christmas, Jack." Lyndon Pollard stuck out his hand. His face looked freshly washed and relaxed, a Sunday-morning kind of look.

"Merry Christmas, sir." Pollard's hand was damp and soft.

"How's your family doing? Your wife . . . Annie, isn't it?"

"Anna, that's right. Good for you, sir. She's fine. They're all fine. Got two boys and a little girl now. How about yours? How are they doing?"

"Oh good, yes. They're growing up fast. Both girls in high school now. You know—boys, cars, and Elvis. What more do I need to say, eh?" They both laughed.

"Are you taking some holidays when we get back to the Peg?"

"Yeah, we'll probably go up to the cabin at the lake for a few days." Pollard looked over his shoulder. "Excuse me, Jack. I need to talk to someone for a sec." He smiled and slid away.

"Nice talking to you, sir." Jack wondered if he'd been too familiar, said too much, maybe. He'd never had such a long conversation with Pollard before.

"Gentlemen! Gentlemen!" It was the dining car steward, Bill Lyman. "Please be seated. Supper is ready!"

A cheer went up. "It's great not having any passengers on board," Jack commented to Lee as they sat.

"That it is," he said. "Gives us all a chance to let our hair down a little." Lee, Sam, and Jack sat with Bob, a waiter. Jimmy, Dutch, and Lou sat across the aisle from them with Pollard. J.D. sat down with Bill. Olie and the waiters would sit last, once everyone was served.

It suddenly hit Jack. *The coloured and whites are sitting together.* It just seemed to happen.

"Bring it on!" yelled Pollard, tapping his glass with his spoon.

Jack looked at the conductor. *I wonder if he's been drinking, too.*

"Yes, bring it on." The others joined in. The clinking and yelling temporarily drowned out the sound of the train.

One by one, the waiters strode in, smiling, each with two heaping, steaming plates.

"Oooh." The appreciative roar of a ravenous crew. Pollard got his first. Hungry eyes followed the plate to its destination in front of him.

"Mmm, this looks amazing," said Sam as theirs arrived. "My mouth's been watering all day at the thought of this bird."

Jack nodded in agreement, paused to say a silent prayer of thanksgiving for the food, his friends here on the train, and his family at home, then dug in.

They feasted on turkey with cranberries cooked in rum and sugar, creamy mashed potatoes with flecks of herbs—Jack didn't know what kind—gravy, buttered peas and carrots, and puréed turnip. They chatted about family and Christmas and holidays and being railway men. The conversation soon turned to railways they'd worked on.

"We had this engineer once down in Kansas—that was on the old Chesapeake, Topeka, and Santa Fe line. Turned out he had terrible night vision," recounted Dutch. "Well, the brakeman was always covering for him, right? And he kinda got sick of that after a while, so one night—I forget where their home base was—the brakeman has his friends draw up a cardboard cow, just black and white, nothing fancy. Mind you, the guy couldn't see worth a darn, so it didn't matter much. And they propped this thing up on the tracks just out of town so he wouldn't be going at full speed. You don't want anyone to get hurt, right? So the brakeman says to this engineer, 'I'm just going for a leak. Be back in a sec.' And the next thing the engineer knows, he's running down a Holstein cow. So he yells for brakes, but the guy's not there, right, and they plough right through this cow. And he's only doing about twenty-five, thirty miles per hour maybe. And the kicker is, the brakeman's buddies are hiding in the ditch, and they're all dressed up in farmer overalls and hats, and one's got a fake beard and all, and they jump up and wave their lanterns, and start yelling and shaking their fists. Well, the poor guy. He finally realized that it probably wasn't a good idea to be driving a train if he couldn't see good at night, right? So he went and got another job . . . I dunno what. But to this day, I'm told, he still thinks he killed a cow on that run." The guys laughed and shook their heads. Dutch sat back, a grin on his face.

Lee put his fork down and took a sip of water. "Did I ever tell you about those crazy Finn loggers used to ride with us up in northern Ontario?" Everyone shook his head, and Lee was off, a tale about rough-and-tumble workingmen too long in the bush, about pay days and booze ups, and, ultimately, the railway police. At each table, stories were being told along with jokes, lies, and, always, laughter. Dinner was over far too soon.

"Excuse me, men." Pollard had pushed his chair back and was standing up. "We would be very neglectful if we didn't show Olie and his crew our appreciation for this splendid Christmas feast they laid on for us tonight. Thanks, guys."

Cheers and applause. "Way to go, Olie!"

The chef, still in his white jacket, stood and bowed with great solemnity. Then he cracked a smile. "Supper's not over yet, boys. We have plum pudding!"

"Oh, yeah!" Another round of applause.

Jack's mouth began to water at the thought of it. The CNR was famous for its plum pudding. In fact, Anna's last words to him were, "George, don't forget to get some plum pudding."

He smiled. *She's the only one who can call me George and get away with it. Imagine! My own wife.* But he knew it was a term of love, and that thought tapped into a raw, lonely feeling lingering just below the surface, a feeling that he didn't want to acknowledge. He drained his coffee and quickly started talking with Dutch across the aisle.

Peter and Lou cleared the tables while a steward wheeled in a serving cart filled with dishes of pudding. Another brought around more coffee.

"I'm not having no more of that stuff," said Sam, "not strong enough." He pulled out his flask and held it out over the table. The others waited while Lee, being senior porter, reached for the flask and took a sip.

His eyebrows shot up. "Whoa," he said with some enjoyment. "What's that?"

"Irish," came the answer.

"I thought you were drinking vodka before," said Jack.

"That was before," laughed Sam.

Lee then disappeared from the dining car for a moment and came back with his guitar.

"Atta boy, Lee," someone called. He pulled a chair away from the table and sat down, adjusted the tuning pegs with his ear cocked to the strings until he was satisfied, removed his pick, and began to play softly, "O, Little Town of Bethlehem." The noise and chatter in the dining car fell like a curtain until all they could hear was Lee over the ever-present sounds of the train. They sat still, suddenly yanked from the merriment of a party into the feeling of Christmas. Jack looked around at the faces—serious, smiling, sad, lonely, some just lost in thought. When that song ended, Lee went right into "Silent Night." He played beautifully, his fingers weaving an old spell over the men. Jack didn't know who it was started humming, but pretty soon everyone was, and then they were singing:

Round yon virgin, Mother and Child
Holy infant so tender and mild,
Sleep in heavenly peace,
Slee-eep in heavenly peace.

"That's very nice, Lee," said Sam when the song ended. "How about 'Rock Around the Clock'?" The men laughed. That was it for the serious stuff. Sam started singing and clapping, and when everyone was going, he stood up and led the group, waving his arms to direct his moving railway choir. Flasks made the rounds at the other tables.

Lou, one of the white dining car waiters, came back with his guitar and sat down across from Lee. The men cheered again.

"Sam," Jack said, "do your B.B. King."

"Yes, B.B. King," cried J.D.

Sam needed little encouragement. With two guitars now and a demanding audience, he stood and launched into "The Thrill Is Gone." Sam poured every ounce of his considerable self into the song. And the men laughed and sang their appreciation. On the last verse, Lyndon Pollard got up, tore off his conductor jacket, and sang with Sam while holding a spoon as if it were a microphone. The men cheered and clapped loudly. The party had begun.

Jack got up to go to the washroom, then stepped out onto the platform again and opened the top half of the door. They were on a trestle crossing a deep valley. The night was clear and stars were out, and a sharp, thin crescent moon had one of its horns hooked on a mountain peak. Jack leaned out into the blast of cold air. The windows on the cars ahead glowed as they arched around a curve—a long string of lights, Christmas lights. He imagined for a moment that the entire railway was a metal necklace strung across the neck of pretty young woman, a richly blessed, good-hearted woman. He thought of Lyndon Pollard singing with Sam. He thought of Lee and the porters and the help they were getting from the prime minister himself. He thought of his sweet, pregnant Anna and their children in their cozy little apartment. For the first time on this trip, Jack felt happy, even hopeful. *I have a good job, and I work with some good people,* he thought. *Sure could do a lot worse.*

Jack turned to go back into the warmth. They were singing an Al Jolson song now. The music was getting louder. It would last all the way to Vancouver.

THE LEGEND of The Great White Pine

"Mmm." Louisa McKenzie licked her lips and turned to her friend. "This rabbit stew is very good, Nancy," she said.

"Thank you. My nokomis taught me how to make it."

"Your grandmother taught you well." Louisa swung the black pot back over the coals and placed another log at the rear of the fireplace so the flames wouldn't burn the stew. "It's getting cold in here," she complained, then laughed. "It was never this warm in the wigwam. Maybe the white ways are making me soft."

Nancy McCargo smiled. "Yes, we have a good life." She looked around the room at the glass windows from Britain, the oil lamps, cooking pots, the iron stove in her bedroom from Montréal—all had come by ship and canoe from so far away.

Louisa's daughter, Margaret, was asleep at her feet in the wooden cradle one of the carpenters had made. She pulled the rabbit skin blanket up a little, rose, and went to the window. Light shone weakly through the frost-painted pictures of trees, ferns, and snowflakes. Rubbing the wavy glass with her fingers, she made a peephole. Past the corn store on its stilts, she could see part of the main square of the fort. It was empty, just drifts of snow trampled by the moccasins and snowshoes of wintering residents. Shadows from three birch trees drew long blue claw marks across the rumpled snow. It was December 25, so the days were short.

"The men won't be home for a couple of hours yet," she sighed. "What should we do?"

Nancy put down the doeskin she'd been cutting with scissors. "Do you want to play another game of Shut-the-Box? You might win this time."

Louisa laughed and shook her head. She returned to the table, picked up her cup of tea, and sipped it. It was strong, black tea from the company store and had come by ship from the other side of the world. Nancy still preferred kinnikinnick tea and liked picking the green leaves and bright red berries. Its fragrance, she said, carried her back to the open places in the forest where she'd found it. In fact, the wintering house was filled with scents from the forest: the birch smoke, the fort-made furniture and plank floors, the cedar branches she and Louisa had placed on the fireplace mantel to freshen the air.

"How about draughts?" Nancy continued. "You did well in that." Louisa shook her head. Both games were still on the dining table. Beside them the flame of a brown tallow candle flickered restlessly in the draughts. "Why don't you finish the dress you're making for the New Year's supper and dance?"

"I don't feel like sewing," Louisa said, brightening, "but I went to the little shop this morning and got some nice ribbon. Won't it be fun to dance again? I love fiddles and fifes. And the pipes! I wonder what the new year will bring, don't you?"

Nancy nodded as she concentrated on her sewing. "More trouble with that terrible Lord Selkirk, I imagine," Louisa continued. "Thank goodness we finally have a peace treaty with the Americans." She stopped and looked at Nancy. "What is that you're making?"

Her friend smiled and set the leather down in her lap. "Some moccasins for your Margaret.

She has seen her twelfth moon and will soon be walking."

Louisa smiled. "She will wear them when she takes her first steps." She leaned forward in her chair and watched her friend cut out a piece, fold it, and begin to sew with sinew.

Louisa was Anishinabek. It meant "the people." Ojibway was another word they used for themselves. Nancy was Cree. They understood each other's tongues and spoke them when their husbands were away. When the men came back, of course, they switched to English. Captain Robert McCargo had taken Nancy for his country wife two years ago. Ever since they began sharing the wintering house with Louisa and her husband, Kenneth McKenzie, they'd become best of friends. The captain was away much of the time, especially in summer, sailing the company schooner across Lake Superior to Sault Ste. Marie.

"What is Robert doing today?" Louisa asked.

Nancy paused. "He was in the naval shed this morning, shaping new planks to replace ones damaged in the hull of *The Invincible.*" White men, she'd learned, like to attach names to their sailing boats. The schooner was now covered with snow at Pigeon Bay, a few miles north of Grand Portage.

"And Mr. McKenzie?" Nancy asked. Her fingers worked a small awl into the leather, making holes for the needle. The first moccasin was almost complete.

"Oh, I don't know," Louisa sighed. "Some of my people from Grand Portage were in to trade this morning, and he met with them. I think he was going over to the farm to see how many geese there are for our New Year's supper. There'll be close to thirty people here for the fête, he thinks." She glanced again at the door. "I hope he brings some milk and butter. The cook says the sugar's getting low."

Nancy raised her eyebrows and nodded to the upstairs loft, where the cook from the Great Hall slept in the winter. "I think our cook has a sweet tooth," she whispered. The two women giggled. They were each only fourteen, and, while accomplished at the work of women, they still had young girls' spirits.

As the wife of the proprietor, the wintering partner at the North West Company fort, Louisa was the most respected woman in the area. She liked being able to buy ribbons, pretty cottons, and silk at the company store. Her husband said that Fort William—here on the Kaministiquia River just upstream from Animike Wekwid, Thunder Bay—was the most civilized establishment west of Montréal, although she did not know exactly what the word *civilized* meant. But none of that mattered now. She was bored. She picked up another shortbread and offered the plate to Nancy. There was one left.

"I will get a sweet tooth from your biscuits," she said, laughing as she took it.

"I know," Louisa said suddenly. "Why don't you tell us a story?"

"Oh, you've heard mine so many times." Nancy stirred the coals under her stew pot with a poker.

"No, you're such a good storyteller," Louisa protested. "Please, tell *The Legend of the Great White Pine.*"

Nancy smiled. She liked that one herself. "All right," she said, adjusting her red leggings and smoothing out her blue dress. Then, picking up her sewing, she began.

"Those of us who have passed quietly in our canoes by the great peninsula that reaches out and touches the Sleeping Giant have often stopped to gaze in wonder at the magnificent white pines that tower over the land there. As the elders have told us, in the legend passed down by their elders, the white pines did not get there by accident."

Louisa leaned back in her chair and pulled the Kashmir shawl over her shoulders, then closed her eyes as Nancy continued.

"Many, many moons ago—perhaps as many as two thousand years, as the white men would count it—a tribe of our ancestors lived on the shore of Thunder Bay near the great rocky peninsula. They had a chief who was a very wise man of great birth. He had travelled far and had seen and learned many things.

"His name was Golden Eagle. He was, at the time of this story, a very old man. He had seen ninety winters and was close to death.

"One day when he felt that his time on Mother Earth was almost over, he called his son, Ti-Baki-Enane, to his bedside. The old man was very weak. He pulled a deerskin bag from under his furs and placed the bag in his son's hands. Softly, he spoke this message: 'Ti-Baki-Enane, my days are few. In this bag you will find many seeds that I have brought from a great distance. Take good care of them, and whenever a new child is born to my people, plant a seed in good earth for it. Soon, great trees will grow from the seeds, and my people will build their homes from the wood. They will also build great canoes, and they will prosper.'

"'I will do as you wish, my father,' answered Ti-Baki-Enane and quietly left the old man to end his days in peace. For years, the young man faithfully planted the seeds whenever a new papoose was born, and soon beautiful white pines dotted the land. As they became large enough to bear cones, Ti-Baki-Enane gathered more and more seeds.

"One night, while he lay asleep in his wigwam, he was suddenly awakened by a strange sound. His wigwam seemed to glow with a bright light, and there, at the foot of his bed of furs, stood the spirits of his father and two other great chiefs.

"The spirit of Golden Eagle spoke very softly. 'My son, you have kept your promise, and we are well pleased. We have come to give you a great duty to perform. Tonight, the greatest child the world has ever known will be born. Pick the finest seed that you have and go to the highest place and plant it at once. All men will see the tree that springs from it, and wonder. Farewell, my son.'

"Immediately, Ti-Baki-Enane arose and, selecting the largest and finest-looking seed, ran to the top of Thunder Hill. There he planted it.

"Truly, this was a special tree, for it grew three times faster than any other, and in a few years it towered at least five times higher than the white pines around it. So tall was it that at night the stars seemed to hang from its great boughs.

"It soon got the name, the Great Papoose Tree, and our people came from miles around to see it. Each visitor would hang a little pair of moccasins or a child's buckskin shirt and other gifts for the children who had lost their parents. Deer and the small animals of the woods would sleep in safety under it, and many a lost traveller would find refuge for the night beneath its friendly boughs.

"This great and magnificent tree lived for almost thirty years, and then one day, one of those terrible storms that sweep across Thunder Bay came and struck it down. Now, nothing remains of this beautiful white pine. But the memory of it is kept alive each year as we place the little gifts for our children under the starlit fragrant bough of our own trees."

Nancy smiled as she finished and looked over at Louisa.

"Yes," Louisa said nodding, "that is a good story."

Nancy picked up the two little moccasins. "See. Gifts for a small child."

"They're beautiful," Louisa exclaimed, leaning forward in her chair to touch them."You are so good at the traditional ways."

"And you are good at the new ones."

They heard the muffled sound of voices outside the door and footsteps crunching in the snow. "They're back," said Louisa. "Now we can enjoy your stew."

"These are not quite finished," Nancy said, rising and setting the moccasins on the table. "I'll sew beads on them tonight after supper. Then I will give them to your little Margaret, in the spirit of the great white pine."

THE *Mitten Tree*

"Ohhhh!" cried Emel as water sloshed onto her dress. She stopped, set the pails down in the dirt, and wrapped her hands in her scarf to warm them.

"Hurry, Omar," she called to her little brother, who was struggling behind her with two jugs of water. "Mother is waiting."

"You filled these too full," Omar complained as he caught up.

A gust of wind swirled dust into their mouths. "It's wash day. Mother needs these," Emel said. Shivering, she picked up her pails and led her brother between the rows and rows of flapping, grey tents.

To Emel, it seemed her family had lived in the refugee camp forever. They were surrounded by a high, wire fence, beyond which was a brown desert filled with low, scraggly bushes and buried landmines. Worn, humpbacked mountains lined the horizon like sentries.

Just as they got back to their tent, Emel's father arrived with a package.

"Where's the food?" her mother asked.

"This is just as good as food," said her father, folding his tall, thin body onto a low stool.

"I'm hungry," said Omar.

"I'm freezing," said Emel. She pulled her tattered blanket tightly around her.

"A-ha," said Emel's father, his eyes sparkling. He gave the package to his children. "Here."

They tore it open.

"Be careful, children. We must save the paper," said Emel's mother.

"Mittens!" cried Omar, as he pulled out a pair of red mittens tied together with a long woollen string.

"Mittens!" cried Emel, as she pulled out a pair of purple mittens that were also tied together with a long woollen string. "Who sent us mittens?" she asked.

Her father shrugged. "I don't know. They just came, boxes of them."

"What will we eat today?" her mother asked. "There's no more flour."

"The relief truck will come later," her father replied.

Emel pulled on her mittens. They were so soft. Her hands felt warm for the first time in weeks. "I'm going to show Mia," she said, racing from the tent.

Omar put on his, too. "I'm going to show Mohammed," he said.

"Don't forget your blankets," called their mother.

Mia and Mohammed had new mittens, too. But theirs didn't have strings attached.

"I wonder what the string is for?" Emel asked later.

"I'll cut it off," said her mother. "It just gets in the way."

That night, as her family slept under their thin blankets, Emel lay awake, twisting the soft, wool string around her fingers. *Why would someone make mittens for us?* she wondered. *Who are they? How do they know we are here in this camp?* But she could find no answers and soon fell asleep.

In the middle of the night, the string from Emel's purple mittens ended up lying across her face. She batted it away and sat up. Moonbeams flooded the tent with light. One end of the string ran right out the door. *That's funny,* she thought.

She pulled at the string, but it wouldn't come. In fact, it pulled back, or so it seemed. Emel couldn't be sure. *What's going on?* she asked herself as she got up, slipped on her sandals, and followed the string out of the tent.

The string wound past the tents where families like hers were sleeping. *How did this string get so long?* she wondered as she followed it hand-over-hand to a hole in the fence that ran around the camp. She stopped, looked this way and that. "Mmm," she said. "This is forbidden." But she crawled through anyway.

The string led across the desert, which she knew was filled with danger. This is strange, thought Emel. *My father would die of fright if he knew I was here.* Yet, somehow, she felt safe.

The string led Emel into the hills, past a camp of soldiers sound asleep beside their dying fires. *They snore even louder than my family,* Emel thought. She giggled out loud.

"Shhh," whispered a sentry, appearing out of the dark. He smiled and pointed up the mountain. "Your string goes that way," he said.

Up a mountain Emel climbed, always keeping hold of the string. She passed a flock of sheep in a pen. Nearby stood a shepherd's house made of rocks.

Perhaps the wool came from here, she thought as she knocked on the door.

"Yes?" asked the very sleepy shepherd with a wavering candle in his hand.

Emel held up the purple woollen string and her purple woollen mittens. "Did you make these?" she asked.

"No," said the shepherd. "But I saw the string today. It goes over the mountain."

"I am following it," Emel explained. "I need to find the person who made these mittens."

"There is snow in the pass, so I will take you," said the shepherd. In a minute he was dressed, and by the light of his lantern, they followed the string. It continued up and up, through the deep snow of the mountain pass.

Funny, Emel thought. *All I'm wearing are sandals, but my feet aren't cold.*

"This is as far as I can go. I must get back to my sheep," said the shepherd. "Good luck."

"Thank you," called Emel and walked down the other side, down into a lush, beautiful valley, just as the sun was coming up. *Momma will be so worried,* she thought. But Emel wasn't worried, and that was strange, too.

Emel kept walking as she followed the string, through forests, around lakes, along rivers, across fields. She passed by a big city. *Why am I not hungry?* asked Emel. *Or tired? This is very weird.*

Finally, the string led her to the shore of the ocean, where it disappeared beneath the waves. *I guess this is the end of the line.* But just down the beach, there was a huge pier and, at the end of it, a very long freighter. *Mmm,* thought Emel. *I've come this far.*

So Emel walked out onto the pier and sneaked on board the ship. "Where is everybody?" she wondered out loud.

She went to the bow of the ship, string still in hand, and tugged. The purple string rose out of the water, a dripping line stretching far out to sea. Suddenly, a loud horn sounded on the ship. Emel ducked and hid as sailors came running and threw off the ropes that held the ship to the pier.

"What are you doing here?" a voice whispered behind her.

Emel whirled around to see a sailor staring at her. "I'm following this string," she explained, "to find the person who made these mittens." Then she held up a mitten and covered her mouth as she began to yawn.

"Uh-huh," nodded the sailor. "I can see by your clothes that you've come a long way. We're leaving now. Why don't you hide in that lifeboat? I'll hold your string for you while you have a nap."

"Thank you," Emel said and she did.

When she awoke Emel was in the harbour of a very big city. "Ohhh," she yawned and stretched. "I feel like I've slept for days."

The sailor was still standing there, the frayed end of the purple woollen string in one hand. "I'm very sorry, but a whale bit it off while you were sleeping."

"Oh, no," Emel cried. "I've come so far, and now it's lost." She wiped her tears with her purple mittens. "Thank you anyway," she said to the sailor and left the ship.

She wandered through the busy city. "Oh!" She jumped at the cars honking, at the sirens wailing, at the drivers yelling. "Woah," she whimpered as the wind whipped her scarf and dress and made her shiver right down to her bones. "Ugh," she moaned as her tummy twisted and turned inside her. *It feels like I haven't eaten in days.*

Emel wandered down a tiny, dark street, sat beside a battered garbage can, and began to cry.

"What are you doing here?" a voice asked. Emel looked up to see a man in a white apron spattered with food.

"I was following the purple string to find out who made these mittens, but a whale bit it off and now I'm lost," cried Emel, wiping her tears from her eyes with her mittens.

"Kids," said the man, shaking his head. "Come with me. You must be starving." And he took Emel into a big, shiny kitchen full of workers in white aprons and caps. She had never seen so much food in her life.

"Sit here," said the man, motioning to a small table in the corner. "Eat this," he said, setting down a huge plate of steaming food.

Emel ate the food like a starving dog. She had never tasted anything so good in her life. "Thank you," she said when she was done. "I have to go find my string now."

Emel walked and walked. She walked to the edge of the city and out into the country and along a busy road with cars and trucks zooming by. Everything in this country was strange. Everything was so big and shiny and noisy. And cold. It began to snow. Emel shivered in her dark dress and pulled her scarf tighter around her face. *Funny. Without my string I feel everything.* She thought of her mother and father, her brother, her friend, Mia. She sat down at the side of the road and tried not to cry.

Honk! The huge sound came from right behind her. Then a giant, whooshing sound. "Hey, young lady. What are you doing there?" Emel looked up to see the biggest truck she'd ever seen in her life. The driver had her head stuck out the passenger window. "You're going to freeze to death wandering around without a jacket. Hop in. I'll give you a lift." She opened the door and Emel climbed up.

"Name's Betsy," the woman said, holding out her hand. "You look like you've been on the road for a long time. Been on the road myself for ten days now. Miss the husband and kids something fierce. Got a boy about your age, a girl probably younger. What those two don't get into! Got three dogs and a couple of stray cats to boot, a few assorted goldfish, and a rabbit we're feeding directly out of the garden." The driver threw back her head and laughed, and continued to talk all day as they drove through some very large and snowy mountains, much larger than the ones Emel had crossed. Emel listened politely, but she never took her eyes off the road as she watched for a glimpse of purple string. It began to snow again, and Betsy turned on the truck's big wipers.

"By the way, where are you going anyway?" asked Betsy finally.

"I was following a purple string," she explained, "but it broke and I lost it, and now I'll never know who made these purple mittens." She held up her mittens to show the driver, taking her eyes off the road for just an instant.

"Hmm, I see," said the driver. "And why do you need to know who made your purple mittens, nice as they are?"

"I want to know why they made them," Emel explained, "and how they got to our camp."

"This string," Betsy asked, "does it look like that?" She pointed to the windshield where a piece of string had got caught on the wipers swishing back and forth.

Emel held her breath and squinted her eyes until she spotted the string. "No, that's yellow. The string I'm looking for is purple, like my mittens." She sniffed loudly.

"Hmm," said Betsy. It was night when they left the mountains behind. They drove for hours across a wide, flat, snow-covered land.

I will never see my string again, Emel thought as she stared out the window. She wasn't looking for the string anymore; she wasn't looking at the stars or anything in particular. Instead, she imagined her family and friends sitting in their tents crying. *I may never see my parents or my brother or my friends again. What a foolish girl I am to go chasing this silly string!*

There was a large, whooshing sound again, and the truck began to slow down. "What's this?" asked Betsy as she pumped the brakes.

Emel turned to look. There were cars stopped on the dark road ahead. Red lights flashed as a man in a uniform waved his arms for them to stop.

"What's the problem, officer?" asked Betsy as they drove up.

"There's a huge tangle of wool tying up traffic," the officer said, shaking his head. "It must have fallen off the back of a truck. I've called for the Scissors of Life. It'll take us half an hour to clear it all away—"

"Did you say wool?" Emel asked. "What colour is it?"

"Colour?" the officer said, rubbing his chin. "Well, I suppose it's purple."

"It's my string!" Emel yelled. Betsy and the officer jumped.

"*Your* string?" the officer asked. But Emel ignored him.

"Betsy, thank you very much for the ride. I have to get out here."

"You're welcome," said Betsy. "Good luck," she called, and Emel closed the door and ran up to the purple pile on the road. There were three cars and two trucks full of people inside the twisted tangle.

"You'll be out soon," Emel said. "Thank you for finding my string." She walked around the edge of the pile until she found what she was looking for.

"A-ha," Emel said. One strand of purple wool led away from the pile and down a road towards a small town just off the highway. "Thank you, everyone," she called as she waved goodbye.

A sign at the side of the road said *Welcome to Elbow, Saskatchewan, Canada.* "That's a weird name," laughed Emel. She picked up the woollen string and almost ran as she followed it into the town, just as the sky in the east began to glow red. Elbow had one main street and two smaller streets on each side, each lined with tidy wooden houses. The purple string led to a little yellow house surrounded by huge banks of snow. Lights were on inside and smoke rose from the chimney.

Emel followed the string to the front door, where it disappeared through the crack at the bottom. She didn't know what to do. *Well, I've come this far,* she thought and pounded on the door with her fist.

"Door's open and the coffee's on," called a voice from inside.

Emel opened the door. Inside was a man in a shiny chair with wheels on it. "Hello, young lady," the man said. "You're going to catch your death of a cold running around like that—" The man stopped. He squinted. "Where'd you get those mittens?"

Emel looked down at her hands. "Someone sent them to me. I wanted to find out who made them, so I followed the string. It came to your house."

"Oh, it did, eh?" said the man. "Let's see. Bring them here." Emel had never seen a wheelchair before. She couldn't take her eyes off it. "Oh, don't worry about this," laughed the man. "It won't bite. Took a walk off a barn roof a couple years ago. Seems like part of me now." He patted one wheel as if it were his horse. "By the way, the name's Oscar." He held out his hand.

"My name's Emel," she said as the man's hand swallowed hers. She held out her mittens. They were a bit dirty.

Oscar held them up close, turned them over. "Yup, these are mine all right. I always do that little squiggle thing in the corner there, eh? See?"

But Emel was too surprised to look. *"You* made these?"

Oscar laughed. "Yeah, what were you expecting? A little old lady in a rocking chair?" He laughed again. "I started knitting after my accident. Made a pair for the wife. She was always complaining that her hands got cold shovelling the walk." He laughed some more. "Hey, a guy's got to help around the house. Made her a scarf, too, and then I started making them for the Mitten Tree."

Emel frowned. "What's a mitten tree?"

"Well, Emel, every Christmas in this town, I put up a Mitten Tree in Happy's store, see?"

Emel looked around. She didn't see anything, certainly not a tree. Not a Happy Store either, whatever that was.

"You don't even know what Christmas is, do you?"

Emel shook her head. "I've heard of Bart Simpson," she said, hopefully.

Oscar laughed and laughed. "You're a real card, kid." He slapped his knee. "I got an idea. Come with me."

Oscar wheeled himself over to the door, pulled a heavy coat from a low hook, put it on, then grabbed a pair of mittens on a string and slung the string around his neck.

"Excuse me," said Emel, "what's the string for anyway?"

"String?" Oscar asked. "Oh, this string. Why, it holds your mittens up when you take them off, so they don't drop in the snow and slush and get all wet. Plus, it keeps you from losing them, too. Unless you lose both of them." And he threw back his head and laughed some more. "Follow me," he said.

Oscar opened a door and led them down a ramp into a dark, cold room. Another larger chair with fat rubber wheels sat in the middle. It had a bendy pole with an orange flag on it and a sign on the back that said *Commit Random Acts of Kindness and Senseless Acts of* . . . Emel couldn't read the rest. It was covered with ice and snow.

Oscar wheeled up beside the big chair and hoisted himself into it. He turned, patted the chair back behind him. "Hop on," he said. "And hang onto me." Then he pressed a button, and a big door raised itself open to the ceiling. Oscar and Emel wheeled out into the snowy driveway.

Emel shut her eyes, then tried to open them. But she had to keep one mitten over her face. "Ohhh," she said, "it's so bright."

Oscar glanced around, laughing again as he turned onto the road. "Yup, sure is. All that morning sunlight bounces right off the snow and into your eyes, eh. You can go blind if you're out long enough."

This is a strange country, thought Emel as they raced down the flat, white street. Oscar honked and waved at everyone out walking and driving. They all waved, honked, and hollered back.

"Merry Christmas, Oscar."

"Who's your friend?" a man asked.

"Name's Emel. We're headed for the Mitten Tree," called Oscar.

"Sure looks good this year," said a little old lady.

"Filling up fast," said another.

This country is weird, Emel thought. Almost every house she saw had a green tree growing inside by a big window, and every one of them was covered with lights and glittering balls and ropes that were shiny and red.

"Are those mitten trees?" she asked, her mouth beside Oscar's ear.

"Those are Christmas trees," said Oscar. He turned to look at her. Emel shrugged. "I'll explain in a minute," he said.

Suddenly, he veered towards a building that said General Store.

"Hold on," he yelled. He wheeled his chair up the ramp, hit the brakes, and slid to a stop in front of the door.

"I'll get it," said Emel as she jumped off and lifted the metal latch. As the door swung open, a little bell tinkled. It reminded her of a goat's bell back home. That seemed like such a long way away.

"Morning, Oscar," called a bald little man with a white apron and a big smile.

"Morning, Happy. I've brought my friend, Emel here, to show her the Mitten Tree. Emel, this is Happy."

"How do you do?" Emel said politely. She had never before been in a store that had so many things. Her eyes didn't know where to look.

"Here," said Happy, holding out a glass jar full of red and white striped shepherd's crooks. "Have a candy cane."

"Thank you," she said, putting it into the pocket of her dress.

"There it is," said Oscar.

"Ohhh," she cried. In the corner of the store, beside some floppy boots and shiny shovels, stood a large green tree. *Just like the ones in all the windows,* she thought. But this tree was covered with mittens, hanging in pairs. Green ones, yellow ones, purple and grey ones, blue ones, and red ones, too. Some of them had snowflakes on them; some had zigzag patterns. There were mittens with two and three different colours of wool mixed together, even mittens with trees and fields of snow and houses. Some of the mittens were tiny, for babies, and some were very large. "It's the most beautiful tree I've ever seen," she said.

"Yes, well," Oscar said, "you see, everyone in town knits mittens and hangs them on the tree. Then we send them off to places in the world where children need them."

Emel picked up a pair of yellow mittens. She stroked the soft wool and held it to her cheek. "Why would you do that?" she asked.

Oscar seemed surprised by the question. "Beats me," he said with a shrug.

Emel turned and looked at him. "You mean you don't know why you made mittens for me and my little brother and all the other kids in our camp? I came all this way to find out, and you don't even know? What kind of crazy country is this?"

Oscar stared at her for a minute, then threw back his head and laughed.

"I'm serious," Emel said, her frown getting deeper.

Oscar frowned right back. "Well," he said, "the winters are real long and cold here, and there's not much good on TV—" He stopped, but Emel continued to glare at him. "I don't know, I guess it's just part of the Christmas spirit."

"What do you mean?" Emel asked, still staring hard. She wasn't leaving without a good answer.

Oscar squirmed in his chair. Happy coughed behind the counter. Emel shifted her weight from one sandal to the other, waiting.

"Do you believe we should love each other and help those who need help?" Oscar stopped and looked at her.

Emel nodded.

"Well," he continued, "so do we. Especially at Christmas. We decorate trees and give gifts to people we . . . you know . . . love."

"Yes, but you don't even know us. You've never seen me before. I'm just a kid in a ragged dress in a refugee camp a long way away. How can you say you love us?"

"Whoa," laughed Oscar. He looked at Happy, who just smiled and shrugged his shoulders.

Then Oscar stopped laughing. His face got very serious. He looked Emel in the eye and said, "You're not so different from us. You got hopes and dreams just like me. I just wanted to help, that's all. No big deal."

Tears welled up in Emel's eyes, and one fat, juicy tear rolled down her left cheek and spattered on Happy's floor. She held up her two hands in her purple mittens. "Thank you for these beautiful mittens," she said.

"You're very welcome, little lady," Oscar replied. "Thank you for coming so far to find me."

"I want to go home now," sniffed Emel.

"I know," said Oscar. "But before you go, want to learn a string trick? Camilla the Clown taught it to me in the hospital."

Emel nodded, swiping away tears with her mittens.

"Okay," Oscar said, "now take off your mitts, and hold out your hands like this."

Emel held them out as Oscar began to wind the purple string between her two hands, around her fingers, back and forth, in and out, until it looked like a spider's web. "The trouble with this trick," said Oscar, "is that it makes you very sleepy."

"Emel, wake up." It was her mother's voice. It sounded very far away.

"Emel!" That sounded much closer.

"No," she muttered. "I want to stay in my dream."

"Dream! How can you dream in a place like this? It's time to get up!" Her mother shook her again.

Emel opened her eyes. She was back in her tent in the camp. *Oh no,* she thought. *I didn't say goodbye to Oscar.*

She sat up slowly. Her purple string lay tangled in her hands. Her father was sitting there watching with a smile on his face. "I know," he said. "Sometimes we don't want to come back from the wonderful places we visit at night."

"Poppa," she cried, "I dreamed I went to a country where they have lots of snow, with trees inside their houses, and special trees covered in mittens."

"That's funny," Omar snickered.

"Mmm," her father said, "it sounds like a very strange country." He looked at his wife. "What do you think it means?"

His wife just smiled and shrugged. "It's a child's dream."

"No, Momma. So many people in the dream were kind to me. Everywhere, people helped me follow the string and find the man who made our mittens. And he showed me a mitten tree. It was covered with mittens. The whole town makes them for kids like us."

"Why?" her father asked. "Why would they do such things for people they don't even know?"

"Because they care, Poppa. The world is full of good people who care." Emel took a big breath and smiled at her family. "It means beyond the fence, beyond the desert and those mountains, there is hope for us, Poppa. We must remember that every day until we are free."

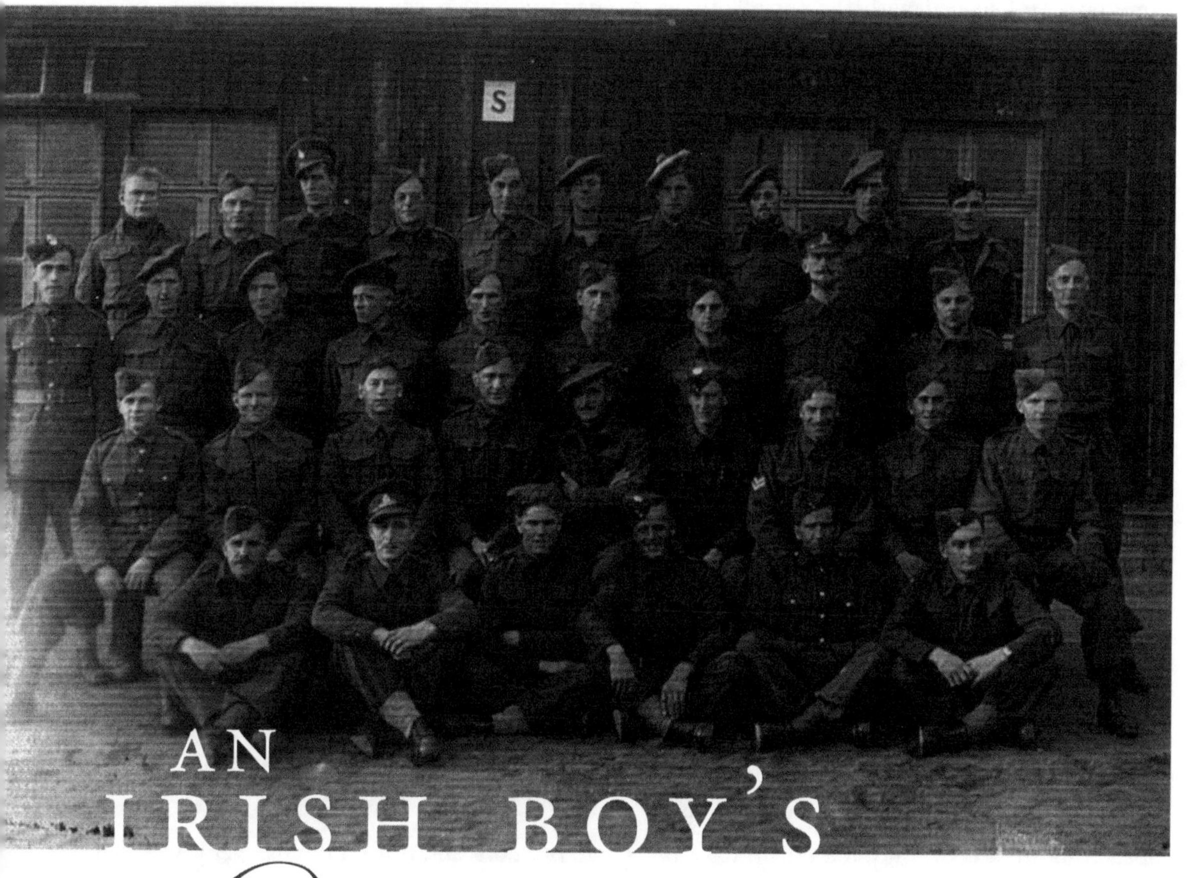

AN IRISH BOY'S *Christmas in Verdun*

I was born at home on Gertrude Street in Verdun, at the Irish end of Montréal. That was in October of '36. Mom told me the doctor came over and helped with the birth. His fee was twenty dollars, which my dad paid off at two dollars a month.

Verdun, Griffentown, Goose Village, Point St. Charles—they should have been painted green on the map. Oh sure, there was a smattering of French Canadians, a few Jews and Poles and what have you, but there must have been a quarter-of-a-million Irish living there in those days. Maybe more.

When the war started, Dad enlisted and left. That was in '39. He was older than most of the men who joined—about twenty-seven. He didn't have to go, but he and his buddies all hung together in everything—so he went. I was only three then, so I hardly remembered him. Just a vague smell of tobacco and a scratchy uniform at the railway station. Otherwise, he was the stranger in the picture on my mother's bedside table. It didn't really bother me not to have my father around. Now my brother, Danny . . . two-and-a-half years older . . . yes, it bothered him. From my point of view, life was great. None of my friends had their fathers either, except for the French kids—not so many of their dads went overseas. But lots of Irish did, and we just never thought things should be any different.

We didn't know we were poor; we didn't know what we didn't have. Everyone else was in the same boat. The only money coming in was what the army sent from Dad's pay.

One day, Mother got a telegram on thin white paper saying Dad was killed in action at Dieppe. It gave his full name, rank, and serial number. Mother refused to believe it. I don't know why—I guess she just had a feeling. I still had my uncles, who were in their teens and too young to fight. Mind you, they were uncles, not fathers, and there wasn't much direction from them, so my brother and I were pretty well free to do as we pleased.

It was a safe, comfortable, friendly area to live. There was no family we didn't know. Montréal may have been our city, but Verdun was our village. There was no danger, no crime among people in the area because everything was solved within our own groups. If something happened, we'd deal with it in our own way. You knew the rules. No one had to enforce them. If you had a disagreement, you solved it immediately. Fists were first choice. Even if the older guys got into an argument on the street and ran back up to the house, our mothers would say, "Go back out." They weren't going to sleep anyway that night, they'd be so uptight. So they'd go back out and finish off whatever it was they'd started. It was totally acceptable. No one ever thought twice about it. And you lived with that because if you didn't deal with it, it affected your whole family. Our neighbours had lived in Verdun for a whole generation or two. So if your father did something, you lived with that. If your big brother did something, you lived with that, too.

The area was all triplexes in three-storey buildings. We lived on the third floor. An outdoor, spiral staircase ran up to the second floor to our door. Then an indoor staircase went up to the third. There was a pull cord, so if someone rang the bell downstairs, we'd pull a cord that stretched along through loops and opened the door down on the second floor. That way we didn't have to walk down all the time to let people in. Anyway, the door was never locked.

Our house was probably built around the turn of the century: solid brick, clean, with a stained glass window in the living room and hardwood trim around the ceiling. A coal wood stove in the kitchen was our only heat for five rooms. They were all coldwater flats. A good percentage of Montréal had already got rid of coldwater flats, but I didn't know that. Our homes would have been uncomfortable to the average person, but it was what we were used to, and we didn't think anything of it. My room was the den at the back of the house, and there was no heat there. I had guppies, and if they weren't hardy enough to skate then they were in trouble because it would just about freeze in winter.

We loved the streets. We'd get home from school and couldn't wait to head back out. All of us kids wore rubber boots, made by Dominion Rubber, with the tops rolled down. Inside we had heavy wool socks that were soaking all the time. If they didn't get wet from the snow, they were soaking from the sweat, because there was no breathing in those things. In school, we used to take everything off in the cloakroom and hang it up, and when we got home, we played around in the snow until it was dark out.

In the war years, all the tradesmen used horses and sleds in winter. Even the city used horses to plough the street. They'd just grade it off into huge piles on the side to make it accessible for the men delivering bread, milk, coal, and everything else. It was great for us because we could build forts right on the street and jump on them from the roofs. We knew the milkman, J.J. Joubert, the Palm Bakery man, the iceman. The iceman wore a piece of canvas or rubber on his back and had to walk with that block of ice on his back up to the third floor, day in and day out, in every house. He didn't get very much for his troubles, maybe fifteen to twenty-five cents max. Sometimes the delivery people would let us work on the sleigh with them to keep us from stealing. If they didn't, as soon as they stopped to make a delivery, we'd grab something and run. Sometimes they let us ride for a couple of blocks, and sometimes we'd go out of town right over to Caughnuwaga, the reserve, or to Chateauguy. That's the only time we ran into the Québécois or the Indians. It was another world. The bad roads and lack of rides kept us pretty close to home.

Everyone kept coal at the back in little sheds that were maybe twelve feet from the houses. The rats always scurried for cover when we went out to get coal in the morning. We never kept the fire going all night. It was too expensive. We'd build it up before we went to bed and let it go out. It was always somebody's job to shovel the coal into a metal coal scuttle. I don't know who did it first, but we used to jump from the house to the shed, because the shed was probably ten feet lower than the building. If you didn't make it you'd hit a corrugated steel wall, and break your leg for sure. But you had to do it, or you'd be considered a real coward. So everyone did it.

The winter was a beautiful time. We never thought of it as being cold. It was just great to have snow. There wasn't the pollution—at least you didn't see it on the snow, and it was always fresh. We never felt cold because we weren't spending all our time in a superheated area, so we were accustomed to it.

I was skinny like most of the kids. We ate a lot of porridge. Bread was dirt cheap. Milk was, too. During the war they used to give you coupons, little blue coupons with holes in them, so you had bread and milk with a little brown sugar on it, and you were living really high. It seemed to keep the ghosts away because we never got sick. We also ate a lot of baloney—which we called "Point St. Charles steak" because the people there were even poorer than we were.

Initially, people settled in areas like Griffentown and Goose Village. Then when you got a little better off, you moved to The Point, then into Verdun. Our fathers all worked on the Great Lakes boats or the Grand Trunk Railway or the Victoria Bridge, where they were coin collectors in the tollbooths. I suspect a fair amount of the coins that were collected went into paying for their homes. Some of the men were longshoremen—dock workers. Or they worked at the abattoir between Point St Charles and the Village. Or maybe for the breweries. The Black Horse Brewery was in "the Griff." There weren't lots of jobs to be had until the war, when the men went overseas.

We shared the things we had, did it without even thinking about it. If there was anything at all, it was there for whoever was around. If we had a gathering and a bunch of people came over to our house, mother sent us out to sell some empty bottles for a couple of cents each to buy a few items. There was always enough food in the house.

Grocery stores put you on a tab because very few people had money. Stores had these thick pads with your name written along the side. They kept a running record of whatever you owed. They never seemed to push you. I don't know how they did that. Most of the stores were owned by the French, like the Brossois family. Old lady Steinberg had the grocery store on Wellington. Not too much was owned by the Irish. We weren't into that. We were pretty much first generation and hadn't established ourselves in any businesses yet.

My dad didn't have any family records, never could find any. We suspected that my grandmother's sister was his real mother. She was the younger sister, and when she got "in the family way," she went off to Australia to have the baby. People were quite embarrassed about it in those days. When she came back, she gave her son to my grandmother. Dad never really knew any of this for sure. It wasn't talked about then.

My mother's mother was Irish. My mother's father came over to Canada with a wife and four children and had one more when they got here. He worked as a cabin boy on the *Empress of Ireland*. When it sunk, he survived and saved a few peoples' lives. We read about him in a book that was published. After the sinking, he didn't hang around. Grandma and her five kids stayed with a family in central Montréal. My mother was the oldest and left home by the time she was thirteen. Grandma put her into a school, a French convent across the road. The family didn't even know it was a convent. That's how little they cared about it.

A lot of my buddies played hockey, but I never played any organized sports whatsoever, not even shinny. My brother, Danny, and I belonged to the Kinsmen Boys' Club, where we boxed. It didn't cost much, and we all used the same gloves. Someone there knew something about boxing and showed us the ropes. We spent parts of our days in winter playing ping-pong and boxing. It was just two streets up and around the corner. It was a great little club, the only one around.

At night and during the day—if we weren't in school—we hopped the buses and went along Wellington Street, which had lots of shops. Sometimes, we went right up to the Montreal Forum. The buses had a drainage ledge below the rear window that we'd hang onto. Once in a while, the drivers stopped and chased us, and when they got back in to drive, we hopped back on. We had these woollen mitts that were always wet, and as soon as we put them on the metal, they stuck. We lost many pairs of mitts that way. You could see a bus going down the street with mitts frozen on the back.

We travelled Wellington from one end of town to the other. There weren't many cars because it was the war, but the few around might belong to some guy who had a decent job or a good business, or maybe to one of the priests—they had the Cadillacs.

During our Christmas holidays, we went to the old movie theatre—we called it "Bugsville"—and paid twelve cents for a movie. The seats were all falling apart, but the movies were great. They catered to everybody's dream. It was nice to see the whole world happy.

One day, mother got a letter from the army. It turns out they'd made a mistake: Dad wasn't dead after all. He'd been shot up badly in Dieppe and lost a lung, but the Germans had patched him up, and he was now in a prison camp, Stalag 8-B, near the Polish border. A little later, we got a letter from him. Dad had been with a special force of one hundred and seventy-six men who landed on the beach at Dieppe. Most were killed immediately. Only seventeen of them lived, seven from the Point.

If we got a tree, we always got it Christmas Eve because they were cheaper then. Otherwise we couldn't afford one. My uncles, who were teenagers and worked on the boats, came back just before Christmas. They'd walk in with a tree they'd swiped off the lot, and Mother would say, "Don't you bring that tree in this house!" Then we'd just go without that year.

My uncles didn't have any direction either. They didn't have a father. One year, mother's oldest brother, Jimmy, brought a tree home that was about twelve feet high. Our ceiling was only eight feet, so my mother said, "That's of no use to us." I knew he must have bought it because she seemed ready to allow it in the house. It must have been cheap because it was too big for most people's houses. "You're going to have to trim it," Mother said. We didn't have a saw, so Jimmy borrowed one from a neighbour, and the next thing we know he brought it back up. He'd trimmed it by cutting the top off. Now we had this blunt Christmas tree. It just goes to show you we didn't know much about Christmas, didn't know that the tree was supposed to be pointed. We laughed about that for a long time.

We spent a lot of time together during the holidays. The fathers weren't around, but we had Mother's two brothers and two sisters. The sisters were younger than Mother, so they loved to play "mother" and take care of us, and we had a lot of tender care. They didn't live with us, but they were around often enough.

Our greatest pleasure was sitting in the kitchen by the stove, where it was warm. Everybody sat there. It was the main area of the house. We took our baths in the kitchen in a galvanized tub. Once a week, Mother would heat the water on the stove in a big pot or kettle, and pour the water in. The oldest got to go first. That was my brother.

Fudge was one of our Christmas treats. My mother and sisters loved to make it on the stove, and we'd all sit around licking our lips, waiting for it to cool. Toys were anything we could get our hands on. A Chiclet box made a great whistle if you blew in it. It used to drive my mother crazy. My Aunt Monica gave me a box once, and I remember them getting into an argument over that.

We didn't go to mass or church, not even at Christmas. We were open to make our own decisions on that. My mother was a Catholic who married Dad in the Protestant church—Grace Church at Point St. Charles. She had no time for Catholicism, so she never pushed us. My father wasn't religious either—and, of course, he wasn't around. In my mother's family, one side were strong Catholics, and the other side were strong Protestants. When the aunts and uncles tried to pick up the children to take them to mass, they'd have to meet them a block away from the house. There was no way they would mix. There was no friendship lost. That wasn't the case in our neighbourhood. All my friends were Catholic and going to church all the time. It didn't seem to have much effect on the way they behaved. They were just as bad as everyone else. But at least they could go get themselves forgiven once a week and start all over again.

On Christmas Eve, we made decorations and hung them on the tree: peppermint candy canes, toffee apples, paper snowflakes, and anything we'd made at school. Mother would give us a nickel each, and Danny and I'd race through the vacant lot across the street—where the snow always seemed ten feet high—and down to a store called Cheerios. They had all sorts of comic books, some second-hand, and you could get two for a nickel. This was paradise. We got our comics, ran home, and read them by the stove. We were in another world.

We always got a letter from Dad at Christmas. He never complained about the treatment he was getting. He felt the Canadians were much better off than the Poles who were in a prison camp right next to them. The Germans also knew that we were taking good care of their prisoners in Canada. Every fall, Mother took pictures of Danny and me down in Lafontaine Park in Montréal and sent them to him in prison camp. Some of the German guards liked to paint, so they hand-tinted Dad's pictures of us, and he sent them back. The Germans used to line up all the prisoners and take their picture, and Dad sent us one of those, too, every Christmas. They were all stamped *Stalag 8-B* on the back.

We didn't have a lot of gifts on Christmas morning. We got up with the thought that we had a few more days off school. That was happiness. We just went out and played, or walked up and down the streets of our city, looking at all the store windows, looking at the covers of sports newspapers and magazines. I can't remember any gifts of consequence. We never went running around saying, "Look what I got for Christmas!" The important thing was my buddies were off, too, so we could play together.

There was always a nice dinner. Mother made roast beef with blood pudding and invited her sisters and brothers over. It was a little more special with people around. Someone bought some cheap kosher wine, and us kids all had a sip. After dinner, we lay around the living room listening to the radio. It was great. My friends and I loved *Boston Blackie, The Green Hornet.* I liked it because I could picture them so clearly in my mind, and my buddies, they had a different picture. At Christmas, of course, they had Christmas music and songs about the war, and sometimes we'd sing along.

I was always considered fairly lucky among my friends. I had a father coming back; they didn't. They'd either died in the war or just weren't coming back—they'd taken off. That wasn't uncommon. Quite a few of my buddies weren't high on their fathers. Their mothers were key. They held the family together.

When Dad came home after the war, I didn't get to see him. He had tuberculosis and went straight into the TB sanatorium at Ste. Agathe. I was too young to visit. My brother was older, so he and mother came back and told me the things he'd said, how the Germans were great dentists because they'd fixed all his teeth, and he never had any problems while he was over there. But he also had white splotches on his wrists because they'd kept him in chains and ropes for a year. I heard mother telling my uncles that he'd escaped twice, but never got very far. The Nazis threatened to shoot him if he tried again. At the end of war, the Germans took them on a forced march for weeks with hardly any food and water. Once again, the buddies from Verdun stuck close together and helped each other. Only one of them died.

One winter day before Christmas, long after the war and after Dad had been transferred to another sanatorium, the doorbell rang. I ran out and looked down to the second floor. A thin man looked up. He wore a long coat and hat, and had a big package under his arm. I went to Mother in the kitchen.

"There's a stranger downstairs," I said.

Mother came out and took a look. "That's your father," she said, and ran down to let him in.

I was twelve at the time. I'd spent most of those years without a father, never even missing him, always surrounded by family and friends. I knew then that my life was going to change, but I didn't know if it'd be good or bad. The package he carried was a gift for my brother and me. It was an electric train set.

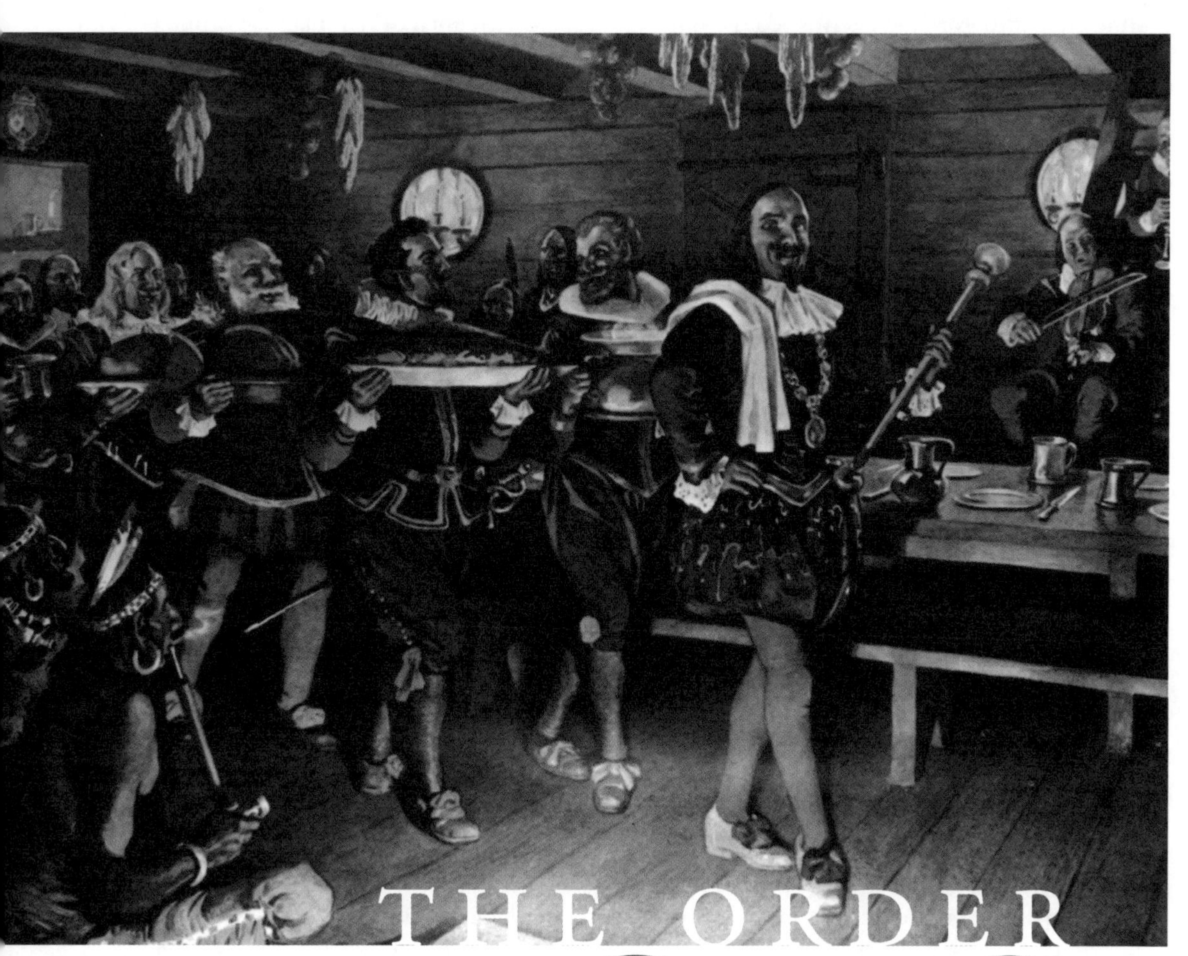

THE ORDER of Good Cheer

"*Mon Dieu!* Are you trying to freeze us to death?" Jean de Biencourt, seigneur de Poutrincourt, stamped his shoes on the frozen ground, his reed torch flickering dangerously close to his hat.

"No," laughed Samuel de Champlain. "Look! We are ready!" He turned, gestured to a man in a stained brown apron. "If you please," he said.

The stonemason-turned-baker stepped forward, shivering and bareheaded. He bent down and touched his own torch to a square of pine needles piled high on the hard-packed dirt. The needles ignited and flashed upward, an orange gash in the black night, lighting the faces of the dozen gentlemen gathered around.

"Bravo!" they shouted.

"Quickly! The others!" Champlain pointed to five more mounds of dry needles. As the baker lit each one, flames shot up to mingle with the papery stars sprinkled across the sky.

"What a spectacle!" exclaimed Louis Hébert, the apothecary, clapping his hands to applaud as well as to warm them. Six columns of fire now illuminated the group, casting grotesque shadows across the courtyard and onto the walls and steep roofs of the log buildings around them.

"But what's underneath the pine needles?" inquired Marc Lescarbot, his long coat thrown open as he stood close to the flames and warmed his hands. One could almost see his keen lawyer's mind turning as he worked to solve the mystery.

"Ah, I think I know," said Francois Gravé, sieur de Pontgravé. He was finely dressed, as befitted a merchant from St. Malo, the very town from which Jacques Cartier had first sailed to the New World seventy-two years before. "You are roasting hazelnuts," he said, a smile of satisfaction on his face.

"No," replied Champlain, grinning. "But that's a good guess. These are, perhaps, nuts of the sea." He pointed to the first pile that had been lit. They watched as the fires died down and black, and curving shapes emerged from the grey ash.

Membertou, the Mi'kmaq *sagamo* and their frequent guest, tilted his lanky frame as he peered into the smoking pile. He nodded, smiling, turned to his wife, and said something to her.

Champlain looked at him. "Kindly tell me if you have guessed what they are."

The battle-scarred old chief grinned. "You call them *les moules* in your tongue."

Champlain grinned. "Well done! You are right."

"Mussels!" exclaimed Poutrincourt. "I've never seen such a thing!" He winked at the gentlemen around him. "It is perhaps blasphemous what you have done to this delicacy, Champlain."

Champlain replied with a laugh. "Then our good king will have to put all the citizens of Brouage to the stake, for this recipe comes from my hometown." He knelt and poked the pine needles with a stick to ensure that they had all burned. "There," he said, standing again, satisfaction glowing on his face, "we have brought another piece of French culture and cuisine to L'acadie. I thought it would be a fitting way to begin our dinner this *Noël.*"

"Will we have to eat standing up and freezing at the same time?" asked Pontgravé, wrapping his black, woollen cloak tightly around him, his words coming in steaming puffs. "I don't remember this custom in Paris." Laughter rippled through the group.

Champlain, feigning disgust, looked at each man, searching for something. "Ahh," he said finally, his eye on his quarry. "Young Charles, would you please lend me your elegant chapeau?"

"My hat!" The young man looked surprised. "But it's freezing. I'll catch my death from the cold."

"And what a grand death it will be in the service of our order. We will remember your selfless gesture fondly in our eulogies—after dinner, of course." The gentlemen roared with laughter as the young man, Charles Biencourt, reluctantly removed his handsome hat and handed it over.

"Bon." Champlain grabbed the large thing and waved it over the smouldering piles, fanning the ashes off the boards and onto the ground.

"So," said Poutrincourt, "the chef reveals his art."

There, resting on six pine boards, all neatly arranged in circles around a centre cross, were black mussels, their shells open like the mouths of baby crows, succulent round tongues of meat from the sea, silently beckoning. "My friends, I present to you *l'éclade!"* More muffled applause from gloved hands. "Now, will some of you be so kind as to pick these up. We must adjourn to the kitchen with haste, where the rest of our meal awaits. And then to the table."

With more bantering and laughter, the boards were retrieved and quickly carried through the nearest door into the cookhouse. The low room was redolent with smoke and herbs and the fragrance of fine cooking. Several bakers and cooks worked at a sturdy plank table in front of the fireplace. Under hanging metal and glass candle lanterns, they put the finishing touches on wooden platters and pewter plates piled high with steaming food.

"Champlain, my mouth is flowing like the river Seine at the sight!" exclaimed Lescarbot.

"Good! I'm flattered," said Champlain. "Anticipation is the best appetizer, *n'est-ce pas?"*

"No," interjected Hébert, "I believe hunger is. Is it your intention to starve us much longer?"

"I see that you are wasting away, Louis, and it disturbs me deeply." Champlain laughed, as he placed a silver metal chain around his own neck and picked up a carved and polished wooden sceptre. "Are we ready, gentlemen?" he asked, rapping the stick on a post. Each man in the group picked up a dish from the table and held it high. With élan, Champlain tossed a folded serviette over his right shoulder, and nodded to one of the cooks, a well-travelled sailor. "Riopelle, will you do us the honour of piping in His Majesty's Most Loyal Order of Good Cheer."

Riopelle, a sturdy man with a ruddy face, produced a wooden flute from his pocket, fell in behind Champlain, and began to play a rousing French reel.

Champlain stopped suddenly, held up his hand and turned around. "I'm sorry, my good man, but as this is the night of the *Noël,* although we have no priests to scrutinize our proceedings on this far and wild shore, I do think we should prefer a tune more in keeping with the spirit of the Holy Nativity."

"Oh, yes, of course, sir . . . please forgive—"

Champlain smiled and clapped him on the shoulder. "Play then, my good fellow, before these men drop their plates out of weakness from hunger."

"This is a pretty carol from Languedoc," said Riopelle, and he launched into "Shepherds in the Fields Abiding." Champlain nodded his approval and led the procession out of the kitchen. At the door of the common room, he stopped and knocked three times with his mace. The door swung open from within, and the procession entered.

The working men, soldiers, and sailors of Port Royal usually welcomed the gentlemen with boisterous applause and stamping of feet as they stood at their tables. But recognizing the Christmas hymn, they stood quietly, their hands folded awkwardly in front of them, as the procession wound around the room. Even the Mi'kmaq men and women, and the scattering of children who usually sat along the walls, sensed something different. One by one, the skin-clad visitors rose, too, smiling shyly as the parade of upper-crust French society passed by, tantalizing scents wafting after them.

Champlain, having circumnavigated the room, stopped at one end of the gentlemen's table in front of the large stone fireplace. A large birch log burned fiercely, casting silver flashes from the chain around Champlain's neck. He reached for his pewter goblet, already filled to the brim with red wine.

"Gentlemen of Port Royal, as it is my honour to be steward on this holy night, it is with great pleasure that I begin our evening by offering a toast to our beloved King of France and of this very ground upon which we stand—New France." Champlain lifted his drink high. "Long live Henry, King of France!" he declared, and the responding cries and cheers of the gentlemen, sailors, and tradesmen bounced off the thick wooden beams of the ceiling.

Champlain waited until the noise died down. "And one more, gentlemen—but surely not the last this evening: to our most benevolent governors, sieur de Monts, who at this moment must surely be suffering the hardships and deprivations of the King's court—" A roar of laughter erupted at the jibe. Champlain managed to keep a straight face, although the twinkle in his eye showed he was enjoying his joke. He turned and motioned to the other end of the high table. "And to our own courageous sieur de Poutrincourt, who proves his bravery not with words, but by his very presence with us." Poutrincourt bowed with mock solemnity at the compliment as Champlain lifted his wine once again. "Long live the sieurs de Monts and Poutrincourt." The men called out the names with gusto—especially that of Poutrincourt, whom they respected for risking his life to endure winter in this new land alongside them.

"Gentlemen, let's eat," called Champlain, and his companions settled down noisily on their wooden benches. Before them, brown tallow candles burned in pine candleholders that had been turned by Habitation carpenters at their foot-powered lathe. Sprigs of pine and red berries decorated the tables. Candle lanterns hung from the ceiling beams and along the hand-planed wooden walls. Shadows cavorted across every hewn plank, every white and tanned and tawny face. The gentlemen had first choice of the plates, which were then passed to the common workers and sailors at the other tables. The Mi'kmaq who squatted along the walls could only wait.

The mussels had been transferred to pewter platters and were plucked by eager hands as they made the rounds. Membertou passed them on without taking any. The Mi'kmaq did not eat mussels. Lescarbot, who'd had a sudden impulse to escape the drudgery of law books for adventure in the New World, reached into a black shell and popped the morsel into his mouth. His eyes looked to the ceiling as he savoured the taste. "Champlain," he said, "this is exquisite! Amazing how so simple a technique can capture the essence of both the forest and the sea, *n'est-ce pas?*" He paused for a moment, then added, *"La terre et la mer."*

"Always the poet," grumbled Champdoré, the boatbuilder, who'd joined the group late. He'd been out hunting, as tomorrow was his turn to be steward.

"And how was your luck today?" Champlain asked. He elbowed Hébert beside him while slurping the juice from a mussel. It was obvious from Champdoré's scowl how his luck had been.

"Not good," came the gruff reply. "I think you and your Mi'kmaq friends have cleaned out the forest around the entire bay."

"In that case, gentlemen, eat heartily," announced Champlain in a loud voice. "Hunter's excuses will make us a thin soup tomorrow." Champdoré smiled grimly, the eye in a storm of laughter.

Champlain turned to one of the sailors, whose duty it was to serve the tables that night. He waved him over. "We are ready for the pipe stuffings. You can start with Monsieur Champdoré there—he needs a little cheering up."

The sailor nodded, went to the fireplace, and retrieved a platter keeping warm by the coals. "Wine, *s'il vous plait,"* called Poutrincourt, and another sailor brought a large jug around.

Champdoré's eyes opened wide as the waiter offered him a pipe. The cheese fritter had been dipped in egg and fried to a golden brown. The boatbuilder picked one up in his thick, scarred fingers and popped it into his mouth. He chewed for an instant, struggling to maintain his scowl, but in the end was defeated. He nodded to himself, then looked to Champlain with a grudging smile. "You may be the king's cartographer, but it seems you can find your way around a kitchen as well." The gentlemen laughed as Champdoré quickly reached for another one.

Champlain received the compliment with a smile and a tilt of his wineglass. "Membertou, what do you think of our little French treat?" he asked of the Mi'kmaq *sagamo.*

The leathery-skinned leader chewed for a moment, then wiped some cheese from his wispy beard with the back of his hand. "Good," he pronounced. Champlain leaned back, smiling with satisfaction. "Just like beaver testicles." There was a momentary silence, then a roar of laughter—not just at Membertou's description, but at the wide-eyed shock on Champlain's face. Then Champlain himself joined in the laughter, and the merriment continued.

"Don't forget to serve some bread to our guests," Pontgravé called out. One of the waiters quickly disappeared and returned with a large basket. He made his way around the room, offering bread to the Mi'kmaq seated on the floor. The French baked every day except Sunday in their indoor oven. Membertou's wife tore off a large chunk and stuffed some in a skin bag. The French invited only the chiefs to sit at the gentlemen's table.

Pontgravé leaned over and whispered to Hébert. "I am sometimes relieved that there are no priests with us any longer," he said. "I enjoy our Mi'kmaq friends in their natural state."

Hébert nodded in agreement. "Can you imagine if there were Jesuits here?" he replied, watching their neighbours visit happily among themselves as they in turn watched the French. "It would be like setting foxes among the chickens."

"My friends!" Champlain called as he stood again, his back to the stone fireplace. "Our waiters are now ready to serve the entrées." He nodded to three men waiting for his signal. They immediately recovered dishes from near the fire and began to serve the gentlemen. "For your pleasure this holy evening, we present partridge with cabbage—" The men, especially the working men, oohed and ahhed their approval. "And," continued Champlain, swelling with pride as the hungry men's appreciation grew louder, "thanks to the generosity of our friend, Membertou, there is venison pie."

The noise level swelled as the plates made their rounds, and the conversation was accompanied by the happy clatter of knives and spoons on pewter plates. The two waiters serving wine were in constant motion. Many casks of good French wine were kept safe from freezing in the wine cellar.

Champlain surveyed the scene with his mapmaker's practised eye, his smile turning briefly to a frown as his eyes travelled the room. Louis Hébert leaned over to speak to him. "Congratulations, Samuel," he said nodding towards the noisy throng. "Your idea of creating this Order of Good Cheer is a brilliant success."

"Thank you, Louis," Champlain replied with a distracted nod. "Something had to be done. We've lost too many gallant Frenchmen over the last two winters to that hideous malady."

"And yet, you seem sombre all of a sudden, for a man who's responsible for this *tour de force.* Is something wrong?"

Champlain looked his friend in the eye. "You, as apothecary, know how helpless we feel in the face of this mysterious *mal de la terre.*" Champlain paused to drain his cup and motioned to the waiter, who filled it up again. "Yet I have come to believe," he continued, "that hard work, cheerful spirits, and good French cooking will prevent this sickness. That's why I thought our little order would provide a tonic. . . ."

Hébert leaned forward expectantly. "Yes?"

Champlain nodded again to the men happily devouring their feast. "Do you see anything unusual?"

Hébert looked carefully around the room. "Only that this fine meal you have so diligently prepared seems to be disappearing quickly." Lescarbot, having finished a conversation with Champdoré, now turned to join in.

"I counted the men," confided Champlain to the two of them. "There are four missing."

"My dear Samuel!" said Lescarbot. "They are in the kitchen preparing your next culinary coup!"

"No," Champlain shook his head grimly, "I sent someone to check."

"Well, then," said Hébert, wiping his mouth with a linen serviette, "it's very clear to me that you've worked them half to death, and they've disappeared in order to earn a well-deserved rest."

"Champlain," called Poutrincourt from the other end of the table, "this pheasant is perfect." The governor pursed his lips as he said it and kissed his thumb and fingers in that French salute to the best of good taste. But his questioning glance told Champlain he was curious about the discussion at that end of the table. The explorer was just about to rise when a sailor came through the door, leaned over behind him, and whispered in his ear. Champlain nodded and got up.

"Excuse me, please," he said gravely, "I have an errand to which I must attend." He nodded to Poutrincourt and left the common room behind the messenger.

"You were right, sir," the sailor said as he held a lantern up for the two of them. "They're in their beds." They hurried across the empty courtyard, past the six black smudges of ash. The thick, glass windows of the common room swirled with light and shadows that spilled out into the trampled grass and dirt.

"How many?" asked Champlain, his face grim.

"Four, sir."

They opened the heavy door to the tradesmen's quarters. It yielded with a squawk on its iron hinges. "Up here," said the sailor as he trod up wooden stairs to the loft.

They stooped under the sloping roof, the air cold and fragrant with the smell of sweat and furs and hay. The floor was covered with rows of mattresses stuffed with grass and reeds. On some of the beds, woollen blankets and furs were tossed carelessly; on others, they were neatly folded. Between the beds were the men's wooden trunks, where they kept clothes and the tools of their trade. The two men walked to the end of the row. A lantern cast a faint light on four shapes huddled on mattresses by a small stone chimney. The sailor held the lamp high as Champlain knelt down at one rumpled heap.

"Good evening," he said quietly, placing his hand on a shoulder. "Are you ill?"

The shape stirred, and a tousled mess of greasy hair turned to reveal a rough, bearded face. "Good evening, sir," the man said, managing a faint smile. "Sorry to miss supper."

"Are you sick?" Champlain asked again, grimacing at the man's awful breath.

"Oui," the man replied, closing his eyes momentarily. "I ache badly, sir."

"Where?" asked Champlain.

The man was slow to answer. Champlain shook his shoulder. "My bones. Everywhere."

Quickly, Champlain turned to the sailor holding the light. "Give me more light." The man lowered the lantern. Champlain pulled off the sick man's blankets, then pulled open his shirt and pulled it sideways to expose his shoulder. "Light!" Champlain barked. "Closer!"

The lantern dropped lower. Champlain raised the man's arm, looked, then covered him back up. "How are your teeth? Do they ache?" he asked.

"No," the man replied, "I don't think so."

"Good," said Champlain cheerfully. "You'll probably feel better in a day or two." He checked the other three men, then rose. "Can I send you some food, some soup perhaps, or wine?"

"Non, merci," came the unanimous reply.

"I'll ask Monsieur Hébert to stop by later," said Champlain. "He'll have a concoction that will make you feel better." Then he nodded to the sailor with the lantern and turned to go. "Goodnight, men. *Joyeux Noël."*

"Joyeux Noël," came one reply.

"God bless you, sir," said another.

The air back in the common room embraced Champlain like a warm glove. The men had had plenty of wine. Their flushed faces and raised voices were proof of that. Their plates were wiped clean.

"Gentlemen . . . men," called out Champlain, his steward's chain back in place around his neck. "I'm sorry to have been called away for a moment. Perhaps we can persuade Monsieur Pontgravé to provide us with a little music."

Pontgravé smiled and nodded his acceptance of the invitation. He rose from the bench and retrieved his lute from a cloth bag hanging from a peg on the wall. The merchant found a seat on a stool near the fire, the light shimmering on his silk shirt as he strummed the strings and made small adjustments to the tuning pegs.

Satisfied, he nodded respectfully to Poutrincourt and began to speak. "This instrument was made by a very famous German lutier in Bologna," he said. "My father brought it back on one of his trading trips. I mention this because the rose you see here" he said, holding up the richly varnished instrument and pointing out the circle of tiny holes cut into the soundboard under the strings, ". . . this rose is fashioned after the rose window of our beloved Notre Dame Cathedral." There were a few murmurs of appreciation from the craftsmen and from those who simply longed for some link to home.

Pontgravé began to play, his head bent in concentration over his instrument, his long hair in danger of becoming tangled in the strings. *"Il est né le divin Enfant."* With the first lilting notes, a respectful silence fell over the men, as aristocrats, gentlemen, tradesmen, and rough sailors listened, each with his private thoughts. Pontgravé played masterfully, his delicate fingers dancing lightly across the strings.

Champlain used the opportunity to slip into a seat beside Poutrincourt. The governor's head bent low as Champlain leaned towards him and announced in a whisper, "The land sickness—it is here."

Poutrincourt's dark eyes betrayed nothing of the awful message. *How formidable you must be at the king's court,* Champlain thought.

"How many?" asked the governor without looking at his cartographer, his gaze instead fixed on Pointgravé, who was now lost in his own music.

"Only four, so far," he replied. "Still in the early stages. But it is only December, and we still have four months of winter ahead of us."

"Good." Poutrincourt smiled broadly and leaned back nonchalantly to take a sip of wine.

A fine actor, too, Champlain decided.

"Have Hébert look at this," Poutrincourt continued. "We must try all of his remedies if we are to defeat this devilish curse."

"Yes, sir," said Champlain, rising just as three cooks arrived to retrieve the platters of meat from near the fire. They stood waiting while Pontgravé finished the carol.

"Thank you, good sir," said Champlain breezily to Pontgravé, "and thank you to your father and to the monks who instructed you so well in the musical arts." Pontgravé smiled his thanks.

"Gentlemen of Port Royal," Champlain continued, "another dish to tempt your palates and keep our friend Champdoré here awake this night. . . ." More laughter, including chuckles from the boatbuilder himself, whose mood had improved considerably. "From the beautiful, verdant forest at our doorstep, I humbly offer roast loin of moose with a savory wine sauce."

With a grand, exaggerated sweep of his arm, Champlain motioned the waiting servers into action. One waiter began to slice the meat. As he worked, another carried a plate of slices and served the gentlemen. Another followed behind and ladled out the sauce made from wine, port, and red currant jelly. The men once again became preoccupied as they fell upon this new dish with gusto.

As he took his seat again, Champlain looked around the room at the happy faces of the men enjoying their feast. *We lost thirty-five—almost half—of our men in that first horrible winter, another twelve last year. How many more will die? Is the melancholy of long, dark winters the true cause? I thought this raising of spirits would help. Perhaps not. I fear only God alone knows. Unless*—Champlain looked over at Membertou, at the small triangular purse he wore around his neck to show that he was an *aoutmin,* a physician–priest, as well as *sagamo—perhaps he knows of some cure.*

Champlain became aware of Hébert, who was watching him with an inquiring look. "After dinner," he said quietly, "we must talk." With that, the steward of the evening drew himself back into the conversation at their table. Membertou was recounting his sighting of French ships when they had first arrived off the coast.

"A young woman of our people once dreamed that floating islands of wood came to our shores," the *sagamo* said. "They had leafless trees and bears that roamed on them. When we first saw white men's ships, we believed the dream had come true. But the bears turned out to be fishermen." Laughter. Membertou continued. "We traded with them—blankets, knives, and fishhooks." No one was eating. All eyes were on him.

A fascinating man! thought Champlain. *Brutal warrior one minute, storyteller in another.*

"Then one day we saw the ships of your Jacques Cartier. Many canoes went out to welcome them and trade." The Mi'kmaq *sagamo* was at least one hundred years old. Champlain guessed that he must have been in his twenties when Cartier first arrived in 1534. "But the sailors fired guns over our heads—we called them thundersticks—so we paddled back to shore. Soon they sailed away." He paused. "I never saw Cartier again. We heard he captured some of our Iroquois neighbours and killed them. We were happy it wasn't us."

"Cartier didn't kill them," Pontgravé interjected. "He brought two boys back to France and taught them French, then returned them to their home the next summer. Cartier came from my town, St. Malo," he explained to Membertou. "The following spring, he took ten people home with him, including those same boys and their father, the *sagamo.*" Pontgravé paused briefly. "They all died a few years later, from the pox."

Membertou nodded without expression. "Yes, many of our people have died from this pox, as you call it."

"We have our own maladies to worry about," Hébert added darkly.

"Gentlemen, gentlemen," exclaimed Champlain, banging his hand lightly on the table. "Enough of this melancholy talk. This is a night to celebrate the holy birth and life everlasting." He smiled broadly. "And what is life without dessert and a warm *digestif?*"

The mapmaker jumped to his feet. "I need you men in the kitchen," he said, pointing to the six gentlemen on the bench nearest to the fire. "Lescarbot, as you are the closest thing we have to a priest here—" The men laughed, for the agreeable lawyer was well known for his ribald humour. "Perhaps you would read the story of the Nativity while we set off in search of delicacies and, of course, more wine." The last was received with loud approval.

Lescarbot, his mischievous smile transforming into a pious frown, rose to retrieve his Bible from the oak mantel. He opened it to the ribbon mark he had placed there earlier, looked up, waited for the men in the room to quiet. "I'll read two passages, the first from Luke and the second from Matthew." He began to read:

At that time, the Emperor Augustus ordered a census to be taken throughout the Roman Empire. When this first census was taken . . .

Champlain and his colleagues stood at the door to listen, for Lescarbot had the rich, mellifluous voice of a storyteller. The room was still, save for the wavering candles and the hypnotic light of the fire. The men stared at their plates, at the candle flames, at nothing as they listened, lost in the beauty of the old and sacred story, or in thoughts of their families at home so far away. After a few moments Champlain and the gentlemen stole away to the kitchen.

. . . and when they saw the child with his mother Mary, they knelt down and worshipped him. They brought out their gold, frankincense, and myrrh, and presented them to him.

Lescarbot looked up, closed the book carefully, crossed himself, then rose and quietly put the

Bible back on the mantle. "Well read, sir," said Poutrincourt as Lescarbot sat down. Slowly, fitfully, the conversations resumed, much subdued by the aura that had enveloped the room. Through the windows, a faint light shone. The sky had cleared and a half moon had risen, its cold, steady light glinting in the wavy glass.

The door burst open. The six gentlemen trooped in, Champlain behind them, marching around the room once again with plates held high. Young Charles staggered with a large earthenware crock, which he quickly set down. "We end this holy evening," called out Champlain, "with prune and marzipan tarts smothered in a frothy wine sauce." Champlain stopped as the men hooted with delight. "You'll be happy to know our cooks soaked the prunes in Armagnac overnight." More laughter. "And," Champlain continued, cheerfully holding up his hand for quiet, "macaroons fresh from the oven." The cheers grew even louder. "Remember, if you find them not to your liking, we will send all of them home with Membertou and his friends." Membertou turned and laughed as well. The warm cookies were being offered to the Mi'kmaq along the wall, who received them happily and took tiny bites to prolong the enjoyment.

"Now drain your cups, if you will," Champlain continued, "and Charles will be happy to fill them with *hippocras* to sweeten your dreams." An astonished murmur rose up from the men as they anticipated the warmed red wine, sweetened with sugar and spiced with nutmeg, cinnamon, peppercorns, and ginger. The perfume from it mingled with the fragrance of almond pastries, wood smoke, and candles.

The desserts were quickly demolished. Old Membertou grew restless and appeared ready to leave. Jean de Biencourt, seigneur de Poutrincourt, rose from his chair at the end of the gentlemen's table. The room fell quiet.

"I have no doubt," Poutrincourt began, "that when word of this evening's exquisite dinner reaches Paris, the good chefs of *rue aux Ours* will be quaking in their boots." Applause and laughter greeted the high compliment. Champlain, smiling broadly, rose and bowed to Poutrincourt and to the men, who cheered all the louder.

"Samuel de Champlain," Poutrincourt continued, "you have set new standards for the Order of Good Cheer. From the bottom of our stomachs, we thank you."

"Three cheers for Monsieur Champlain," a sailor cried lustily. And the men, Champdoré included, responded with a rousing chorus.

Champlain rose again. "Please also include in your thanks all the cooks and bakers and hunters," he said, "and Membertou and our Mi'kmaq friends who keep us so well supplied with meat from the forest and from the sea." Again cheers boomed off the wooden walls.

Poutrincourt, still standing, cleared his throat. "Gentlemen, it is time to pass the chain and staff of office to the steward for tomorrow." He turned to Champdoré, smiling. "I don't envy your position, sir, but I wish you good luck."

There was laughter as Champdoré rose smiling and walked to the end of the table to meet Champlain. Champlain took off his chain of office and placed it around the boatbuilder's neck. Then he handed him the sceptre.

"My friend," Champlain said, reaching for his goblet, "I toast your success tomorrow. Here's to good food, good company, good health—and the Order of Good Cheer." He and Champdoré clinked their cups and drank as the men cheered and raised their own.

"I think this company would be quite satisfied with the leftovers from your dinner, instead of my meagre offerings," Champdoré said with a good-natured grin.

"No, it's not true," laughed Champlain, slapping his friend on the shoulder. "I am hungry already, just thinking about tomorrow."

When they were seated, Poutrincourt rose again. "Let us close this *Noël* with a prayer." There was a shuffling as the men turned in their places and bowed their heads. "Our dear God in Heaven. Thank you for the many blessings you have bestowed on our beloved France, her king, and on our humble habitation in this outpost. . . ."

Champlain, Hébert, and Membertou stood outside the habitation watching moon sparks flash on the ruffling bay in front of them. Membertou's wife stood in the dark behind him.

"Tell me, Membertou," said Champlain, "why do you only have one wife when some *sagamos* have as many as seven?"

Membertou chuckled. "She is as good as seven," he said, "and she is the only one who would stay with me." The three men laughed as they turned and began to walk towards Membertou's wigwam. His camp was just down the shore in the shelter of the forest.

Champlain pulled his heavy cloak tightly around him. "My friend," he said, "Hébert and I want to ask you a question about Cartier." Membertou stopped and turned. Champlain could not see his face in the dark.

"Yes?"

"It's about this *mal de la terre* that killed Cartier's men—and so many of ours these last two winters. Cartier said the Iroquois taught them to make a medicine, a tea that cured them. They made this tea from the branches from the *annedda* tree. Do you know it?"

There was a long silence as Membertou tilted his head and considered the question. Champlain felt the cold seeping through his French-made shoes. A single snowflake flashed briefly in the air like a shooting star.

Finally, the Mi'kmaq *aoutmin* and *sagamo* shook his head. "That name is not known in our tongue."

A chill of disappointment ran through Champlain. "If you have any medicine that might help, would you give us some? Four of our men have the sickness now."

The news hung there in the dark between them. Finally, Membertou spoke. "I will." And he turned to go.

"Bonsoir," he called out as he and his wife walked towards their home in the forest. "You make a good *atoctegic,"* he said over his shoulder.

Champlain laughed at the compliment. *Atoctegic* was the Mi'kmaq word for chief steward.

Then Membertou stopped and turned, a dark shape against the dark forest. "Cooking is the job of women," he called. "The best cure is a good wife. That's what you French need." The *sagamo* turned and walked away.

Hébert and Champlain watched them disappear into the dark. "Perhaps he's right," mused the apothecary, "but that won't help us now."

Champlain turned to Hébert. "Let's go examine your supplies again and try to find some remedy for these men." He left unsaid one chilling thought: *the future of New France depends on it.*

As they turned and walked back towards the dark walls of the habitation, the sound of Pontgravé's lute and the men's singing came thinly through the cold air.

MERCY *Flight*

NEWSPAPER CLIPPING

(The Sault Star, Tuesday, December 23, 1941)

LOCAL PILOT LEAVES ON MERCY FLIGHT

BOY WITH BROKEN LEG AWAITS AIRLIFT

While most people were winding down from work to enjoy Christmas, local pilot J.C. "Buzz" Beaudette took off from Sault Ste. Marie late yesterday afternoon on a medical mercy flight to Hawk Junction. Beaudette, with the Ontario Air Service, is due to pick up a six-year-old boy struck down by a truck in Franz early yesterday.

The name of the boy is not known although it's reported that his leg is badly broken. The patient was brought to the Red Cross Hospital in Hawk Junction on the Algoma Central Railway train Monday afternoon. Doctors decided that the boy should be sent to the Sault as soon as possible. Hawk Junction is about 110 air miles due north of the Sault.

Weather conditions at the time were favorable, but the forecast is for snow squalls and deteriorating visibility as a low-pressure system moves into the region. "Buzz" Beaudette, one of the Air Service's most experienced pilots, is flying a 300-horsepower Buhl Airsedan, purchased from the now-defunct Buhl Aircraft Company in Michigan and assembled here. He was expected back in the Sault last night.

NEWSPAPER CLIPPING

(The Sault Star, Wednesday, December 24, 1941)

MERCY PLANE MISSING IN SUDDEN STORM

PILOT'S WIFE CONFIDENT HUSBAND IS SAFE

A winter storm that struck the area late yesterday may have forced down a plane on a mercy flight carrying a boy with a broken leg from Hawk Junction to the Sault.

Gordon Portland of the Ontario Air Service (OAS) says Jean-Claude "Buzz" Beaudette was due back in the Sault last night. He was carrying six-year-old Donny Redfeather of Franz, who was hit by a truck in that community on Monday morning. Also on board was Annie Redfeather, the boy's mother.

"Buzz is a seasoned and careful flier," says Portland. "I think he's probably landed on some little lake and is just waiting for the weather to clear before he resumes his flight."

Officials say the storm hit Hawk Junction at about 8:00 p.m., shortly after Beaudette took off. The flight to Sault Ste. Marie would normally take just over an hour.

"I didn't sleep much last night," said Mrs. J.C. Beaudette. "I was thinking of Buzz and that poor boy and his mum. Buzz is very capable, and I know they'll all be okay. I just hope he's home for Christmas."

The Dominion Weather Office says the storm, which has already dumped more than three inches of snow on the area with northwest winds of forty miles per hour gusting up to seventy, is expected to last at least another seven to ten hours.

With visibility reduced to only a few hundred feet, the OAS cannot launch any kind of search. "As soon as it clears, we're off," said Lefty Andrews, an OAS pilot and friend of Beaudette's. "The boys are chomping at the bit to go."

NEWSPAPER CLIPPING

(The Sault Star, Friday, December 26, 1941)

AIR SEARCH LAUNCHED FOR DOWNED PLANE

Three aircraft belonging to the Ontario Air Service (OAS) began to search this morning for Sault pilot J.C. "Buzz" Beaudette and his two passengers. Christmas has been delayed at the Beaudette home, while children wait for their father.

Their plane, a Buhl AirSedan, may have been forced down Monday night by the storm that ended late Christmas Day, preventing a search from being launched earlier. Beaudette's passengers are Annie Redfeather of Franz and her six-year-old son, Donny, who has a badly broken leg. They were being flown from Hawk Junction to hospital in the Sault.

The search will concentrate on the area between the Sault and Eton, the rail station at mile 120 on the Algoma Central Railway. The stationmaster is reported to have heard a plane fly overhead shortly after 8:00 p.m. Tuesday.

Beaudette and his passengers have now spent four nights, including Christmas, in the bush. It's hoped the experienced flier simply landed on a small "lily pad" lake and is waiting for good weather before he takes off again. Temperatures during the storm dropped to –26°F at night.

"We haven't opened a present, and the turkey is still in the freezer," the pilot's wife, Suzanne Beaudette, Westaway Road, said yesterday. "Our three kids are little, but they know all of us, including Santa, are waiting for Daddy. Buzz will be our Christmas present this year."

The air search is being led by Gordon Portland, director of the OAS. Other pilots include R.B. "Lefty" Andrews and A.S. "Scotty" McInnis. G. H. Sawyer, J.P. Reynolds, and T.R. Bathgate will act as spotters.

On Christmas Eve and again during Christmas Day masses, prayers were said for Beaudette and his passengers by his priest, Father August Ruisseau of Precious Blood Cathedral.

NEWSPAPER CLIPPING

(The Sault Star, Saturday, December 27, 1941)

NO SIGN YET OF MISSING BEAUDETTE PLANE AND PASSENGERS

There's been no sign of the Buhl aircraft piloted by J.C. "Buzz" Beaudette and believed forced down by bad weather Monday night while on a mercy flight from Hawk Junction to the Sault. Beaudette was carrying six-year-old Donny Redfeather, who was suffering from a broken leg after being hit by a truck in Franz early Monday. Also on board was the boy's mother, Annie Redfeather, 24.

Three Ontario Air Service (OAS) planes have been searching the area between the Sault and Eton since yesterday morning. OAS director, Gordon Portland, said a decision will be made tomorrow about whether the number of planes involved and the search area will be increased.

NEWSPAPER CLIPPING

(The Sault Star, Monday, December 29, 1941)

PILOT AND PASSENGERS SURVIVE MERCY FLIGHT WRECK

BOY, 6, 'STABLE'

HIS MOTHER AND BEAUDETTE HURT

After five stormy nights in the bush by a "lily pad" lake, then a trapper's cabin, Pilot J.C.

"Buzz" Beaudette, Annie Redfeather, 24, and her six-year-old son, Donny, are in hospital in the Sault.

Beaudette's Buhl aircraft had made a forced landing in total darkness when the storm struck during a mercy flight from Hawk Junction to the Sault late on December 22.

Donny Redfeather, who was being flown to hospital with a broken leg after being hit by a truck in Franz last Monday, is in stable condition suffering from the effects of hypothermia and severe frostbite to his feet.

Buzz Beaudette received a nasty six-inch gash on his head when he went through the windshield of his plane as it crashed into a tree at the end of the tiny lake. Annie Redfeather, the boy's mother, suffered cracked ribs and a fractured left arm.

Furs Save Boy's Life

"We're all very lucky to be alive," said Beaudette, "especially Donny.

"He was wedged in the back with a bundle of furs his father had trapped. His mother was planning to sell them to pay for the hospital visit. I think they probably saved his life."

Dr. V.H. Mainprize of Plummer Memorial Hospital says the boy's condition was critical when he arrived, but it has since stabilized.

"He was already in a lot of pain before the plane crashed," Dr. Mainprize said. "How he made it, I don't know. We're worried about saving his feet, which are in pretty bad shape. He didn't have any shoes or boots with him after his accident."

"Scrap" of Canvas, Sleeping Bags, Furs Keep Survivors Alive

After the crash, Beaudette and Redfeather used the plane's canvas nose tent to build a small teepee in the bush. Two old sleeping bags and the furs kept the three of them from freezing in the –21°F temperatures and howling winds. The trio lived on berries and bulrushes, and drank bush tea made with melted snow by Mrs. Redfeather.

"Young Donny was in a lot of pain, and he'd moan and cry out as he drifted in and out of consciousness. Mercifully, he was out a lot of the time," said Beaudette.

On Christmas Day, a trapper on a nearby lake, Pierre Verhelst, and his wife, Kathy, smelled smoke from their fire and came over on snowshoes to investigate. Verhelst returned with his dogsled and ferried the injured boy, his mother, and Beaudette back to the couple's log cabin on Loon Lake.

"I'll tell you, those two coming through the snow, it was like seeing ghosts. It was a great Christmas present," said Beaudette.

Pilot and Trapper Thanked

Once Donny Redfeather was made comfortable in the Verhelsts' bed, Pierre hauled a large pile of wood onto the ice to make a signal fire for when the storm ended.

Then, although visibility was still limited by blowing snow, he left by dogsled for Ranger Lake, about 60 miles to the south, to send word to the Sault.

The next day, December 26, Mrs. Verhelst lit the signal bonfire and kept it going. It was the smoke from that fire that was spotted later in the day by Teddy Bathgate of Superior Airways and Ontario Provincial Police Constable Glen Williams. Mrs. Verhelst had also tramped an SOS into the snow beside the fire.

"We owe the Verhelsts and Teddy and Glen a lot," said Beaudette. "I want to thank them and all the OAS (Ontario Air Service) guys for all they done. Little Donny was a real trooper, but I don't think he would have lasted much longer."

Beaudette Describes Bush Ordeal from Hospital Bed

"When I woke up, I was lying in a snow bank in front of the plane," said Beaudette, looking chipper as he smoked a cigarette in his bed at Plummer Memorial Hospital with 23 stitches in his head.

"I don't know how I missed that tree when I went through the windshield. Thankfully, the prop had been broken off by the time I went by," he added with a grin.

Beaudette's misadventure began in Hawk Junction on Monday night.

"We were late getting away," he said. "We were a little low on fuel, but there was a problem with the pump on the fuel truck. It was a little after 8:00 p.m. when we finally took off, and of course it was pitch black."

Beaudette, exemplifying the mettle of the men who fly for the Ontario Air Service (OAS), used his ingenuity to meet the challenges that life in the north presents these pilots.

"The moon was up, a pretty little crescent moon, and I followed the glint of moonlight on the Algoma Central Railway tracks for a while. When the storm hit, I couldn't see them anymore, so I took her up to forty-one hundred feet, but it wasn't any better. I decided to outrun the storm and headed inland towards Ranger Lake, and that worked for a while. But in the moonlight I could see the storm catching us and knew I had to make a landing.

"It was real dark when I brought her down on this little white patch of a lake. I knew we had only one crack at it. I think we brushed a couple of treetops going in.

"After that, the skis hit hard and bounced, and then I woke up in a snow bank with blood running in my eyes."

When Beaudette came to, he found Annie Redfeather still in the front seat of the plane, battered, bruised, and in shock. The pilot helped her out, not knowing she had a fractured arm.

"Annie only speaks Cree, and it was dark so it was hard to communicate," said Beaudette.

Once he found his flashlight inside the cabin, Beaudette checked on Donny, who lay hidden under the pile of furs. "He wasn't making a sound. At first, I didn't know if he was dead or just unconscious. When I realized he was still alive, I decided we'd leave him there until we figured out what we were going to do. Least he was out of the wind and snow."

Like all bush pilots, Beaudette carries a canvas nose tent that is used to shelter the aircraft's engine in freezing winter weather. He retrieved the tent from the cargo bay along with two old sleeping bags, and an axe.

"Annie and I looked at each other, and she pointed to the bush, so we found some dead spruce sticking out of the ice and made a little teepee in the shelter of some cedar trees.

"I knew her arm was hurting bad, but she wouldn't let that stop her. When we got the tent set up, we went back for Donny.

"It was hard getting him out of the back, and when he cried out with the pain, it just about broke your heart. We got him into one of the sleeping bags—Annie took the other—and we put the furs under us on the snow. It wasn't too warm, to say the least. The wind was howling pretty good, and none of us slept too much that night."

Annie Redfeather A Hero, Says Pilot

"If it wasn't for Mrs. Redfeather's bush skills, we'd be in pretty bad shape," says Beaudette, with admiration in his voice. "She was right at home out there and knew just what to do."

According to Beaudette, the morning after the crash, he and Mrs. Redfeather built a fire. Then she disappeared into the woods. She came back with leaves and made bush tea in a tin can Beaudette had in the back of the plane.

"We needed tea to warm us and to lift our spirits," said Mrs. Redfeather, speaking from her hospital bed through an interpreter, Father George Beaupré, who's spent many years at Oblate Missions in the north.

"I saw burnt trees at the end of the lake and dug in the snow where I know the bushes grow after a fire."

She shrugged off the injury that kept her from using both hands. "The tea was good," she said.

The blizzard continued for three more days, and the survivors had no food with them.

"Just five crumpled cigarettes and two old sticks of Juicy Fruit I found in my jacket pocket," Beaudette said with a laugh. "Annie and I shared the cigarettes, and Donny had the gum, which we gave him in little pieces."

On the second day of their ordeal, with the storm still raging around them, Mrs. Redfeather again left the tiny tent and went in search of food.

"I went to the swampy area and gathered some bulrushes that were sticking out of the ice," she said in her soft-spoken Cree. "On the way back, I found some kinnikinnick that the bears had left for us."

"When she got back to the tent," Beaudette said as he picked up the story, "she had me split the bulrushes open and pull out the pith, and we put that into our tin of boiling water. She threw the berries in there, too. It was a pretty watery soup, but it sure did the trick. I tell you, we felt much better after that.

"By Christmas Day, we were bored, cold, hungry, and really missing our families. Donny was in a lot of pain, too. He speaks some English and kept saying, 'My leg hurts.' I only had a few aspirins in the first aid kit, and he went through them pretty quick. We didn't realize his feet were freezing in that thin old sleeping bag, because he just had socks on and couldn't wiggle his toes on his broken right leg."

To pass the long hours during the storm, Redfeather and Beaudette told each other stories. Donny would translate when he was able. "I loved listening to Annie even if I didn't have the foggiest notion of what she was talking about," said Beaudette. "It was comforting to all of us."

Trapper Misses Christmas Goose in Race to Alert Authorities

"It's a Christmas Day I'll never forget," laughs Pierre Verhelst, the Loon Lake trapper who along with his wife, Kathy, found the plane wreck survivors on December 25. Speaking by telephone in Ranger Lake before returning home, Verhelst credited his wife with making the discovery.

"We went out for a snowshoe because we were getting cabin fever," the trapper recounted, "and the wife smelled smoke. From the wind direction, we knew there wouldn't be anybody out there, especially that day, so we went over to have a look. We could hardly see their tent for snow piled up around it, but they had a small fire going and were making tea." The trapper laughed again. "You should have seen the look on their faces when they saw us."

While Kathy Verhelst stayed and helped care for the three by giving Donny her sweater and building up their fire, Pierre hurried back to Loon Lake and got his sled dogs and sleigh.

"We took Donny and his mom first and then went back for Beaudette. He claimed he could walk, but the drifts were deep, and he was pretty shaky from that gash on his noggin.

"Once we got Donny settled in, Kathy started preparing to feed them Christmas dinner. That's when I left for Ranger Lake to get the word out. It was still blowing pretty good, but the dogs know the route like the back of their hand. I camped on the trail and got there in good time Sunday morning. By the time we got through on the phone, three planes had already taken off. So they sent another one, but I guess by then that pilot had already seen our smoke.

"The wife had a goose in the oven when I took off," Verhelst said with a chuckle. "Guess I'll head back and see if there's any left."

NEWSPAPER CLIPPING

(The Sault Star, Tuesday, December 30, 1941)

Doctors Amputate Crash Victim's Toes

Local Merchant Pays for Medical Care

Six-year-old Donny Redfeather, who survived almost a week in the bush after a plane he was on crashed-landed during a storm, had three toes removed yesterday morning by surgeons at Plummer Memorial Hospital in the Sault.

Dr. V.H. Mainprize says the boy, who was being airlifted to hospital in the Sault with a broken leg after being hit by a truck December 22, is in good condition. "With his leg broken, Donny couldn't do anything to keep circulation in that foot. We were able to save his two biggest toes," said Dr Mainprize. "His leg has also been set and is now in traction."

Dr. Mainprize credited the boy's courage in enduring the ordeal. "He's a brave boy and very tough," he said.

The pilot of the flight, J.C. "Buzz" Beaudette, who'd received a six-inch cut to his head, is now resting at home. Donny's mother, Mrs. Annie Redfeather, suffered cracked ribs and a fractured left arm. She is still in hospital, but is expected to be released soon.

Dr. Mainprize said a local merchant has offered to cover all the hospital expenses incurred by the Redfeathers. The man has asked that his donation be kept anonymous.

A LETTER *From New France*

My dear, sweet Catherine,

I write this letter from New France with the comfort of knowing that early next summer I will deliver it to you personally and safely, and will be able to cheerfully warn you of its chilling and wretched contents. If God is with me, I will read it to you under the apple tree at our beloved Limoëlou, or perhaps on our favourite walking path along Rochebonne Beach, gazing out over the Atlantic Ocean across which our Father has so benevolently delivered us yet again.

Failing that, it is also possible that this frail parchment will never be gazed upon by your gentle, loving eyes, but will rest here with our remains in this wild, Godless place, and will decay in a nameless and unknown grave in the forest with our bones. Yet it gives me such comfort to reach out to you tonight that I must continue, although the freezing ink conspires against me.

It is the *Noël,* the holiest of nights in the civilized world. I think of you in the cathedral at St. Malo, lighting a candle among the rows of wavering flames, and praying to St. Christopher and all the saints for our safe return home, just as I pray for you this moment. I can see you now as you tilt your head, as if you are hearing a distant whisper, your red hair spilling out from under your shawl. It is only me sending you my love as, like a wandering pilgrim, I watch you from the shadows while the monks softly sing their Latin verses in air pungent with incense.

Our own grim candles gutter in the freezing drafts that pierce our walls like savages' arrows. One hundred and ten souls are congregated here, huddled beneath blankets and scraps of fur, more miserable perhaps than even the most wretched guests in François I's dank dungeons. The log walls of our fortress are plastered with ice, blasted by a ferocious, knifing wind that contains such moans and howls, I wonder if we are not on the wrong side of the River Styx. At night, our brave sentries can endure their frigid watch upon the palisades for only a quarter of an hour before they must retreat to the hearth and fairly throw themselves into the smouldering fire in their frantic hunger for heat.

We find ourselves perched near a great gullet of a river that flows out of this frozen, wild land. Our rough, log fortress sits in Ste. Croix harbour. His Majesty's ships are drawn up close to shore and have been locked in ice since November, their masts and yards sheathed in icicles like some macabre frozen Calvary. There is not much snow, only a foot deep, but the protective moat we dug about our fortress last fall has disappeared beneath the drifts. All around us lies a dark and endless forest, where at night the freezing trees snap with the ferocity of an army of Spanish fusiliers.

We are not alone. A thousand savages live close by in a community called Stadacona. These are the very same heathens from whom we delivered those two young boys who returned with us to France last year after our first voyage. You were right to doubt the sincerity of the one called Taignoagny. Since he and his brother, Domagaya, departed our ship here, he has steadfastly worked to turn his father, Donnacona, against us. The savages now mistrust our intentions, and there is much disaffection among them.

This summer we journeyed southwesterly up the great river without their services as guides and translators, finally landing at a large community of four thousand. Their town, which they call "Hochelaga," is near a mountain which I have named Mount Royal in honour of our king. Standing on its summit there in the glory of the moment, celebrating the achievements of France, I confess to you our strong disappointment at seeing, farther up the river to the west, a great, long, foaming cauldron of rapids through which no king's ship nor even bark canoe can safely pass. It is almost certainly not the passage to the Orient for which we so fervently search. With our adventure now tinged with regret, we left the mountain, some of my men so fatigued from the climb in their metal armour, that several of the stronger savages carried them down on their backs. Fearing malicious intent on the part of these people, we declined their invitation to a feast and retreated to our boat, rowing hastily downstream to our bark and sailing back to this place.

In our absence, a party of men built our winter habitation in which we now find ourselves locked as though in a jail. Our wine is frozen solid as is all of our ships' food. The rivers and lakes are frozen, too, so that we must melt snow for our drinking water. The early winter and lack of deep snow has made the animals of the region difficult to hunt so even the savages are hungry. They are also afflicted with a mysterious pox. Almost daily we watch as shaggy columns of fur-clad savages carry yet another body out to their graveyard. There they hoist the bark-wrapped corpse onto a wooden platform and leave the devil's own black scavenger birds to do their raucous, grisly work. These simple people see gods under every tree and stone and in every animal and thing that lives, yet I pity them, for they do not know the comfort of our Lord's promise of life everlasting in a glorious Heaven.

Recently, within our own lodge, there has been a new sound to join the moaning of the wind. Some of our brave French men have the dreaded *mal de la terre.* This is not a new malady for sailors, but I fear that God's wrath at their sinful ways will threaten our own enterprise. Even now, a dozen men are incapacitated, lying in their log bunks with swollen legs and arms, great black and blue blotches on their skin, flecked with red spots the size of flea bites. Their gums are reduced to a stinking jelly that at night oozes blood over themselves and their blankets.

I and the King's gentlemen have been busy attending to them with our best efforts, bleeding them, exhorting them to pray to their Holy Father, to say their rosaries and renounce the many devilish sins that plague them now. However, I fear that some are beyond hope, and their deaths may leave us with weakened defences against our neighbours, and perhaps even without the necessary numbers to sail our ships back home to France.

This then is how we spent this evening of the Holy Nativity: the majority of able men supping on a caribou stew and fresh-baked bread, and dropping rosy shards of frozen wine into our cups of melted snow-water. With no priest to say a mass or make the blessing, I offered my own inadequate prayer for deliverance from the clutches of winter, savages, disease, and the wide, tempestuous ocean that separates us from our beloved country. After our meal, we sang several favourite hymns and a few of the less ribald tunes the sailors knew. Then the evening drifted into stories and talk, and as shadows hovered on the glistening walls, we spoke of the ones at home who love us and of the meals we will eat when we return. Once again, I was reminded of how love of God, love of country, and love of family are the three pillars upon which a happy life rests.

Lest this seem too forlorn and morbid a letter, I hasten to assure you that there is still great hope in our efforts here. Donnacona has spoken to us of fantastic wealth in the form of metals and precious stones that are to be found in a land called Saguenay to the north. He has told us of communities of white men who live and dress as savages near a large inland fresh-water sea, of a race of one-legged people, and a land of rich vegetation to the south of the great river. These reports promise to excite the King and, I hope, will whet his appetite for further exploration and discovery to bring glory to his name and all of France.

As I write, I am also deeply aware of your own solitude in our home and regret deeply that God has not seen fit to bless our happy union with children. Therefore, along with this letter, I will present you with a young savage girl who has been given to us as a gift and sign of friendship. Once she learns to speak French and has received the necessary instruction from the monks, perhaps she can be baptized as a Christian and received into our home as the daughter for whom your heart longs.

Oh, how I wish I could gaze upon your beautiful face at this moment, to see your delight, to comfort you in my arms. I pray for you and send my prayers winging over this frozen land, across the tossing Atlantic to the warm fires of our hearth. I pray, too, for your dear mother and the soul of your dear departed father and for my own parents, whose constant worries have always fuelled this sailor's longing for home.

To the glory of God, France, our king, and to you, my sweet wife, I remain faithfully, loyally, and eternally yours,

Jacques Cartier
Nova Francia
December, 1535

MIRACLE AT *Forty Below*

"Oohh, Daddy," Shamimu exclaimed, "it's beautiful."

Her father, Drossan Sabiti, stepped back to admire the new lights, tiny red and green ones. They cast swatches of colour onto his flowing *boubou,* the traditional Kenyan robe draped over his mountainous frame. He dwarfed the Christmas tree.

"Cool," said Peggy, his oldest daughter.

"Qu'est-ce que tu penses?" Drossan asked his wife, Colette, who was nursing Bonfils on the couch. Their two-and-a-half-year-old, David, cuddled beside her, thumb in his mouth, eyes fixed on the lights.

"C'est beau, très, très beau." She looked at her daughters. "Hurry, they be here soon," she added in English. Drossan's three younger brothers and sister-in-law were on their way. The aroma of goat stew wafted in from the kitchen. A feast in the making.

"It is hard to believe it was three years ago today that we first arrive here, non?" Drossan's round, black face split open in a white gash of a smile.

Colette shook her head as she reattached Bonfils to her breast. "December 12. I don't even like to think about that," she said.

I do like to think about it, Drossan thought. *That's when the miracle happened.*

Drossan stirred. His body was tilting. He opened his eyes, grabbed the arms of the seat, and looked around. *Where are we? Nairobi? Paris? Toronto?* Then he remembered: *No, we are in the middle of Canada somewhere.* It came as a surprise, and he sat up, fully awake.

Colette was still sound asleep, her head against the fuselage beside the plane's window, a blanket over her bulging stomach. He turned his big frame and looked behind him between the seats. Shamimu was reading an airline magazine while Peggy stared out the window.

Drossan looked out, too, as the plane continued to bank around its turn. Rows and rows of glowing white spots spread across the ground below. Drossan nudged his wife. She opened her eyes, looked at him. He pointed to the window. "Saskatoon, *je pense.*"

Colette cupped her hand against the glass, then turned to her husband, a quizzical look on her face. "Everything looks so white. What is it?"

Drossan shrugged and leaned forward, his heart beating faster now. This was their new home, and they knew almost nothing about it. All four of them peered out the windows as the plane landed. The flashing lights of the runway flew past, and between them, a carpet of white.

"What is *that?"* Peggy asked from behind.

"It's covering everything!" Shamimu said as she leaned across her sister. "Maybe it's salt."

"Maybe," nodded Drossan, his eyes wide as the plane taxied to the terminal. He had read about snow in books; he had seen it in films, but, still, he wasn't sure about this. There was so much. It seemed . . . impossible.

"It might be manna from heaven," added Colette switching to Swahili, "like when God made a miracle for the Israeli people."

The plane came to a stop. They watched people in huge coats with fur-lined hoods shuffle around on the tarmac, some driving small carts pulling trailers for luggage. Their breath came in great white plumes like mist from a waterfall. Fog filled the air. The door at the front of the plane opened, and a blast of cold air rolled down the cabin aisle.

"It's so *cold,"* said Drossan, standing now with his family, drawing out the word as he grimaced and scrunched up his shoulders. The line of passengers began to move. *What kind of country have we come to?* Drossan wondered.

"Fffff!" Colette sucked in her breath as they walked up the sloping corridor that led into the airport. They were all shivering.

Who will meet us? Drossan wondered. *Will those people from the church be there, our sponsors?* He gripped his daughters' hands as they walked along a glass wall inside the terminal. Below them were crowds of strangers dressed in massive coats and wool hats and scarves. The fear of danger, of dying, that he hoped he'd left behind rose up inside him. It clawed at his guts, at his throat, as they rode down the escalator and walked through the sliding doors.

"Mon Dieu!"

Tears filled Drossan's eyes. He stood, frozen, at the sight. Memories flooded back. Machetes flashed through the air, like in his nightmares. Slicing sounds, screams, men, women being pulled from their beds and flung to bloody floors. The soldiers of Mubutu Sese Seko. How many times had he imagined it? More than a hundred bodies—his mother, father, brothers, sisters—their entire family left to the flies and vultures in the killing fields and streets of Zaire. Eight years in a Kenyan refugee camp had done nothing to dull the pain. Not even Colette's swelling stomach with the promise of new life. And then, the bang of that white man's rubber stamp on their application to Canada. And another on their passports in Toronto. Only then did they dare to breathe deeply, freely at last. Now Drossan stood in his *boubou,* tears streaming down his face. He threw his arms open wide.

"Ahahahahah." His big booming laugh echoed through the airport. People stopped and turned to look.

"You are alive!"

His three brothers—Kiza, Sangu, and Biosubula—and his sister-in-law—Kashindi—stood there with grins on their faces. They came together in a rush of arms and coats and kisses and tears.

"We thought you were dead," Colette cried. "They told us they'd killed all our families."

"We escaped. We've been in camps, too. The church here sponsored us. We didn't know you were alive either until . . ."

"I can't believe it," said Drossan, holding the face of Kiza, his youngest brother. "I thought I'd never see you again." He raised his head to the ceiling. "Praise God, it's a miracle."

Like an island in a river of travellers, the Sabiti family stood laughing, crying, touching one another. "Where's your luggage?" Sangu finally asked.

"We don't have any," Drossan replied.

Kashindi had winter coats for the girls. "Here, put these on. You're shivering," she said to Peggy and Shamimu.

Drossan looked around for the first time. Through his tears, he saw two people watching them. *Who they are? They don't look like police or spies.* They were holding more coats. They smiled at him and came over.

"We're Robert and Lynn from the church," the man said.

"Welcome to Canada," Lynn added. There were tears in her eyes, too.

Drossan laughed again. Another deep belly laugh. Then he gave them both crushing hugs. "Thank you," he said, "for bringing us here."

Robert sniffed, then laughed. "The car's just outside. Here, you better put these on." He handed Colette and Drossan each a coat.

Drossan waved it off as he strode towards the exit in his cotton *boubou.* "No, thank you. I don't need one." The automatic doors swished open, and they walked into a billowing wall of ice fog.

Drossan stopped. His mouth opened. His eyes went wide. His hand went to his throat. He gasped. He grabbed Collete's hand and, with the girls, ran back inside the terminal.

"I can't breathe," he said in a croaking whisper. His brothers were all laughing. *How can you laugh? I am going to die!*

Colette coughed. They looked at each other. What have we done? their eyes said.

"How can anyone *live* in this cold?" Colette asked.

"You wear these," Biosubula said, pointing to the parkas Robert and Lynn held. "Put them on."

"It's forty below," said Robert.

Drossan just looked at him. He had no idea what that meant.

They almost ran out this time, hurling themselves into the cold night. Every parked car was running, sending up swirling clouds of exhaust.

"Daddy," cried Shamimu. She stopped, bent down, and picked up some snow. Then she licked it.

"Yes, yes," Drossan said. They all stopped, picked up some snow, licked it tentatively.

"It's not salt," said Peggy. Everyone laughed.

The four of them piled into Robert and Lynn's car. The rest followed. Drossan didn't want his daughters out of his sight. There was conversation, but he was too distracted to listen. Looking through the frosted windows, he saw tiny houses covered with snow. He thought of Kenya, so beautiful, so green, and warm. *There is nothing special about this place. Kenya is better than here.* The disappointment grew, a cold, grey weight.

They drove across the city, through a neighbourhood with bigger homes, then stopped. The Sabitis followed Robert and Lynn up to a stucco house.

They walked in. The bright, white kitchen had a table and chairs. In the living room, there was a big black couch, a TV, chairs, lamps, a huge bookcase. In the bedrooms, the beds were made. There were dressers and closets full of clothes. They walked in a trance back to the kitchen. Lynn opened the cupboards. Colette's hand went to her mouth. They were crammed with dishes, cups and glasses, pots and pans, brightly coloured boxes and packages and cans of food.

Drossan looked at Robert and Lynn. "Your church—" He stopped and shook his head. "You are so good to us."

Robert just smiled and pointed to the fridge. "Go ahead."

Drossan opened the door. The light came on. "Oh my!" He clapped his hands to his cheeks. Milk, eggs, cheese, butter, lettuce, celery, tomatoes, juice. "I must be in a dream," he said, tears brimming up as he looked from Robert to Lynn to Colette, his daughters, his brothers, his sister-in-law.

Finally, after everyone left, they climbed into bed, exhausted. Drossan fell into a restless sleep. In the middle of the night, he awoke. He thought for a moment he was back in the camp. *The food!* He crept out to the kitchen and stood in front of the fridge. *Am I dreaming?* Half crouching, he reached for the handle . . . and pulled.

It is still there! Bathed in the glow of a forty-watt bulb, Drossan was filled with amazement. *Thank you.*

The next morning, the Sabitis opened the drapes of their living room window. "Wow!" The white snow sparkled; the sky was a deep blue. The houses across the street were bigger and nicer than the ones they'd seen last night.

"I'm freezing!" moaned Colette, lying on the couch under two parkas. She'd slept with them on top of her—under the covers—all night.

Drossan checked the wall thermostat that Robert had shown him. "It's up as far as it will go," he said, shrugging his shoulders. He sat down with a sigh. "What will we do?" He looked around the room at his family.

"Maybe we should go back to Toronto," said Colette, sitting up, putting the parka on, and pulling the hood over her head. "They said it is warmer there."

"You look like the Inuit, Momma," Peggy laughed.

Colette looked at her. *"Qu'est-ce que c'est?"*

"They're people who live up north in Canada. It's even colder up there."

"How can that be?" said Colette, wrapping her arms across her chest and folding herself into a corner of the couch.

In the next few days, the Sabitis did not go outside much. Robert and Lynn brought more clothes and food. The minister from the church and his wife came by. Drossan's brothers visited every day. No mention was made of leaving. Drossan felt trapped, lost. The weather warmed a little. At least that's what people said, but the Sabitis were still freezing.

The phone rang. Drossan answered, spoke briefly, and hung up. He was puzzled. "Robert and Lynn are coming," he said. "They are bringing over a Christmas tree."

Drossan went to the window and looked out at the drifts of snow in their front yard. *Where are they going to plant this tree? The ground is frozen, non?*

Soon there was a knock at the door. They laughed when Robert brought the tree right into the living room. It filled the house with a strange scent. The Sabitis just sat and watched as Robert and Lynn showed them how to decorate it.

"Are you ready?" asked Robert grinning. He plugged in the electrical cord. All the lights came on.

"Ahhhh!"

"Merry Christmas!"

"Oh, yes," Drossan said, nodding. "It's just like we see on TV."

"We are in Canada now!" cried Peggy.

This was their third Christmas tree, and it was almost done. "If we could go back home right now to live, would we?" Shamimu asked as she handed her dad the white angel with silver wings. Drossan looked around the room at his wife and children. He nodded to Colette.

"Robert, Lynn, that church, they made this place warm for us," she said. "I am so thankful for them. Otherwise we go somewhere else."

"They never let us down," agreed Drossan, "not once."

Colette shook her head. "No, this is our home now. Canadian people are very peaceful, very kind to us."

Drossan turned and carefully placed the angel on top of the tree. "Every day, I thank God we are here," he said quietly.

A knock at the door.

"Here they are!" the girls yelled as they jumped up and ran through the kitchen to the side door, David trailing after them.

Drossan looked out the window. Biosubula and Kashindi waved as they walked up the sidewalk. Large flakes of snow were falling. *Like salt. Like manna from heaven.* Drossan smiled. *They are beautiful,* he thought, *very beautiful.*

THE *Monkey Doll*

"Is it there? Did you see my doll?" Henni asked, but her parents only laughed.

"Just wait till tomorrow," said her mom, smiling as she took off her heavy coat, wool hat, and mitts. "You'll see soon enough."

"It's not soon enough at all," moaned Henni. What if the doll she asked for wasn't there, and they got her something else, something she didn't . . . didn't love?

"If you go to bed now, morning will be here faster," said her dad, laughing as he pulled off his big overshoes with the straps, the good ones he wore to church on Sunday.

"No, Daddy, please!" she cried. "Was Mr. Schumacher there? Did you see him? Did you talk to him?"

Her father laughed. "Yes, he was there. But no, I didn't talk to him. I'm just a worker who can't speak English so good yet like you. But I did see a table full of hockey sticks and pucks. I think your name was beside one, is that not right, Pirkko?" There was a twinkle in his eye.

Henni sighed loudly. *It's not fair!* They'd just come back from the grown-ups' social at the school. The parents had seen all the Christmas gifts that Mr. Schumacher had bought for the children. Tables and tables of them. Beside each gift, she knew, would be the name of the lucky child who'd receive it. *They know what I'm getting!*

Henni went to bed, but didn't turn out the lamp. She sat in her flannel nightgown, thinking. Last year, she'd asked for Tiddly Winks, but got a game of checkers instead. That was fine. She and her dad played every night after supper, if he wasn't working night shift at the McIntyre Mine—Mr. Schumacher's mine. The year before, she'd received a wooden top. It was on her bookshelf. This year, when Mrs. Ashworth wrote the grade three students' list of gifts to choose from on the blackboard, she knew immediately which one she wanted. She wrote it down. The Eaton's Beauty Doll.

Henni looked at the picture she'd cut out of the catalogue. *Belle.* That's what she'd call her. Belle was just so . . . so beautiful in her satin dress with the lace collar and pink ribbon tied in a bow. Henni closed her eyes and imagined combing Belle's curly, blonde hair. When she opened them again, it was morning and her mother was calling.

It didn't even bother Henni that it was thirty-nine below. Or that she had to eat oatmeal porridge for breakfast again. She quickly bundled into her woollen snow pants, boots, wool hat, a scarf wrapped around her nose—and off she went, almost running in the dark to the big, brick Schumacher Public School. It was the last day of school before the Christmas holidays. *Today I get my Belle,* Henni thought. It was the best day of the whole year.

Henni floated down the gleaming, wooden floors into her classroom and took off her coat and snow pants in the cloakroom just as the bell rang. Her friends, Miriam, Reva, and Karen, were already in their seats. She ran to her desk across the aisle from them, right behind Big Franky.

"Isn't this great!?" whispered Miriam as Mrs. Ashworth closed the door after the last straggler had entered the room.

Reva didn't say anything. She just held up both her hands to show them—her fingers were crossed. Henni knew that all her friends had asked for Beauty Dolls, too.

After a warning from their teacher about being quiet and polite, they trooped down to the auditorium. The other classes were on their way, too. The auditorium was really just a large room made by pulling the folding walls of the two Kindergarten rooms open, making a space that included the hallway between them. They took their seats on rows of wooden benches and chairs, everyone turning around to look. There were the tables along the back and sides of the room, one for every grade, each loaded with gifts. On the grade three table there were hockey sticks, games of chess and Chinese checkers, tin wind-up toys, round tubes of wooden toys, boxes of puzzles, a funny-looking monkey doll made out of socks, and, there, looking for all the world like beautiful young ladies . . . a row of Beauty Dolls. Each present had a white card with a name beside it.

They're even more beautiful than in the catalogue, Henni thought.

In walked the principal, Mr. Parsons, and with him—Mr. Schumacher, a round little man in a tweed suit with a short white beard. "He even looks like Santa Claus," Henni whispered to Miriam.

Mr. Schumacher sat at the front beside the Christmas tree decorated with snowflakes and tinfoil bells and red paper chains that each class had made. Henni could see that everyone was just as excited as she was. Kids kept turning around, whispering, and fidgeting. Mrs. von Stritzky played a few carols on the piano, and everyone sang cheerfully. Then Mr. Parsons rose, coughed a little, and spoke.

"Students of Schumacher School," he began, "once again we are very pleased to have the founder of the McIntyre Mine with us today, the man after whom this town and your school are named—Mr. Schumacher. As you know, every year he donates money to buy each one of you a Christmas gift. That is the true spirit of Christmas. Would you please join with me in welcoming Mr. Schumacher and thanking him for his generosity?"

There was a roar as 270 kids applauded and cheered. Some of the older boys even whistled.

I wonder which Beauty Doll is mine? thought Henni. *I can't wait to hold her.*

Then it began. The Kindergarten classes went first. In single file, they walked up to Mr.

Schumacher who held a large glass jar filled with candies. Each student took one and thanked him. Then they were free to go to their class table, search until they found their name and their gift.

Henni, Miriam, Reva, and Karen held hands as they waited, too excited to speak. Finally, it was grade threes' turn. "Thank you, Mr. Schumacher," Henni said, and they shook hands. Her eyes fixed on his red and cream tie as she took the candy.

"You're welcome," he said. "I hope you have a wonderful Christmas and a very good year at school." Henni popped the striped licorice into her mouth. It was all she could do not to run to the table at the back. Miriam, Reva, and Karen were already there, cuddling and cooing over their new Beauty Dolls.

"Where's mine?" she asked out loud, but no one was listening. She looked around. There wasn't another one on the table. *Oh no!* A terrible feeling grew in her stomach as she looked around the table. It was getting barer by the second. She stood there, fighting the tears, feeling her lower lip quiver. *My doll's not here.* She even looked under the table, to see if it had fallen off. "Mrs. Ashworth, there's been a terrible mistake," she wanted to say.

"Where's your Beauty Doll?" asked Miriam, holding hers like a newborn baby.

Henni shook her head. "I don't know." Two big tears rolled down her cheeks. Miriam pointed. There was only one gift left on the table—the sock monkey doll. Henni walked over as if in a dream, a very bad dream. There was her name—Henni Kokonen—on the small white card. Slowly, she picked up the doll and went back to her seat. She couldn't look at anyone.

When all the children had their gifts, school was dismissed, and everyone rushed out the door. "Do you want to come over?" Miriam asked. "We're going to play dolls."

Henni just shook her head. "I have to go home," she lied. She didn't want to play with her stupid, ugly monkey doll. Her face burned. She felt like she was going to be sick. She took her time in the cloakroom, waiting for all her friends to leave, then walked out of the school, in no hurry to get home.

As she trudged along the street, she held the doll by a leg, dragging one of its long, thin arms in the snow. Tears flowed down her cheeks. She stopped to wipe them away with her mittens. *Oops!* She'd dropped the monkey. It lay in the snow, its button eyes staring up at her, big fat lips grinning. Henni giggled. She couldn't help herself. "Get out of there, you dumb monkey," she said as she picked it up and brushed it off.

She held it closer to her as she walked. *It's not a Beauty Doll,* she thought, *but it is cute.* She sniffed back more tears.

Just then she heard a car squishing through the snow. There weren't a lot of cars in Schumacher, so she turned to see who was coming. It was a big black one, and she jumped a little when she realized who it was. Mr. Schumacher slowed and rolled down his window.

"Henni?" he asked through his white beard.

"Yes," she said, surprised to see Mrs. Ashworth sitting in the front seat.

"Are you all right?" he said, kindly, squinting his eyes.

Henni felt the tears well up inside her. She bit her lip, trying not to cry again. "Well," she said, "yes. I . . . I wanted a Beauty Doll, but—" She stopped. She didn't want to be ungrateful. "This one's nice," she said, holding up her monkey.

"A lot of children would be very happy to have a doll like that," said Mr. Schumacher.

"Oh, yes," said Henni quickly, wondering why they were talking to her. "It's . . . it's cute." She couldn't think of anything else to say.

"Alice Bukowski would be happy with a monkey doll," piped up Mrs. Ashworth, rising in the seat to look at Henni. "She asked for a Beauty Doll, too, but she was away sick today. . . ." Her voice trailed off.

Henni's stomach made a somersault. She stared at Mr. Schumacher, at Mrs. Ashworth. She sucked in her breath, held it, not daring to trust her ears, not daring even to think.

Mr. Schumacher laughed at the look on her face. "Henni," he said kindly. "There was a mistake." He smiled at Mrs. Ashworth. "We didn't order enough Beauty Dolls. One of you will have to take the monkey."

"Oh!" cried Henni, covering her mouth with her mitten. Mr. Schumacher had a Beauty Doll in his hand. *Belle!* He held her up and looked at Henni.

"Do you want it—or should we take it to Alice?" he asked, his eyes all crunched at the corners. "We're headed there now."

"Yes," Henni said quietly. She wanted to yell it. "Yes, I want—" She stopped herself. *No, no!* a voice inside her said, a tiny voice. *Alice is my friend. And she's sick . . .*

"Then here," said Mr. Schumacher, handing the Beauty Doll out the window.

"I . . . I . . . I mean," Henni stammered. "I mean, thank you, but no, I think I'll keep this one."

The doll hung in the air for a brief moment. Then Mr. Schumacher smiled and pulled it back inside the car. Mrs. Ashworth shook her head. "That's very generous of you, Henni. Alice will be very happy."

Henni couldn't speak.

"Someday you'll remember this," said Mr. Schumacher kindly, "and you'll know what a gift it was." He shifted the car into gear and stepped on the gas, easing it forward slowly in the crunching snow.

"Merry Christmas, Henni," said Mrs. Ashworth with a wave. "I'll say hi to Alice for you."

"Merry Christmas," said Mr. Schumacher as he wound up his window and drove off in a cloud of steam and exhaust.

Henni watched the black car drive out of sight, then looked down at her monkey doll again, at the silly grin on its big fat lips. She hugged it hard. *Maybe I will go over to Miriam's,* she thought. And she started to run.

THE *Lost Herd*

"Can't even see the gawl-darned barn," Ty Corbett muttered as he stood at the window. Outside was a blur of white on white, snow hurtling against the fence, the posts, splattering, disintegrating into swirling bits and pieces, wispy cyclones chasing their tails across the yard, sifting over buried hedges and shrubs, shifting. Snow bunching up against itself in restless, growing drifts. The long, thin branches of the weeping birch whipped like a ragged flag, its white trunk gleaming with a fresh coat of ice and snow. Beyond it, nothing.

"What'd you say, hon?" Stephie poked her head out of the kitchen. Her grey hair hung in two braids over her new suede and denim shirt, the one gift from him she'd opened this morning. There was a spot of flour on her right cheek and a red apron over her denim skirt. The scent of roasting goose filled the living room.

"Storm's gettin' worse." Ty shifted his weight onto the other boot as he nodded towards the window, standing in that solitary, self-contained way of horsemen when both feet are on the ground. "This one's bad." He looked at his bride of forty years, shook his head.

"What'll the herd do, d'ya think?" She came over to him, reached out, touched his arm, an unconscious intimacy that neither of them noticed.

He turned away from the window. His pale blue eyes glittering like marbles, reflecting lights from the Christmas tree by the fireplace, its riot of presents still intact. Perry Como was singing "Let It Snow"on a long-playing record they'd got for their new stereo/console TV. Stephie's question wasn't a real question—she was about as good a rancher as he was, knew the way of things and animals, probably was even better with animals. It was her method of helping, knowing that talking was at least something, better than staring out the window like a caged animal.

"The smart ones'll stay by the feed, bunch up behind those willows down yonder." He paused as he pictured cattle shifting, jostling into each other for warmth. "The ones out on the edge might split off 'n' drift downwind lookin' for shelter." He stopped, not wanting to think about what the result of that might be.

Stephie stood up on her tiptoes and planted a kiss on his leathery cheek. "Well, I'm happy the kids aren't stuck out on the road in this." She turned, walked briskly towards the kitchen, as if trying to infuse the house with a new and confident energy. "Come 'n' have a coffee."

"In a sec," he replied, going to the stone fireplace, stooping to throw another log on the fire. He straightened and caught his granddad looking down at him from the crackled, dark oil painting above the mantel. He'd been a lawyer for the railway, came out for a look around and never left, started the Circle C ranch, hired one of the railway poster artists to do his portrait. Tyson Corbett the First had big dreams. So did T.C. the Second, until the Kaiser's boys unleashed a storm of lead into a muddy, rat-filled trench in France. The colonel, a lawyer, too, had paid the ultimate price for getting up close to his men. Tyson Corbett III, aged sixteen, inherited almost eight thousand acres in that instant, waited seven years to marry the girl next door—next door being ten miles away—and had been happy more or less ever since.

Happy, that is, if he was out on his horse, leaning on the saddle horn, watching a few hundred head of Herefords dining on fresh spring grass on a gently rolling prairie; not happy cooped up like some fatted Christmas goose waiting for the axe to fall.

His hand touched the crisp, white Stetson perched on the leather arm of the chesterfield, Steph's gift to him. Ran his finger along the braided leather band. "You needed a hat for good," she'd said as they sat in their robes by the fire this morning, listening to the wind screaming by at seventy miles an hour, the house creaking, shuddering from time to time. Thirty-eight below. Wind sucking the snow out of every secret place, its icy fingers redrawing the terrain of southern Alberta like one of those flour and salt maps the kids used to make in school.

Amanda had called first. The archaeologist. Professor. Unmarried. More interested in dead dinosaurs than living men. "Why couldn't she have come out earlier?" he'd complained. "Why'd she have to leave it till the last minute?"

"She's writing a paper. For the Smithsonian!" Steph had said. "It's a huge honour for her."

Tom was another matter altogether. Although he hadn't been saddled with his ancestors' given name, he'd got the legal gene. Was a hotshot young lawyer in one of those slick Calgary law firms. Oil patch business got him dark suits, pretty blonde filly—Charlene—new Caddy every second year. And two young boys—Travis and Clint—who ate, breathed, and slept hockey. They were storm-stayed in Calgary, too.

"Sorry, Dad," Tom said when he called again this morning. "The boys are really bummed out."

Bummed out? Sounded like one of those Beach Boys, or those hippies yapping about Americans in Vietnam. His coffee was waiting for him on the pine kitchen table. Black. Steph was basting the goose. She looked good bent over the oven door like that. The heat was pleasant.

The radio was on top of the fridge. He turned it on. It was four o'clock.

And now the news: Buckingham Palace says the Queen has approved the design of a new flag for Canada. A spokesman says official recognition of the Maple Leaf flag will come in February. . . .

Ty tuned out for a moment, took a sip of his coffee, listened to the wind instead. He grimaced, threw the coffee in the sink. It was old, burnt.

In Saigon, the death toll from the Christmas Eve bombing at the Brinks Hotel has been confirmed at two—both U.S. military officers. The blast is being blamed on Viet Cong terrorists. One hundred and seven Americans were injured. . . .

Ty went to a cupboard, took down the bottle of red wine they'd opened last night. California. Ty always tried to support western businesses, on either side of the border. He yanked the cork out with his teeth, got a couple of Steph's special crystal glasses.

"Want one?" he asked, as she closed the oven door.

She smiled, nodded, her faced flushed.

He poured two glasses.

Here at home, the blizzard that started yesterday continues to disrupt Christmas travel across southern Alberta. RCMP closed the TransCanada highway near Canmore this morning. Whiteout conditions have been reported from High River to Pincher Creek. The storm—one of the worst in years—is expected to last at least another thirty-six hours. Winds will continue from the northwest with gusts up to seventy miles per hour. Temperatures tonight are expected to reach minus forty. Police are advising motorists to stay off the roads—

Ty clicked the radio off. "Let's go sit by the fire."

"Worried?" she asked when they were settled.

"Yup."

"How long can they last in this, Ty?" She always used his name when she was feeling something. That was their livelihood out there walking around on four hooves. And it didn't matter that the cattle were raised to end up in a Safeway meat counter. They were still living creatures. Both of them hated seeing the animals suffer.

Ty shook his head. "It's a killing wind." He paused. "Some might be down now." He took a drink of the cabernet, nice and dry, stretched his scuffed boots towards the fire. It pained him deeply to be sitting in the house like this, to not be out there on his horse, driving them back home or into some shelter. But a man'd die in minutes or just get lost and wander till he froze to death. Either way, it wouldn't take long. There was nothing to do but wait. Steph, curled on the couch close to him, pulled a crocheted blanket over her.

"Maybe you can get out tomorrow," she said, staring into the fire, taking a sip. Normally, they'd have toasted "Merry Christmas." Nothing merry about tonight.

"Jeez H—!" The drift against the barn door was hard as rock. Ty put his head down, strode over to his shop, got the pick. It was morning, though that was hard to tell—still storming, not quite as bad. The weather man'd said it would last all day, but the wind would only be gusting up to fifty miles an hour. "Only fifty!" Ty had muttered at the radio. He had so many clothes on, it was hard to swing the pick, but in minutes he got the door clear. Inside was a dark refuge filled with the frosty smell of horses and manure. All four horses had their heads over the doors of their box stalls, waiting. "Hey, fellas." He'd mucked them out yesterday, given them their Christmas mash. Steph had cooked apples and oatmeal. It was back to regular chop this morning. Ty thought they looked disappointed as he poured it into their wooden troughs. He cleaned their stalls quickly, listening to the creaks and groans of the barn as he worked, a conversation that Ty usually found comforting. Not today. Three barn cats watched as he threw the manure into a wheelbarrow and dumped it into an empty stall. He replaced it with fresh straw, hay, and water for each horse.

"Eat up," he said, slapping his chestnut, Rusty, on her flank. "You're gonna need it today, girl." When she'd eaten and had a long drink, he led her out of the stall. Working quickly now, he brushed her out, the horse's steaming breath mixing with his own. He threw the biggest, thickest wool blanket he had over her, set the work-worn saddle on her back, reached for the cinch under her warm belly, tightened it up good. Then he tied on the lariat, his Winchester in its case. He led her out the back door, into the lee of the wind, just to let her size up the situation before he pushed her into it. She balked anyway when she saw the storm. A grim, grey-white thing, still raging.

Ty Corbett swung onto his horse with a groan. Two pair of wool long johns, jeans, overalls, two pair of thick, wool socks, shirt, sweater, peaked black wool cap with earflaps, fur-trimmed hood of his old winter parka over that, wool scarf tied around his neck, woollen mitts inside his stained leather work mitts. *Gawd, I can hardly move.* His clumsy winter boots found the stirrups. He nudged Rusty with a heel, clucked his tongue automatically as he neck-reined her right with a thick-mittened hand.

"Let's go, girl."

Into the whirling snow he rode, out through the empty corrals, past the high, rectangular stacks of hay bales, and angled cross-wind towards the caraganas. He was used to snow, the sting and bite of it, but this . . . He grimaced, tilted his head into the wind so the hood would shelter his face. Rusty didn't like it either, wanted to go downwind. He pushed her west until they got to the barbed-wire fence—or what used to be a fence, for nothing but the post tops and, once in a while, the top barbed wire showed above the drifts. On a normal day, Ty Corbett could see a good distance from where they were, on a slight rise in the land. Today, it fell away to nothingness in the south. Ty followed the drifted fence line, kept it to his right, till they reached a corner made by another fence coming up from the south. He turned downwind then, put the wind to his back quarter. He thought of Steph back in the ranch house. She'll be pacing already, stopping to look out every window, wishing she were out there. But Ty had refused her offer and knew that she was secretly thankful.

Rusty plodded through the snow, sometimes up to her belly in soft drifts, other times breaking through hard crusts up to her knees. Every few minutes she shook her head, dislodging the snow that froze around her eyes. Ty gave her a pat. "Atta girl." A small willow loomed out of the whiteness ahead, then another. They became a clump of shadowy, twisted trees. Then poplars rising above them, bare and forlorn. And behind them, a reddish blur—cattle.

What a sorry lookin' sight! The Herefords were bunched up like he figured, their backs covered in snow frozen to their coats. Their white faces drooped. Small icicles hung from their mouths and nostrils. The snow blew in around their legs and made drifts beneath the cows. Only their shifting feet kept it packed down. Bits of uneaten hay lay scattered in the snow. Ty circled around behind them, counting. "Damn," he muttered, the word swept away like a cigarette ash. There were forty, maybe fifty head max. That meant another hundred or so were out there somewhere. Ty was thankful his winter herd wasn't bigger. Like all ranchers, he sold off a good portion of cattle every fall after a fattening summer of grazing. It'd been a good year. They'd made some money. Kept the best cows and heifers as breeding stock to build up the herd. That's what was out here now. He wished he could do something for them, but he had to find the others first. *How much longer can the poor buggers last?*

Reluctantly, Ty turned Rusty downwind again. He still couldn't see more than fifty, sometimes a hundred feet, but Ty knew the land. As long as there wasn't a whiteout, he wasn't worried about getting lost. Frozen to death, yes, but not lost. That, of course, could change in an instant.

He followed the fence line south, keeping away from long drifts that submerged the posts. There was an alkali draw ahead, a low place with soil too sour to grow willows or poplar or anything else, that would give a little shelter to a storm-caught cow. Trouble was, the fence turned there, went around the white-mud slough. In the featureless landscape, Ty felt the draw, more than saw it, felt his seat slide forward in the saddle as Rusty went down the slope.

There was a smudge in the whiteness ahead. Ty set his teeth. It was a heifer, a two-year-old by herself, snow halfway up her belly in a drift by the fence. Circle C brand on her rump. She stood motionless, her eyes covered with ice and frozen shut, her rear into the wind, tail almost buried in the drift. "Come on," he yelled, his voice dry and flat as sandpaper. "That's no place for a girl." Nothing. Not a muscle moved.

He reined in Rusty, swung his right leg over her rear as he dismounted, wondering vaguely how many times he'd done that in his life, stopping to help some calf or cow in trouble. He waded awkwardly through the snow. "Hey, girl," he said, approaching her head. She still didn't move. He reached out, swiped at the ice over her eyes. It stayed there. He scraped harder, then banged at the casing with his clenched fist. "Sorry 'bout that." A chill feeling rose inside of him, and it wasn't from the cold. The broken chunks clung to the hair on her white face. He picked them off one by one. "Now you can see," he said, and he waded around to the back of her. *Her teats may be frozen.* He swept the snow away from her rear end, so he could give her a push. The business end of her tail was caught in the hard drift. He grabbed it in his mitt, pulled.

"Shit."

He stared at it for a second, the frozen thing like a broken stick in his hand. He threw it down in the snow, the stub white and red, too frozen to bleed. The heifer hadn't flinched.

Grimly, Ty waded back to Rusty who stood waiting, her rump to the wind. He unsnapped the rifle case, pulled out the 44-40 Winchester. He turned, worked the lever action, heard the cartridge click into place. As he raised it to his shoulder, he wished he hadn't knocked the ice off the heifer's blue-black eyes. In the wind, the shot sounded like a kid's cap gun.

The cold rose higher inside him now, seeping in around his neck, along his spine. His fingers were freezing, his double layer of mitts no better than driving gloves in this wind. He pounded his hands on the saddle horn, wriggled his toes, which were hurting, too. *Damn socks are too tight.* He rode around the alkali slough, wishing for a nice hot coffee, but he hadn't brought any—it was too cold to stop, to pull a hand out to open the thermos. He was hurting now, hurting for that poor dumb animal, afraid of how many more he'd find. Ty rode downwind, guiding his horse with the pressure of his knees, a slight movement of the reins on her neck. He tried thinking like a half-frozen cow, tried figuring where a storm-driven herd might go.

For the first time in his life, Ty wished his grandfather had found a different place, one with more creeks that carved sheltering coulees out of the prairie where proper trees could grow. Maybe one in the foothills to the west, with sharp bluffs overlooking quick, little gravelly rivers with grassy flood plains and scattered forests of conifers. He shook his head, wriggled his body to shuck off the shivers.

"Let's check out the crick," he said out loud to Rusty.

They turned and angled southeast across his land. They'd gone only about two miles so far, only about a mile and a half from the ranch as the crow flies. The creek was a couple of miles away across nothing but grassland. No fences. Not much for trees. But there was a small cut on the north side of it, on an elbow where the shale from spring floods had been sluiced away over the years. Below that'd be out of the wind a little. He knew it. But did the cattle?

An hour later, and they still hadn't reached it. Ty wondered if he'd missed it. He was now officially cold, stone-cold right to his bones. *Sixty-three is too damn old for this.* He worried about Rusty, his best horse, twelve years old and getting on. He rubbed his hand along her mane, shook the snow out of it. *Just don't step into somethin', girl.*

He heard it then. Off to his left and ahead. There it was again. A cow, bawling. *For Pete's sake.* Ty wondered if the cattle had smelled them. They were downwind. Rusty stopped. Ty looked down. Her front hooves were on the brink of a small bank. The crick was frozen, of course, sifted deep with snow. He pushed Rusty down to the bottom, then turned her left, picked their way through the low bushes and drifts, following the broad, white line as it snaked along, over a couple of beaver dams. It felt good to get that monstrous wind off his back, its sharp claws out of his skin. The light seemed better, too. He looked up. Clouds were thinning. *Maybe she's played herself out.*

There they were—the huddled shapes of cattle. Right where he thought. *Good.* He felt the relief rise up inside and realized he hadn't been breathing much. The snow sifted down on them from over the crest of the bluff. A fine powder filled the air, went into his eyes and up his nose. The cattle were covered with it, but it was soft, and they were out of the murderous blast. They stirred from their tight huddle, began to mill as he rode up to them, then around, counting again.

Gawl-darn it.

There were only thirty-eight, maybe forty head. A sour feeling scuttled the hope before it had a chance to catch, sent it spiraling back to the bottom of his gut. Another forty head were still out there somewhere, drifting with the storm, most likely to the south. But the awful thing was, there was no shelter downwind, nothing for miles and miles but barbed-wire fences, several of them.

Ty Corbett got down from Rusty, dropped her reins in the snow. "Have a drink, girl," he said, meaning eat some snow. He went around to the lee side of his horse, stomped his feet in the snow, shook his legs, flapped his arms to get warm. *Should've brought some coffee.* He had a quick leak instead—downwind—then mounted up.

Ty turned Rusty south again. They plunged through drifts on the other bank, back into the wind tunnel of driving horizontal snow. They were four miles from the house now and its warm, fragrant kitchen, the snapping fire. Steph might be reading, curled up on the couch. A cup of tea or hot chocolate steaming on the coffee table he'd made—a slab of pine, gleaming with varnish. She might even have a nap if she could, if she weren't too worried about the cattle. And him.

The two of them drifted downwind now, downstream on a freezing current. That lull he sensed had been just an illusion. The wind seemed harder than ever, driving flakes and dirt that stung like BB-gun pellets, then stole the air out of his nose and mouth. He was even colder now. Ice picks jabbed up and down his spine. Ty shrunk down inside himself as they ploughed on, swinging this way and that, looking for dark shapes on a shapeless plain, something that didn't belong, out here in this at least. His mind wandered, to the old-timers' stories about the blizzard of '07. About a herd driven into a ravine on the Bartley place, cattle pilling on top of each other like at a buffalo jump. So packed in, it took thirty years for them to rot down to sun-bleached bones. He'd ridden over to show the kids once. They'd called it Death Valley.

They went on for an hour, then two. Ty looked at his watch once and was surprised it was two-thirty. In a couple of hours it'd be dark. That wasn't the worst of it. He knew every step they took downwind had to be retraced—into the wind. Like the early skiers who, after every long, hurtling run, had to climb slowly back up the mountain. Home would be a tough place to get to. Even without cattle.

They came up to a fence, what was left of it under drifts. Ty turned Rusty to the right, to the west again, putting the northwest wind on their faces. They followed the fence for a while, until they came to a place where it disappeared under a drift. He stopped and stared into the snow, trying to read the story. This group had probably peeled away from the first ones he'd seen, run with the storm down to here. Trapped against the fence, they stood, the snow piling up under them. They would shift, move, pack it down as they slowly froze, until the snow rose to the height of the fence. Then they went over, drifted down to the next one. He urged Rusty over the wire. She didn't want to go. In the trackless snow, he pointed her downwind again. That's the way the cows would travel, little square-sailed galleons wallowing across a stormy sea, wind nipping at their sterns.

They were six miles from home, then seven. Ty came to another fence, went back and forth along it for half an hour. The light was fading now. Ty wondered if he should head home or ride on over to the Hansons' Triple Bar. He could phone Steph if the lines were still up. And say what? That he'd failed? *Just a little bit longer.*

A couple minutes was all it took.

Oh, my dear God.

He winced, turned his head away. Sucked in a cold breath. Rusty snorted, shook her head, jingling the bridle. She was spooked as well.

After more than sixty years of living on a ranch, Tyson Corbett thought he'd seen just about everything. The cattle had bunched up at a fence all right, packed in tight like sardines. They were half buried in the drifts that formed around them, but for some reason, they hadn't trampled the snow down and gone over the barbed wire. Maybe just too cold. They'd stayed put, their faces turned south as if towards some Promised Land—one they couldn't see. Thick crusts of ice and snow covered their heads. Huge icicles drooped from their noses and jaws, thick as stalactites, pulling their heads down to the rising snow. Freezing them in place like displays in some mad museum diorama. The cows at the back of the bunch had given shelter to the ones at the front. But their rear ends faced into the wind. And they had paid the price. The blowing snow and dirt from exposed prairie had blasted the hair right off their hides, had sanded the bare skin into leather, then peeled it off and rolled it back a foot or more, rubbed the exposed meat and muscle until it was black and glistening—frozen solid. Drifts piled arse-high around them, their tails and back legs covered. It was hard to tell which ones where alive and which ones weren't. In the deepening gloom of dusk, new snow pelted the lost herd—a cruel, satanic benediction.

Something clicked in Ty, shoved the shock, the horror back down, like a bullet pushed backwards into a magazine. He nudged Rusty, reined her right. She didn't want to move. He kicked her, pulled hard on the reins, in action now. He rode to the west side of the bunch, pushed Rusty up to the front by the fence. "Hiyah," he croaked. And he yelled again. The animals were too numb to move. He pushed Rusty right into them. "Hiyah, let's go." This time he cried as he yelled, the tears freezing instantly on his face. He brushed them off with a mitt then charged the cows again. They wouldn't move.

And then he realized. *They can't see! They won't move if they can't see.*

Ty looked around, saw a broken fence post leaning against the good one that replaced it. He backed Rusty up, reached down, yanked the grey, weathered thing out of the snow. Again he pushed Rusty towards the herd. Crack! He hit a cow over the head. The force of it shattered the casing of ice. The cow shuddered, shook its head. One eye was clear. Crack! Crack! Like some demented clergy dispensing blessings to a crowd of Christmas pilgrims, Ty swung the post again and again. The cows, relieved of their icy hoods, stirred from their frozen trance. They staggered in the drifts, slowly began to move along the fence. Half mad now in the dark and freezing wind, Ty clobbered his beasts to freedom, laughing out loud once at the awful heartbreak of it.

Dislodged and moving slowly, Ty pushed the cattle east, then turned back, left them for a moment. Five shapes still stood in the trampled snow, their heads down, wind-butchered haunches facing north. He pulled the Winchester out again, rode up close.

Bang. Ca-click. Bang. Ca-click. Bang. Ca-click. Bang. Ca-click. Bang.

The anaesthetist himself was numb.

The way back was a blur of time and space, of shuffling movement and stupefying cold. The cattle refused to head into the wind. Ty thought he'd try it anyway—they were eight miles from home—but they turned away. So he drove them northeast instead, pushed them like a sailor as close to the wind as they'd go. And later, when the left side of their faces and eyes were freezing up again, he tacked, and swung them back west, always fighting them north, pushing them in a zig-zag pattern to gain ground, towards the waiting shelter of home.

Ty stopped. Struck dumb by the wind and cold, he leaned forward, buried his face in Rusty's mane, in her neck. His feet were frozen, his hands frozen, his face numb and long past raw. Without conscious thought, he fumbled with his mitts, tugged them off, stuffed them into his crotch on the saddle, then shoved both bare hands under the blanket against Rusty. He stayed like that for a while, with no sense of time. Only the arrival of dull pain told him the heat was working, his hands were thawing. He was dead tired, so tired he was afraid of falling asleep, of falling into the soft and downy snow, succumbing to the warm invitation of death that lurked at the fringes of his thoughts. He shook himself, sat up, went to pull his mitts back on, fumbled with them. *Damn!* He dropped one. In an instant he was awake. Rusty whinnied, sidestepped.

"Whoa, girl."

He was in trouble. All the stories of dead ranchers came flooding back, their ghosts hovering like spectators in the snowy gallery, looking down at him, watching to see how he'd get out of this one. A dropped mitt, a spooked horse, and he'd be one of them. Ty held the reins tightly as he lowered himself to the ground. He bent down, then fell to his knees. There it is. Between her feet. His hand was numb again as he tugged it on, pulling the leather with his teeth.

Ty gave up trying to drive the cattle. Hunched over in the saddle, head down, the reins slack, he gave Rusty her head. She plodded forward, carried him into a white nightmare of a land that was without form or direction or time.

It was hours later, or minutes, he couldn't tell, when the pin-prick of a light flickered up ahead. *A flashlight? Star? No, yard light!* Ty roused himself. Then the light disappeared as they came up back of the bale stacks, then in a dark wind shadow. They were at the barn. He slid stiff-legged off his horse, clinging to her for a moment till his legs got some feeling back. Staggering to the door, he opened it, drew Rusty inside, then closed it on her. He weaved towards the hay bales, crawled between the corral bars, pulled at the corner of the stack. An avalanche of bales tumbled down, sweeping him with it. Ty lay back and laughed—a ragged, croaking sound—then staggered to his feet. All this was automatic now as he threw the bales over the fence, climbed back through, tore off the strings, kicked the bales into loose slabs of hay for his cattle straggling in. Back in the barn, he wiped off Rusty, gave her fresh water, a big helping of chop, threw a horse blanket around her, the kind they use on race horses, fastened the strap.

"Thank you, girl," he said patting her. "Good job."

Blinding light roared from the windows of the house, hurting his eyes. Steph was a silhouette at the door.

"Good Lord," she said as he shuffled in. "I thought you were dead."

She walked him like a zombie, blinking, into the kitchen. "Sit." She pulled out a chair. He plunked down, boots and all, a frozen hunk of meat. She swatted ice and snow off his hood, his parka. "Oh, Ty!" she said, unknotting the scarf. She pulled off the hood, his cap, threw them on the floor. "Did you find them?"

He nodded. "Most of 'em." It was barely a whisper. "'Bout forty drifted down almost to Hansons'—"

"Hansons'!" She yanked his mitts off, threw them onto the pile.

"Had to shoot six," he said, looking at her. "Brought thirty back, maybe. We'll probably lose some more." Ty glanced up at the clock over the sink. "Turn the radio on."

"What?" Steph tugged at the zipper on his parka. It was frozen. Like his fingers.

"The radio," he repeated. "Please, turn it on." It was ten o'clock. Ty needed to know how bad it was out there, as if to confirm that this wasn't some awful dream.

"Just a minute." She tugged the zipper. "There." It came free. She yanked it down, pulled him out of the sleeves. He shifted in the chair to help. She turned the radio on, then rushed out to the living room.

. . . worst storm to hit the province in fifty years. The RCMP says ranchers have been particularly hard hit. The ditches and fences are lined with dead or dying cattle, Inspector Dan Stevenson of Hanna says. . . .

Stephie reappeared with a blanket. "Here." She wrapped it around his shoulders, then knelt, undid his boots, and pulled them off. Like a statue, Ty sat listening.

Donna Waters, president of the Calgary League of Animal Rights, says the ranchers who left their cattle out in the storm should be sent to jail . . .

"What!" yelled Ty, standing suddenly in his bare, unfeeling feet. Steph rose beside him.

A woman's voice came over the radio.

It's a crime what these poor animals are going through. They should never have been left out there. Those ranchers should be locked up.

Ty walked over, twisted the button hard. He felt like throwing up. Went over to the sink, stood there with both hands on the cool enamel.

"How can she say that?"

He raised his head, stared at the black window. An old man stared back, shaking, in pain.

"Oh, hon." Steph reached out, touched his arm. "She doesn't know what's she's talking about." She tugged his arm. "Come, sit down."

He folded himself back into the chair.

"How can people have so little understanding?" His voice broke. His back slumped like a clobbered cow. "I'm quitting, Steph. That's it."

“No, Ty!” She went up behind him, grabbed his shoulders. “Don’t let her get to you. You’re so much better than that.”

Ty Corbett’s body shook as he wept. Steph folded her body over his cold back, wrapped her arms around him.

“This is who you are. *You* brought those cattle in. Lots didn’t. You heard. The ditches and fences are full of them. Not ours. You saved most of them. You did it.” She paused for a long moment. His chilled body soaked up her warmth. “You’re the best man I ever met, Ty.”

Her warm tears ran down his leathery neck. He reached up to her, his thawing fingers touching her hair.

THE ONE WHO *Became a Wolf*

Johnny Tuu'luuq spotted the *iglut.* They were right where he knew they'd be—under the bright star he'd been following for the last half-hour. A tiny speck of light came from one of three domes squatting on the snow. His dogs saw it, too. They jerked the caribou harness, pulling the *kamotik* hard as they raced towards home. As he got closer, the seal gut window in his parents' *iglu* took shape. The lamplight drew faint, white lines around each block of snow across the roof. It always reminded him of a turtle he'd seen in a book at school. His father's dogs leapt out of their snowy beds and barked their greeting. Johnny dismounted from the back runners, stomped the anchor into the snow, and bent to untie his panting team. He retrieved a few chunks of frozen meat from the sled and tossed them gratefully at the animals. It unleashed a snarling storm of fur and teeth.

The hunter threw his *kakivak*—his spear—high onto his dark *iglu,* perhaps harder than he needed to. The sharp iron point landed with a *ka-chunk.* It was safe there, away from the dogs, who'd chew the wooden shaft to slivers in minutes. His gut also felt chewed up. His teeth were clenched at the thought of the task ahead. He pulled the musk-ox robe off his *kamotik,* slid the seal off, too, then turned the sled upside down and propped it against his *iglu* so the runners wouldn't freeze to the snow. Grabbing the seal by a flipper, he crouched and descended through the sunken door into his father's snow house.

They were all there, smiling: his children, his wife, his parents, his grandmother, swimming in the pale light of the seal oil *kullik.*

"Daddy!" Johnny knelt on the icy floor as little Kenojuak climbed down from the snow bench and ran to him.

"Hey, *Nanook,"* he laughed. "Bear" was a good nickname for a five-year-old hunter.

The boy turned to look at the seal. "You got one!" he said, sticking his finger into the wound on its neck, then putting it to his mouth, sucking the frozen bits of blood.

"Hello, father . . . mother . . . grandmother," Johnny said in Inuinnaqtun. He nodded respectfully as he stood up. He pushed back his frost-rimmed hood and stepped towards his wife. Effie smiled as she set their daughter, Lucy, on the fur bench and rose awkwardly.

"Hi," Johnny said, touching his forehead to hers, touching his nose to hers, breathing in her warm breath, her comforting scent.

"You have been gone a long time," she said. It was not an accusation. Her brown eyes were filled with concern. The lamplight glistened in her oiled black hair.

"Yes," he nodded. "The hunting was not good."

It felt warm in the *iglu.* Outside it was thirty below. Johnny pulled his *atigi* over his head, hung the caribou parka on a peg, then reached for Lucy. "How is my little girl?"

"Where were you?" she asked, stroking the few long whiskers hanging from his chin.

"I was hunting," he answered. "See." He pointed at the seal. Kenojuak was bent over it, staring at its glassy round eyes.

Johnny turned to his father. "How was the hunting for you?"

Enook shook his head, lowered the metal file and knife. "The airplanes must be frightening the game away," he muttered. "I broke my knife." He motioned to the shortened blade. "I was careless."

Johnny saw his father glance at the seal. He knew his father would understand in an instant the story of the kill—how he had waited all day for it, scraping the ice with the scratching bone to lure the seal to the breathing hole. He would know from the wound in its neck whether the kill had been quick and clean. The missing chunk by the tail would tell him how hungry Johnny and the dogs had been. He would picture them eating out there on the ice. He would also know from the size of it that there was no more meat outside.

"Mother," Johnny said, greeting her with a rueful smile. "This is just a small one, I'm afraid." He shrugged his shoulders.

"It is enough," his mother said. A steel needle flashed in her hand as she tugged gut thread through her mending—his father's hunting bag.

"Sedna is unhappy with you." Suqualuk stirred from deep in the caribou robes. She glared at him, her grey, stringy hair hanging limply around her toothless face. "Did you give that seal a drink of fresh water after you killed it?" she asked, her voice a dry wind over frozen gravel.

"No," Johnny laughed. "I don't believe in that."

"No wonder you are an unlucky hunter," she said. "Not like your same-named-one." His Uncle Johnny, after whom he was named, was away hunting on the ice with Johnny's brother, Aglak, and their families. "Sedna chases all the sea creatures away from you."

She spit a yellow gob onto the icy floor and sat back with a satisfied nod.

Enook coughed, then resumed filing the blunt end of his knife. Johnny turned to warm his hands by the *kullik.* The stone pot suspended above it was full of black tea. It smelled good and strong. The meat bags hung limp and empty on a peg beside the lamp.

"The Black Robe came by," Enook said matter-of-factly.

"Which one?" Johnny tried hard not to sound surprised.

"Father Lemer."

Johnny silently cursed his bad luck. He had not wanted it to be like this. He waited. The *kullik's* light burned cold now, the warmth suddenly gone out of it. The walls of the *iglu* closed in, no longer comforting. It was now a cramped, frozen place. Silence. Johnny suddenly knew what it felt like to be a seal, waiting, waiting, desperate for a breath of air, getting the cold iron of a *kakivak* through the neck instead. He glanced at his wife. Effie's head stayed down as she fussed with the sealskin *kamiks* on Lucy's feet.

"Father Lemer wanted to baptize us," Enook continued slowly. His father was a patient hunter. He would draw this out. Johnny sat down beside his wife, picked up Lucy, held her in his lap. His mother, Eunice, her weathered face a mask, turned her back to him as she knelt down at the cutting plank. She lifted a scrap of hide. A boiled caribou tongue lay stretched out under it, grey with flecks of dried green herbs his mother collected in summer. Johnny felt his mouth water.

"And what did you say?"

"I said we would think about it." Enook glanced at Suqualuk. "The white man's Creator is powerful. This Jesus—I think that is a good story."

Suqualuk hissed her contempt. "We have all the stories we need. Kiviuq, Sedna—these spirits made the ancestors happy."

They don't make you happy, grandmother. Johnny suppressed a smile.

Enook nodded, his black eyes peering from deep crevices in his round, dark face. Eunice's bone-handled *ulu* rocked back and forth as she cut the caribou tongue. "It is their Jesus' birthday today," she said, not looking up, the knife thumping and slicing in a timeless rhythm. "I saved this for us."

"The Father left a book so that you could read us stories." Enook nodded to an indent carved into the wall where a small black Bible sat. *Tswppt!* His grandmother spit her comment, onto the wall behind her this time.

"He also said he saw you in Ikaluktutiak." The hunter had struck.

A shiver ran down Johnny's neck. He looked at Effie whose brown eyes met his and urged him on. The *ulu* stopped. His mother's back waited. His father made no pretence at filing. His hunter's eyes glowed like embers in a summer campfire, waiting.

"I have been thinking about this for a long time," Johnny began. "Then a few days ago, I met Noah Agluk and his family on the ice. They were moving to Ikaluktutiak." His father's eyebrows raised slightly at the news. Johnny continued. "The Americans are building a new settlement on the west side of the bay. That is why all these big airplanes are flying around."

Enook nodded. "Father Lemer told us. He is very upset. The Black Robes just finished their stone church, and now the community is moving across to the other side."

"You know about this?"

Enook nodded. "But we do not know about you. We do not know what you were doing there."

Johnny swallowed hard. "We want to move to the settlement, father. To the new one." The words clanged like the ship's bell in the stone church, like the bell in the school chapel he remembered in Inuvik. Forlorn, signalling the death of something.

Effie shifted beside him, leaned into him slightly. Her touch gave him courage. "The Americans are building a huge thing that takes pictures of the sky." Johnny did not know exactly how radar worked, but his parents would understand even less. "They will be able to look through clouds and fog and storms to see if there are any airplanes coming, or rockets with bombs." His mother sat back down on the bench, having rendered the tongue speechless. She twisted the cord on her *atigi.*

"Inuit do not have airplanes and bombs," Enook said quietly, a whisper, like snow moving on snow.

"No, no, the Americans are afraid of the Russians who live across the ice. The *Communists?"* It was a new word to them. "They are afraid of war, of the rockets that might fly over our land on the way to America."

There was more silence as Enook thought about this for a moment. "You would take pictures of these rockets?"

Johnny shook his head. "No, Father—there might never be any." He shrugged. "I would get a job. The Americans told me there are many kinds of jobs. They will pay me money. We will live in a wooden house. There will be enough food to eat. There won't be hunger times for my family."

"That is good," snorted Suqualuk, "because the airplanes will frighten Sedna away from Ikaluktutiak, too. It will no longer be a fair fishing place." That was what the name meant in their tongue.

Enook stared at the ice floor. Then he looked up at Johnny. "You are not a good hunter," he said matter-of-factly. "That day the airplane took you away to school, I watched it climb up into the sky like a silver bird and disappear. And every day when we were out on the land I would look up and think of you, and wonder when you were coming back home to live with us. And finally you did. You have learned many things about how the white man lives, and you had to learn again how we hunt, how we live off the land. But *illiquusiq*—our ways, our habits—that is something you carry here." Enook jabbed a stubby finger to the side of his greying head. "But you do not have it here." He thumped his chest over his heart with a closed fist.

Johnny looked at his father and mother. "When I went away it was different. But when I came back it was different, too."

Enook nodded and thought for a long moment. "Perhaps there is room in our hearts for only one way," he said finally.

Johnny took a deep breath. It was as close to acceptance as there would be from his father.

His mother raised her head. "When will you go?"

"Not for ten days."

Her face brightened. She got up and put the sliced tongue on a tin plate, handed it to her mother first. Suqualuk took a piece. Eunice set the plate down on the furs. She and Enook took a slice, then Effie, then the children. Johnny waited till last, as a hunter should.

The matter was settled. Conversation resumed, fitfully. They talked as they ate about other things: the weather, hunting, the growth of the children, when the new baby might come. When the caribou tongue was gone, Effie picked up her knife and cut chunks of fresh meat from her husband's seal and handed them out. They chewed it happily, sucked hungrily at the blood that ran down their fingers.

After they had eaten, Johnny remembered something and dug into the skin pouch he kept on a string inside his caribou shirt. "At Christmas, the whites give each other candies," he said, opening the bag. "I brought some for you. Here."

He held it to his father. Enook took a white ball with red swirls and carefully licked it. He nodded and licked it again. "I remember I had one like this once," he said, "from the missionaries." He popped it into his mouth.

"Just suck on it, don't chew it," he said to his mother as she picked one from the bag. "You might break a tooth. Grandmother, you don't have to worry about that." For the first time that night there was laughter in the *iglu.*

The children, their eyes big, reached into the bag. "This one's blue," cried Kenojuak.

"So is mine," said Lucy holding it up to show her mother. "See, like a seal's eye." They licked them, too, as their grandfather had done.

"Suqualuk, would you tell us a story?" asked Effie later, as they sipped their tea from chipped, blue enamel cups. A small gust of wind dislodged some snow by the smoke hole. It sprinkled down on them like a blessing. "It is a good night to hear one of your stories."

Suqualuk hesitated at first. Johnny thought she was refusing, but she was only waiting for her family to settle in among the fur robes on the bench. Lucy and Kenojuak snuggled against their parents, who leaned back onto fur robes pushed against the walls.

"This is the story about someone who became a wolf," the grandmother began. "She was called Qisaruatsiaq. The story was told to me many years ago by Saali Arngnaituq." Johnny nodded. It was the Inuit way to credit each song or story to the person who made it or passed it on. "A long time ago, when there were no white men in the country . . ."

The children soon fell asleep. Johnny remembered doing the same thing so many times. Suqualuk's story was about an old woman who deliberately separated herself from her community and slowly became a wolf. Johnny smiled to himself. He knew the story was directed at him. It was her way of saying that in leaving them to join the white men's community, he would become a wolf, changed forever.

When the story was over, Johnny and Effie said goodnight and left their children undisturbed to sleep with their grandparents. They emerged from the *iglu,* stopped, and looked up. The *arsanirit* swept across the vast Arctic sky, streaks of white and green and pink that painted the snow with shifting swirls of colour.

"Our ancestors are playing soccer," Effie said quietly beside him.

"The old ones believed that the lights are the torches of our ancestors' spirits," said Johnny. "They are guiding souls to a land of happiness and riches."

"I like that story better," said Effie. He could hear the smile in her voice.

Please guide us to happiness, too, Johnny Tuu'luuq prayed silently. *I am descended from you, from this land. I will carry that with me wherever we go.*

INCIDENT at Gold Rush Creek

"Bag of pond scum!"

"Brutish oaf!"

"You lice-infested vermin!"

"Oh, shut your gob!"

The Percy boys were going home. It was Christmas night. Well, Boxing Day morning, really. Moon shadows lay across their snowy path like fallen logs, tripping them occasionally. The scrape and swish of snowshoes was the only sound in the still, crackling cold. *Almost* the only sound.

"Filthy swine!" yelled Cyrus Huntingdon McIlmoyle Percy—formerly of London, San Francisco, and, most recently, Claim Number 357 on Gold Rush Creek, near Granville, Yukon Territory.

"You miserable, scuttling crustacean!" replied Vincent Meriwether Everett Percy, also formerly of the addresses listed above, and younger brother of the idiot listed above.

The sad truth is the Percy boys were—how shall I say?—tipsy. No, they were more than tipsy. They were pie-eyed, plastered, three sheets to the wind, drunk as hoot owls. After a night of observing Christmas festivities at the establishment known far and wide as the Granville Hotel. Saloon. Dance hall. Poker palace.

"You shrieking magpie!" Cyrus tossed the *bon mot* over his shoulder as he shuffled through the snow. Staggered really. His huge buffalo coat was unbuttoned, flapping open like his mouth, his fur hat wildly askew so that the leather string hung down across his nose like a rat's tail.

"Putrid polecat!" Vincent called out. His words echoed through mountains bristling with the ugly stumps of trees cut down by gold miners, and used to build their sorry huts and line their greedy little mine shafts.

Cyrus chose that very moment to look back at his half-witted brother and stepped into thin air—off the bank of Gold Rush Creek. Like a furry avalanche, he tumbled down the slope—rear end over tea kettle, as they say in polite circles—landing in a deep and fluffy drift.

"Bollocks!" He writhed fitfully, spastically, struggling to untangle his snowshoes and right himself.

"Hahahaha!" Vincent stood on the crest of the bank, gloating in the light of the almost full moon. "Serves you right, you clumsy jackass."

"Rrrrhhh." Growling like a cranky grizzly, Cyrus brushed himself off, turned and resumed his trek along the well-worn trail across the snowy creek.

Whump. The ice cracked beneath him. A common sound, especially when there's four feet of black water racing past underneath, gnawing away at the ice like a beaver. Still fuming and spitting snow, he shuffled on, stumbling, half crawling up the bank on the far side.

Whump. The ice cracked again, behind him.

Almost simultaneously, there was a loud and heartfelt "Agghhhh!" and an even louder splash.

Now a splash is not a good thing to hear out there, in the winter, at four-thirty in the morning, when you're half cut, and a snowy half-mile from the dead fire in your wretched little one-room cabin. And did I mention that it was twenty-three below? Probably not. Well, it was. Balmy by local standards, but still not a good time to be swimming in the Yukon Territory. And with a full load of clothes on, to boot. And speaking of boots, this particular pair being attached quite firmly to a pair of snowshoes. And being of a web design, not exactly seal flippers. No, not helpful at all.

"Help!" Vincent Percy yelled, quite emphatically.

Cyrus' first instinct was to laugh. And that is exactly what he did. "Ahahahahah!"

His brother was too preoccupied to share in the amusement. Bug-eyed as a bullfrog, Vincent thrashed and flailed about in the dark circle of rushing, chilling water. His hat had been dislodged and lay flopped on the ice like a drowned muskrat—which it had been at one time.

"Serves you right, you clumsy jackass." Cyrus mimicked his brother's very recent jibe, and it was quite well done, really.

"I-I-I c-c-can't swim! The current—" Vincent's bare hands clawed at the jagged ice around the hole he'd got himself into. He'd lost his mitts somewhere—who knows where? Meanwhile the rushing current was tugging insistently at the lower part of his body, intent on carrying him downstream for a mile or so, under the ice, to give him a wash, a rinse, and a darn good thrashing on the rocks at Dead Man's Falls. If he didn't get snagged first, that is, on some submerged branch and held still for the fishes to nibble on, until the spring floods finally released him and sent him tumbling, leaping over the aforementioned falls.

Cyrus removed a mitten, stroked his grizzled and still quite *snowy* beard—then proceeded to fill his pipe, strike a match, and light it, looking for all the world like some sourdough Father Christmas puffing away on the bank. "Seems to me you've got yourself into a bit of a pickle," he said finally, smoke encircling his head like a wraith.

"Cyrus," gasped Vincent, as he continued to slosh noisily, "it-it-it's s-s-s-so c-c-cold." And he seemed quite sober as he said it.

"You should have thought of that when you took your bath earlier tonight," said Cyrus, slipping his mitten back on

"What—" croaked Vincent, before he was pulled under, only a bare hand remaining clenched to the dripping edge of the hole. He reappeared, spewing a mouthful of water onto the ice. "Are you talking about?" he finished, punctuating his question with a gasp.

"You took too long," Cyrus yelled. "You always take too long. The water's always cold when I get in. And did I mention filthy?" The note of indignity rose in his voice.

Vincent, his head dripping, dark hair plastered to his round English head, little icicles glittering by the light of the silvery moon (which would be full tomorrow), kicked mightily as he tried heaving himself onto the ice. "Well, you get the short straw all the time," he sputtered. "That's why the water's tepid. It's only tepid, by the way, not *cold,* you stupid ninny." And he fell back into the clean and disagreeably frigid mountain stream, with a smaller splash this time.

"Yes, we both know you bloody well cheat. That's why you get the long straw." Cyrus hurled the accusation back at him. He wiggled his toes inside his boots, which were still attached, of course, to his own snowshoes. It was getting cold out there just standing around, jawing.

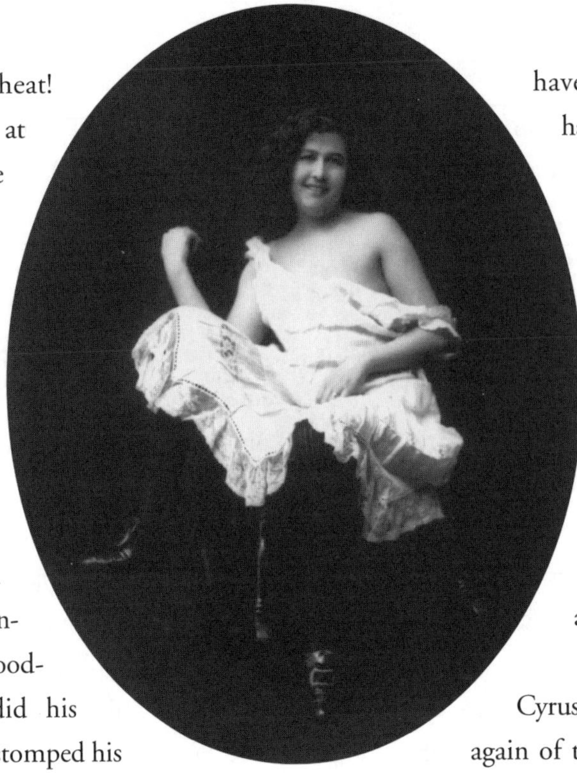

"Cheat? I don't cheat! You're just unlucky. Like at cards." The words were barely uttered before the drowning man succumbed yet again to another head-dunking, but not before he added, "Like at love."

The cruel taunt echoed across the naked hills. Cyrus winced. "Unlucky! You cad. You good-for-nothing—" He did his own bit of sputtering, stomped his snowshoe in the drift he was standing in with little effect. "You stole my woman, you charlatan!"

Vincent paused for a moment in his struggle to survive, which at the moment seemed unlikely. "Do you mean Priscilla? I didn't steal her. She couldn't stand the sight of you!" And he immediately resumed his flailing and thrashing.

"What do you mean? She winked at me all evening!" Cyrus was warming now. Anger can be as good as a crackling fire.

"Hahahaha—" Vincent's mocking laugh was drowned out by an untimely dunking in the cold tub of running water in which he soaked. "Please don't make me laugh!" he gasped upon reappearing. Yet from some great inner reserve he found the strength to laugh again. "You silly, self-deluded imbecile! She's supposed to do that. Wink and nod and coo in your ear, sit in your lap. Did she sit in your lap? Well, did she?" The nod would have been imperceptible had it not been for the thin, chill light of the moon hovering above them like a monocle, the only witness to this sorry spectacle. "Ahahaha," Vincent laughed again before his grip slipped off the ice, and he disappeared into the watery abyss.

"Poppycock," muttered Cyrus, deeply wounded, aware again of the intoxicating scent of Priscilla's cheap perfume in his beard, the memory of her warm, almost hairless lips on his love-starved ears. He pulled off a mitt again, fumbled for his pocket watch, flipped it open. There was a sudden surge of water in the hole, and Vincent emerged like a whale breaching, blowing.

"Blimey!" Vincent expostulated, notably weaker this time. "I'm dying."

"According to my calculations, you should have been dead minutes ago," said Cyrus, snapping the timepiece shut, restoring it to his pocket. He had a sudden urge then to go finish the job himself, push the idiot's head down until . . . but, no, he'd grab the poke around his brother's neck first, the leather pouch in which he kept his nuggets and flakes of gold, yank it, snap the cord, then push him under. Yes, then he would have it! The gold the silly nit would otherwise squander so lavishly on Priscilla and countless other frilly girls, the many friends for whom he'd buy whisky, mere acquaintances, even total strangers who wouldn't remember his name the next morning. And then, of course, there were the all-night poker games. The stupid, lazy spendthrift. Yes, he'd finish it off right here and help himself to the spoils. But a nagging thought hung over him like a pair of long johns on a clothesline. That would cross a line, wouldn't it? Pass from being a tragic but common enough accident on a backcountry stream, into the less murky waters of murder. No, he should let nature, good fortune, and a lot of cheap whisky do its dirty work for him, keep his hands clean. Unsullied. Metaphorically speaking, of course.

"Excuse me," cried Vincent pathetically. "I'm drowning here."

"Go ahead," said Cyrus. "I was just thinking about the gold I'll inherit after your inevitable expiry."

"Expiry?"

"Yes, your miserable little death. I don't know whether to walk back into town and report this unfortunate accident now or continue on to the cabin, light a fire, and pry up that floorboard where you keep what's left of your pitiful stash."

"How do you know where I keep my gold?" Vincent aroused himself and desperately hammered at the ice with his elbows, trying to break it and work his way to shore.

"I discovered it weeks ago, when you were lingering in the outhouse, trying once again to avoid doing the dishes." He laughed uproariously, quite madly in fact.

"Dishes!" Vincent thundered from his watery grave-to-be. "I do my share of the dishes!"

"Hah!" cried Cyrus. "You don't do your share of anything. Who's the one who chops the firewood, melts snow for water, washes and puts his socks and underwear away—instead of leaving them to hang about for days as public proclamations of his disgusting failure to maintain a modicum of personal hygiene?" Cyrus stopped, panting heavily. Outrage was hard work.

"A modicum?" snorted Vincent, catching yet another momentary—but I assure you, quite precarious—hold on the serrated edge of the ice. "There's a ten-pound word to toss off from your snowy, snooty perch up there, you toff. You're always *up there,* aren't you, big brother? While I'm down in the muddy mineshaft tending the fire, melting the frozen gravel, mucking it into the lift box. And what are you doing? Lollygagging around. 'Oh, look at the eagles,' he says. 'Oh, two ravens just flew by.' Drinking cup after cup of tea. Practising your penmanship in the snow. And every once in a while hoisting the box. Don't talk to me about lazy!" And with that, he allowed himself to be dunked once again by the river gods or at least the minor ones who inhabit rushing little creeks.

"You pathetic pipsqueak of a windbag," rejoined Cyrus with gusto, so much inflamed that he was forced to take off his buffalo coat and toss it onto the snow. "I stand out there in the cold all day long, waiting for you to fill the box, and you dig a little, have a smoke, dig a little, take a pee, and I'm jumping around freezing in the raw, biting wind and the double-digit minus temperatures of this icebox of a country, and you're down there in the warm and shelter, leaning on the spade, thinking about last night's poker game or some floozy, and secretly pocketing the biggest nuggets that happen to catch your bleary, bloodshot eyes."

"Windbag?" croaked Vincent faintly, finally showing signs of giving up the ghost. "You're the gaseous one who fouls the bed so badly it curls the hair on the musk-ox hide. Then you steal the covers and leave me freezing in the polluted air in just my underwear." Yes, he was growing decidedly weaker now, his head slipping lower and lower into the dark water, quite spent perhaps, more from hurling vitriol in this verbal joust than in the unsuccessful practice of self-rescue techniques. "You, you odorous fart," he said quite limply before slipping away in the dark with a sigh. A feather plume from his last breath rose into the night like a spirit, a fitting emblem of his final words.

"Good riddance," muttered Cyrus. And yet, as he stood there sucking his pipe back to life, gazing at the black hole, that portal to the netherworld, he was surprised at the sudden silence, at the oppressive emptiness that descended on him like a cloud. Go for the gold, he thought to himself, brightening. He retrieved his heavy coat from the snow and trudged away without a look back at the grim black spot on the snowy creek.

"Here you go, then," said Cyrus Percy, his eyes lowered, as he handed over a brown paper package tied rather festively with a red, wool string. "You might want to put these on presently."

The recipient, perched on a chunk of tree stump, huddled by a glowing iron stove, shivering under a frayed four-point Hudson's Bay blanket, his bare feet immersed in a galvanized tub of water that was decidedly warmer than tepid. Vincent Percy, alive and in the flesh—although it was still rather bluish and blotchy flesh, and certainly not yet in the pink—looked up with a smile. "I don't know what to say, brother."

"I think you've said quite enough already for one night," said Cyrus, grabbing the one decent chair they had between them in the squalid little cabin, pulling it closer to the stove, away from the line of dripping clothes that hung across the dim room, the only room. "Go ahead, open it."

Vincent, now thawed sufficiently to move his fingers after a sopping, half-mile romp back to the cabin, quickly untied the wool and carefully set it aside. "Oh," he exclaimed with a touching mixture of delight and surprise. He pulled out a pair of red, home-knit socks, one perhaps only slightly larger than the other. "When did you make these?"

Cyrus cleared his throat, splashed a little more of Muktuk Fanny's bootleg whisky into his glass, a former jam jar. "While you were in the outhouse," he muttered, "or sometimes when you were digging in the shaft, I'd run back and knit a line or two."

"Jolly good," said Vincent, holding them up, then quickly removing his feet from the tub and reaching for the burlap sack that passed for a towel. "Think I'll put them on right now." But then he stopped himself. "I've got something for you, too," he said quietly.

"You do?" Cyrus seemed genuinely surprised. And why not?

"Yes—go look in my rucksack." He pointed to a filthy canvas bag hanging from a wooden peg on the damp and frosted wall.

Cyrus opened it, took out a white flour sack with something hard and round inside. He let out a long appreciative whistle. It was a tobacco container, carved from a birch log, lid and all. "When did you do this?" he asked, every bit as incredulous as his brother had been just moments before.

"When you were dumping the lift box on the pile." Vincent beamed at his own canny secret. "I had it down the shaft with me, hidden, and carved it between loads."

Cyrus extended his hand. "Thank you, brother. Merry Christmas."

"Merry Christmas." Vincent smiled.

"No hard feelings?"

"Just in my toes. They hurt like the dickens."

Cyrus leaned back and laughed.

"I must ask you one question, though," said Vincent, pouring himself a generous splash of whisky. "Just why did you come back for me?"

Cyrus eyed his drink as he swirled the amber liquid around the bottom of the jar. "Well," he said, "every bloke with half a brain knows that creek only has four feet of water in it. You could have stood up at any time. I thought people would think I killed you, and they might string me up for a crime I didn't commit. So you see, brother, I wasn't saving your sorry life from your own drunken stupidity. I was saving mine."

"Is that the God's truth?" Vincent looked skeptical. And why wouldn't he?

"It's as close as you'll ever get." The effect of Cyrus' scowl was undone somewhat by the merest hint of a wink.

"Then I suggest a toast," said Vincent, raising his glass. "To brothers."

"To very rich brothers," Cyrus added.

As they laughed and cheerfully clinked their jars, light from the moon setting on the mountaintop leaked through their one filthy window and bathed itself in the whisky. In the bottom of their glasses, it shone like gold.

Tim

This is where my friends, Stan and Theresa, live. They're nice. They have a dog, Luca, that I walk twice a day. She's a golden retriever. I just walked Cocoa. She lives across the street over there in that big brown house. She's a chocolate Lab.

The doorbell doesn't work, so I have to knock loud. Mmmm, boy, this wreath sure smells nice—just like a forest smells, I guess.

Hi, Theresa. Merry Christmas to you, too.

Luca Bella! Are you so happy to see Tim? Yes, you are. Such a beautiful girl. That's a nice kiss. I love you, too. Yes, I do.

You're having a party, eh, Theresa? Oh hi, Stan. You're having a party, eh? That turkey sure smells good. I bet Jamie and Katie can't wait for Santa Claus to come. Did they write him a letter? I used to do that with my mom.

Did you know I got a new couch? I got a picture of it. It's in my photo album right here. Just a sec, I'll show you. See, Luca, there you are. And there's your friend, Cocoa. There's my new couch. It's orange. The people at the Salvation Army gave it to me. And some dishes and a new hot plate, too. My old one wore out. I guess I already had my Christmas, eh, Stan?

We better get going, Luca Bella. Wanna go to the park? Do you? Where's your leash, girl? Oh thanks, Theresa. I got something for you right here in my pocket, Luca. A Christmas treat. Yes, I know you can smell it. See you later, Theresa. Bye, Stan.

Look, it's snowing. Isn't it pretty? The flakes tickle my nose. How come they don't tickle yours? They're so big and fluffy. I'm so glad it's snowing. It just wouldn't be Christmas without snow. That's what everybody always says.

Wait! Luca! Don't go around the lamp-post that way, you silly girl. You're all tangled up. There we go.

Look, they're having a party in that house, too. See the people all dressed up? I like to look in windows at night. The lights look so warm. Sometimes people are just sitting reading the paper or talking—or maybe playing the piano. It's a nice street.

See, that's my house over there. It's not really my house. It's a rooming house. That's my room way up there—the top window just under the roof. It's dark now because I'm out here. The pigeons live right outside my window. Every night they sit there and coo, and I fall asleep. I always look out in the morning and see people going to work. I can see if it's raining or snowing, so I know what to wear.

Virgil hates the snow. He's my new friend—from an island somewhere, somewhere warm. He lives across the hall, but we share the same bathroom. He drives a streetcar. His wife died. Sometimes he cries at night. The pigeons don't keep me awake, but sometimes the crying does.

And that house—I walk their dog, Zoe. I got a picture of her, too. But they went skiing and put Zoe in a kennel. I miss my dogs when people go away. They gave me a Christmas card with a twenty-dollar bill inside, so I bought some liver treats for my dogs. I know you love them like crazy, don't you, Luca? They sure must be good. I haven't tasted them myself. I know some people eat dog food, but I don't.

Listen . . . see how quiet it is now. The snow makes everything so quiet, just like the city got tucked in under a big soft blanket. Don't you love that, Luca? No screeching tires. All the cars just whispering along.

We're almost there. Maybe we'll see some friends. Sometimes there are lots of people with their dogs. They just stand around and talk, and the dogs run around chasing each other all over the place. And they always like to play right by your feet. You have to be careful. Remember how they knocked me over one time, and I hurt my leg again?

Look, Luca! Here's your park. Oh, there's no one here. We've got the whole place to ourselves. I guess everybody's at home. Okay, there you go. Go find a squirrel. Thatta girl . . . look at her roll in the snow. A lot of dogs do that. I don't know why. I guess it just feels good. We'll just walk around the park a few times 'cause there are no other dogs to play with. See. Sniff, sniff, sniff. That's all she does. And she has her favourite trees to pee on. Stan says she's just marking her territory. She thinks she owns this whole park. Isn't that funny?

I'm older than Stan, but he's my friend. Sometimes I feel like he's my dad. That's funny, too, eh? I never knew my dad. He went away before I was born. That's what my mom said.

I could watch my dogs all day. Hah, that's what I do anyway. Even if I had a TV—which I don't—I'd rather watch my dogs. Oops, she's having a dump. Got my plastic bag right here. See. I always carry lots of extra ones because you never know how many times a dog is going to poop. Sometimes it's only once, and sometimes it's three times. I always carry extra bags. Some people don't. They just pretend they don't see what their dog did. Or else they kick snow over it and walk away. And then I step in it. I hate that.

Boy, it's really snowing. It looks just like one of those glass balls you shake, and the snow floats around and comes down on a tiny house inside.

Hey, there's Bobby. Hiya, Bobby! Bobby!

Guess he didn't hear me. Looks like he's in a hurry. Maybe he's going to the mission. He used to be a window washer. You know, on those high-rise buildings downtown. Until he lost his nerve. That's what he said. Now he just drinks. I drank with him, once or twice maybe, but I don't do that anymore. I forgot to walk my dogs. That's bad. So I don't drink anymore after that. Not much anyway.

Here, Luca! Come! Time to go home, Luca Bella. Time to snuggle in. It's getting colder. I can feel my fingers are getting cold. Are you cold, girl? We'll take the shortcut through the alley. You've been such a good dog, Luca. See, if we walk fast we get warm. We get home faster, too. There's our street. Boy, the cars look like big lumps of cookie dough and like someone sifted flour all over everything.

Looks like all the people are still at the party. I can open the door because I have my own key. Everyone says they trust me. So I use the key when nobody's home.

Hi, I'm Tim. I'm the dog walker. This is Luca. Here, Luca. I have to wipe your feet, little girl. That's a good girl . . . lift your paw. Okay, go find Stan and Theresa. Go find the kids. See you tomorrow, girl.

Oh hi, Theresa. I thought you were busy. Thank you. What is it? It's warm. Oh, I love turkey and mashed potatoes. I'll have this for my Christmas dinner tomorrow. I got a new hot plate. Did I tell you? I'll heat it on that. Thank you, Theresa. Merry Christmas. Goodnight.

Boy, you can hardly see these steps, eh? I'm glad I just live over there. I wonder if Virgil is up. Maybe he'd like some turkey and potatoes. We can sit on my new couch and have some. I won't bother him, though, if there's no light under the door. He'll still want some tomorrow.

I wonder if the pigeons will be awake.

RAIN ON *Gold Mountain*

"I'm going out for a smoke," Lee said, setting his black iron on the hot stove with a clunk.

His wife nodded, swiped at her glistening forehead without altering the course of her own iron. It ploughed along the back of a white man's shirt, a black ship smoothing a wrinkled sea.

Lee fished for a hand-rolled cigarette in the yellow tobacco can under the counter, got a wooden match, and opened the door. A wave of cool air wrapped itself around him, washed him, rinsed him. He breathed it in, felt it on his steaming, sweating body, felt it sink into his greying hair, his stooped shoulders, his tired, tired bones.

Rain roared down a spout beside him and spattered noisily on the sidewalk. Rain splashed off the broad backs of delivery horses, standing, waiting. The streetcar tracks glistened in pock-marked pools of light.

A car chugged by, shiny and black. A new Model T. The driver sat up straight and dry and white. People rushed by like a river, *guailow* mostly. White men, *white ghosts.* He felt invisible in the dark doorway as he watched them push past, heads down, hanging onto broad-brimmed hats, clutching the closed throats of woollen coats. Fearful of catching something, a sniffle that could bring death in a week or two. They carried shopping bags—some cotton, some brown paper, darkening, wet—bulging with groceries and gifts. Black umbrellas swirled by, shiny as buttons, sliding downstream towards home. Everyone was hurrying. The clock on the fire hall tower said five-thirty. He would close the door in half an hour, lock it. Keep it locked for a day. Tomorrow was Christmas.

He struck the match against a dry brick, enjoyed the brief flare of it, a firecracker, a tiny celebration for a day off. He lit the twisted end, pulling deeply, sucking the flame into the tobacco. His exhalation, a ghost swallowed up in the misty night. An image flowed into Lee's mind then. It came uninvited, took him by surprise, as it did from time to time. Was it thirty-nine years ago already?

He had been waiting for her in his tiny, dark room, in bed, his clothes on. Ting's candle had beckoned like a lighthouse beacon. "They've gone," she'd whispered. He'd heard them singing Christmas carols, heard them leave for church or for a party, he didn't know which, he spoke so little English then. Only nineteen, a dollar-a-month houseboy working for a British Royal Navy officer with a big moustache and booming voice. His conquered wife and skittish children were bossed around like sailors on one of his ships anchored out there in Esquimalt harbour.

Ting, the maid, had been there when he arrived. She'd been brought over as a prostitute, but ran away. The officer's wife had found her, taken her in. Now Ting had befriended him. Lee's railway work had ended, the track laid, the job done. The white construction bosses had broken their promise to pay the workers' fares back home. Like thousands of labourers, he'd been worked half to death, lied to, left to fend for himself. *Kuli,* the whites called them—to eat bitterness. It was a cruel slur and a bitter truth.

It had been raining that night, too. A man with a horse and wagon had picked them up, taken them along the muddy trail slashed through the forest to Victoria. They caught a ride on a fishing boat to Vancouver, bought tickets to Toronto with all their savings, then went to a tiny Chinese restaurant on the brawling waterfront. The owner had seen that they were young and afraid. Perhaps he'd seen, too, that they were in love. He fed them, gave them blankets, let them sleep on his floor.

The train trip through the mountains had been a nightmare. Lee told Ting about the workers, about picking up the pieces of bodies after the explosions, the blasting accidents. The whites were sewn into canvas bags and sent back on a cart or buried in some meadow with a wooden marker. The dead Chinese—or whatever parts of them they'd found—were often just flung over the cliffs, the sides of steep embankments. The men turned their backs as the ravens feasted. They cursed their bosses who cursed them back.

The Chinese knew that the Canadian prime minister had called them rats. "Well, they do come and so do rats," Mr. Macdonald had said. Lee explained to Ting that to white people "rat" meant filth, garbage, their lives worth nothing. The Chinese had come to Gold Mountain, as they called it, for the work, the wealth that was promised. Every railway tie, every bump, every click was a worker's bone, he told her—a tooth, a leg, a jaw, a rib. He spit out the window when they passed Craigellachie. Not a single Chinese had been invited to watch them pound the last spike. Lee didn't relax until they reached the prairies. But by then Ting was sick.

There was a doctor on the train, a kind man, but when he saw her fever, the pale colour of her skin, he shook his head. Lee looked after her, wiped her face with a wet rag, fed her thin soup when she'd eat. She died in his arms outside Winnipeg. He held her until Kenora. They took her away then, said they'd look after her small, stiff body. Numbly, Lee continued on, wondering if she, too, had been dumped beside the tracks. When he got off in Toronto, he vowed never to take another train, and he never did. Not even a streetcar.

He slept in stables, in parks, then walked into this very laundry one day and got a job scrubbing clothes in tubs out back. Eight years later, he bought the business, married Mai, the butcher's daughter down the block. The neighbourhood grew up around them. So did his family. Five daughters and three sons. They all worked in the family business, even two sons-in-law. With so many mouths to feed, there was little money. Once a week, Mai's father sent a boy over with a dripping, brown parcel: pork knuckles, brisket, and chicken gizzards. Lee felt fortunate, surrounded by his loving family. Had not Master K'ung himself said, "Loving hearts find peace in love."

A *guailow* brushed by him and went into the laundry, a big white man in a hurry. Lee threw the butt of his cigarette onto the sidewalk, watched its smoke curl up into the rain, until it was snuffed out by a wet, black boot. As he turned to go in, a loud voice inside said, "Just find my shirts!" The window was covered with steam. He opened the door. Mai's face was creased, her eyes dark. She held a piece of paper in her hand, shook her head at him, helplessly. Lee walked in, smiled at the glowering giant hovering over the counter like a warlord.

"I can't find them," Mai said in Chinese. Lee took the ticket from her, smiled again to the stranger—he did not remember seeing him before—and went to the wooden shelves to search the stacks of paper packages tied with thin, white string. In the steamy room, Lee felt his face grow warm. He would be ashamed to lose a customer's clothes. It almost never happened. Mai rubbed her worn hands as she watched him search. There it was. Finally. With a sigh of relief, Lee put the package on the counter, then waited for the man to pay.

"Merry Christmas," Lee said, bowing respectfully to his customer.

The man just looked at him, threw the money on the counter, then turned to leave. "Bloody chinks," he muttered and went out the door.

Lee followed him, closed the door and locked it, then wiped a circle of steam off the window. He watched as the man stopped on the street and waited for the clanging streetcar to pass, then scurried across—a white ghost disappearing in the rain. Lee wondered if the man was a Christian, if he prayed to his dead Christ, if he was rushing home to a celebration.

He thought of something else that Master K'ung, Confucius, had said. "You are not able to serve man. How can you serve the spirits?"

Lee turned and saw his wife's tired eyes, the stinging hurt on her face. It never got any easier for her. "Go upstairs and make the rice," he said gently. "Tell the children in the back to stop. I'll be up in a couple of hours."

As her slippered footsteps retreated up the stairs, Lee picked up a hot black iron, brought it down with a clank. It had taken many years, but he had finally learned not to eat bitterness, learned to toss it away instead like dirty wash water. Did not their Jesus say, "Turn the other cheek"? Did he not say, "Forgive"? There were many sacrifices to be made for their children. Some day, Lee thought, they will have a better life. They will be accepted. His iron ploughed along the back of a white man's shirt. A ship smoothing a wrinkled sea.

LES HABITANTS du Richelieu

"How is your picture, monsieur? Do you like it?" Édouard Letendre turned away from his card game and towards the man busily sketching in a chair near the window. It was dark outside. The window was sugared with frost.

"Yes, it's going well," said the artist. Cornelius Krieghoff had his leg crossed, balancing the pad of paper on his knee. He made a couple of quick strokes with his pencil, then looked up. "Excuse me, but your brother can see your card. I'd be sorry to think that my presence caused you to be unlucky at your game."

"Antoine! Ah, yes! Our wily voyageur doesn't need any more help. He learned every trick in the book on his canoe trips to the northwest."

"No, no, it's not true," protested Antoine. That provoked a chorus of laughter. He scratched his head through his red toque and grinned slyly.

"It's all too true," said Ferdinand, his brother-in-law, sitting beside him. "We learned long ago not to bet too much with Antoine, or the seigneur will never get his rent." More laughter.

"It's a pity that you can't be here for the *Noël* tomorrow night," said Édouard, plunking down his ace and bringing groans of displeasure all around. He turned again to the artist. "You are very welcome to stay with us."

"Thank you for your invitation, but we have commitments—although we are enjoying your tremendous hospitality."

"He wants to get back to Montréal to the swell city people," croaked Virginie, Édouard's mother, who stood by the stove cooking and watching her grandson play with his dog.

"No, on the contrary, madame," Krieghoff protested. "We must return to our little home in Longueuil. My brother, Ernst, is arriving tomorrow from Toronto. We'll go across on the ice bridge to the city to get him. Otherwise, we'd happily remain here in the warm embrace of your family, as you have made us feel so much at home. Don't you agree, Émilie?"

"Oh, yes. I love it here," his wife said quietly, as she played a card. "My family are farmers, too, you know, at Boucherville." She often sat in during her husband's painting and sketching sessions to "balance the scene," as he put it. "You are fortunate to live in this parish. The Richelieu River is so beautiful."

"It reminds me of my childhood," added Krieghoff, pausing to smile at their daughter, also named Émilie, who'd been playing with a dog under the table. "The castle where we lived in Bavaria was near a river." He motioned outside with his pencil. "My room was near the top, and I spent hours looking out the window, watching the shadows of clouds race across the hills and forest, watching the workers in the fields—life unfolding before me. . . . Perhaps that's why I became a painter. To capture this fleeting beauty."

"Yes, yes," nodded Édouard's uncle, Prosper. "My favourite season is winter, when there is deep snow in the forest." He stood by the table with his pipe, watching the game, his brother, Alphonse, beside him. "The long, blue shadows on the snow, the quiet. It is very serene."

"Ah," said Krieghoff, nodding. "Your eloquent description makes me long for the hunt and a good fire at night in camp."

"We must do that, then," replied Prosper, and his brother nodded. The two old bachelors lived on the next farm along the river to the south, having settled there at the same time as their brother, Bernard. Bernard, Édouard's father, was intent only on playing with his new granddaughter, Marie-Hélène, and her sister, Eugenie.

Prosper continued. "You know, my nephew, he makes good money working in the forest during the winter for the British American Land Company."

Krieghoff nodded, trying to capture the expression on the speaker's face, his vitality, his character.

"Does the forest keep you employed all winter?" Krieghoff asked, looking up at Ferdinand, his pencil poised and still for an instant. He had not been paying full attention to the conversation.

"Oui, we're cutting wood like crazy for railway ties—lots of oak and pine for all the new buildings in Montréal and Québec."

"It's hard work, no?" the artist asked.

"Very hard. We work six days a week. Not on Sunday, of course. Fortunately, we are close and able to come home to see our family. Otherwise, it would be a long time between visits."

"And, Édouard, you say you had a good harvest, a profitable year on the farm?"

"Yes, it's true," he replied, turning, holding his cards close to his chest this time. "We had a good crop of oats and barley, not so much wheat. We sold a cow, a couple of sheep, a pig. Our chickens are laying well. Our oxen are healthy and my horses, too, so it has been a good year, thanks to God."

"That *curé* who was just here, does he come often to visit?" Krieghoff's question was to no one in particular.

"He knows that we thresh our wheat next month," offered Édouard. "It was a good harvest this year, and he'll want his tithe, as usual." There was good-natured laughter around the table.

"Father Benoit doesn't need our tithes. He is the richest man in the parish," grumbled grand-père Bernard, finally paying attention to the adult conversation.

"Of course he is," offered Antoine. "He has more fields, a bigger wood lot, more cows, horses, and pigs than anyone in the parish."

"And a pretty little housekeeper," added Ferdinand.

"Enough! Enough!" hissed Virginie, as she hung a cloth to dry on a line over the stove. "These are unkind thoughts so close to the *Noël.* Mary, Mother of Christ, forgive us," she said, crossing herself and glancing at the Madonna's likeness on the clock.

"Will you go to mass tomorrow night or Christmas morning?" It was Émilie who asked this time.

"Both," answered Eduoard. "With what we give in rent every year for our pew, we have to show up to make it pay." He grinned wickedly as laughter erupted once again.

Madeline shook her head in dismay at her husband's humour. "We'll have a nice lunch at the rectory with our friends in the village. Later, we'll have a big fête here with all our family."

"We killed a pig for that," Ferdinand added.

"And, of course, we have a new batch of rum," said Antoine.

"It's a fine rum, very fine," laughed Krieghoff, pausing long enough to have another drink. He set the cup down with a sigh. "Speaking of rum, perhaps you heard the story of an acquaintance of mine, Lord Kerr? He's an aide to the Governor-General." They shook their heads as Krieghoff chuckled. "Well, he'd been drinking rum at the Shakspeare Club, was 'into his cups' as the English say, and rode his horse up the steps and right into the new Bank of Montréal."

"No!" Antoine laughed. The card game stopped as the Letendre family listened. The new bank was one of the grandest buildings in Montréal.

"Yes," laughed Krieghoff, "he refused to get down and conducted his business right from his saddle." He shook his head, still laughing. "Thank goodness he's not Roman Catholic—he'd be taking his horse into Notre Dame!"

"Our beautiful cathedral!" said Madeline, a horrified look on her face. The men laughed loudly at the story.

Antoine got up to freshen their guest's drink from a stoneware jug. "And how will you celebrate the *Nativité?*"

Krieghoff lowered his sketch pad. "I'll go to mass with Émilie—I don't take communion, of course—then we'll spend the rest of the day with her family. Except for Ernst, the rest of my people are in Germany. She has a very large family, so it is always delightful."

Émilie joined in then. "We like to take the children tobogganing, and my mother always cooks a huge meal. Cornelius will entertain after dinner on his violin or guitar. Which will you bring, *mon chère?*"

"You are a man of many talents," exclaimed Édouard.

The artist laughed. "I'm equally rusty on both. I've been so busy with my painting."

"When Cornelius first came to America, he made his living playing music," Émilie said. Her husband shrugged.

"I sense you are being too modest," said Antoine. "You should bring your instruments next time you come."

"Yes, yes," agreed Édouard. "Come back for New Year's. We all go to the tavern for a real party then. There'll be fiddles, plenty of dancing."

Krieghoff laughed. "That sounds like fun. I accept. We'll show my brother how to properly bring in the New Year." He folded a paper over his sketch and stood up, stretched his legs and arms. He glanced at the clock on the wall. *"Chérie,* we should go. It'll be very late when we get back."

"Are you sure you won't stay with us?" Édouard seemed disappointed.

"Yes, sadly, we really must go," Krieghoff replied. "But we will be back in just a few days."

"Bon. I'll get your horse from the barn, then." Antoine jumped up from the table, pulled his *capote* from a peg on the wall, and went outside.

"Thank you for this wonderful afternoon with your family," Krieghoff said, shaking hands with Édouard and Madeline and all their family.

"Can we see your picture?" asked Alphonse, who had spoken hardly a word all afternoon.

"Of course. It's just a rough sketch. I'll paint from this when I get back." Krieghoff folded back the covering paper and held it up to show him.

"Hmm, it's good," the old man said with a nod.

"Thank you. If you like it, then I will have it framed and bring it back for you." Krieghoff took his coat and helped little Émilie with hers.

"That would be very nice."

"Then we will say *au revoir et Joyeux Noël.*" The sketch pad tucked safely under his arm, Krieghoff, his wife, and daughter opened the door and stepped outside.

"Joyeux Noël, friends. Safe journey home." Their hosts crowded out on the door stoop. The cutter stood ready, its lanterns ablaze. Antoine held the little Canadien horse by its bridle. The Krieghoffs climbed in, pulled the fur robes over their laps. Cornelius took the reins, clucked at the horse, and they drove onto the snowy track that followed the river north, sleigh bells jingling in the crisp still air.

"Until next time," they called, waving over their shoulders as they went around the bend of the river and into the night.

LORD Stanley's Cup

"What a grand day!" Frederick Arthur Stanley, Baron of Preston, looked up at the cloudless Ottawa sky as he settled into the seat of the cutter beside his wife. "Far too nice to be in church."

Lady Constance Stanley swatted his leg playfully under the fur robe she had pulled over their laps. "Wave, darling," she said as the driver clucked the horses. The vice-regal cutter pulled away from St. Bartholomew's Anglican Church amid the tinkling of harness bells. A crowd of well wishers stood on the steps, seeing off the governor-general and his family after the Christmas morning service. A second cutter with more of their children and aides followed behind.

"Let's have a skate after lunch, shall we?" Algernon suggested from the front seat. At seventeen, he was the sixth of the Stanleys' eight surviving children.

"I have a better idea," said Isobel, his sister, who was only a year younger. She was swathed in elegant furs from head to foot, her hands disappearing into her muffler. "Let's have a hockey match. Ladies against the men." Isobel played on the Rideau Ladies team, which enjoyed occasional exhibition matches.

Lord Stanley laughed. "But you don't have enough players on your fair side, my dear."

"Yes," cried Isobel. "We've got Alice, and we'll get my friend Lulu to join us. I'll send the cutter around to pick her up. You'll play, too, won't you, Mummy?" She turned around, her eyes dancing with excitement at the challenge.

Lady Stanley turned to her husband in his fur coat and hat. "Yes, of course I will, dear. It's a wonderful idea." She gave him a wink.

"George," Isobel called to the driver as they turned into the gates of the governor-general's estate on Sussex Drive, "can you stop for a moment. I want to talk to the others."

"Yes, ma'am," he replied, reigning in the two horses, festive in red and green garlands. As they stopped, the second cutter drew up beside them, puzzled looks on the face of the driver and his passengers.

"We're challenging them to a hockey match after lunch," Isobel called out. "Mummy's playing, too."

Edward Stanley grinned and clapped his gloved hands in anticipation. "This will be the easiest win ever." At twenty-six, he was the oldest of the Stanley clan and an aide to his father.

"It will be good practice for our tournament coming up," added Arthur, one of the best players on the Rideau Rebels hockey team.

"Alice, you'll play, won't you? We need you," Isobel said to Edward's friend.

"Yes, of course," said Alice, her eyes flashing under her black mink hat.

Edward Stanley looked at his father's aide, Lord Kilcoursie, in the front seat. "Freddie, you must come to witness this rout."

"I wouldn't miss it for the world," he said, "as a spectator or participant."

"Good. Settled. Race you back to the house," Edward called, urging the driver to send the horses speeding off. The driver complied with a gentle touch of the whip, and while they weren't racing, both cutters sped up the driveway at a rapid pace.

Two hours later, after a leisurely Christmas lunch at Rideau Hall, Lord and Lady Stanley led their family and entourage on foot through the snow to their massive outdoor rink. The caretaker had flooded it again that morning. The smooth surface gleamed in the clear, cold light. The rink was more of a large pond than a geometric shape—a large open area with small islands of oak and maple off to the sides. A bonfire of massive logs burned near shore to warm the skaters. The players headed for the wooden benches there to strap skates onto their boots.

Lulu, Isobel's friend, and star of the Rideau Hall women's team, was first to step on the ice. Captain Wise, one of Lord Stanley's staff, set out the curved ash sticks he'd carried down, then threw out the hard India rubber puck. Lulu grabbed a stick and went gliding down the ice to warm up, circling round the islands, easily turning backwards and forwards in her long skirt and coat, swooping across the entire rink, weaving around the flags set in the ice that marked the goals at either end.

"Lulu, you soar on ice like a bird," the governor-general called, "a swallow on skates."

"Thank you, Lord Stanley," she replied, stopping smartly by the benches to resettle her fur hat.

"Are you sure you men aren't having second thoughts?" said Isobel as she stood up, testing the tightness of the straps. "It wouldn't do if word were to get out, Daddy, that you and your male heirs were defeated by members of the weaker sex."

Lord Stanley laughed as he selected a suitable stick. "That's why I invited Philip," he said, waving to the publisher of the *Ottawa Journal* and who was walking down the path, skates in hand. Philip Ross was a friend and accomplished hockeyist who often promoted the new game in his newspaper. "He'll ensure that the correct facts are published. Gentlemen, let's put these foxes to the chase." Lord Stanley skated off with his sons to warm up.

"It's the cocky pheasant that gets shot first," Isobel called out as a rejoinder.

The game commenced with the men—Lord Stanley and his sons, Edward, Arthur, and Algernon—conceding first possession to the ladies.

Isobel, Alice, Lulu, and Lady Stanley moved up the ice. Isobel slid the puck over to Alice in the middle as the men backed up. "Here!" Lulu yelled, darting between Algernon and Arthur. Isobel shot the puck to her, but Edward, anticipating the pass, intercepted it.

"Look out, Mummy!" shouted Edward as Lady Stanley frantically skated back to guard their goal. Edward picked up speed, ducked his head left as he approached his mother, and when she turned awkwardly that way, he dodged to the right, slipped by her, and slid the puck easily between the flags.

"Hooray!" shouted Lord Stanley. "The sterner sex has drawn first blood."

"Good show!" shouted Lord Kilcoursie from the snowy sidelines, as he, Captain Wise, and Philip Ross applauded.

Laughing at herself, Lady Stanley dug the puck out of the snow bank. "Alice," she called, "you be goaler this time. I have a score to settle." Resolutely, she skated up the ice, Lulu and Isobel crossing in front of her. She swerved to the side of the rink, where the puck momentarily disappeared in the snow. Edward lunged at it and fell off balance, just as Lady Stanley recovered it. "Isobel!" Quickly, she fired the puck to her daughter, behind Algernon and Arthur, who were, inexplicably, at the centre waiting for a pass.

"Go!" yelled Lulu, racing to catch Isobel as she streaked towards the goal, pushing the puck on her stick, only her father between her and the flags. Now it was Lord Stanley's turn to backpedal. As Isobel raced by him, he stretched across the goal, reaching with his stick. Isobel whirled around and passed the puck back to Lulu, who had a clear shot.

"Ahhh" cried Arthur as he threw himself on the ice across the goal. Lulu hesitated, then simply flipped the puck over him. It soared between the flags and into the snow.

"Hooray for our side!" Isobel shouted as she raced to hug her friend. "Well done, Lulu!"

Lady Stanley joined her then, too, laughing and out of breath. "Good show, girls."

"Good show?" said Lord Stanley, rising to brush snow off himself. "That was one of the prettiest goals I've seen yet."

The family game continued for a few moments more. The men recovered their aplomb and quickly took the lead with goals by Algernon, Arthur, and Edward in quick succession. Then, the three men on the sidelines were invited to join and the spirited "scratch" match continued.

Later, as they undid their straps on the benches by the bonfire, Edward looked thoughtfully at his father. "I've been thinking," he began, his cheeks flushed and rosy like the others', "this game of hockey is very much like the country."

"Oh," said Lord Stanley, as he pulled at his boots, "in what way?"

"It's rugged and energetic, full of raw, youthful spirit. I'd even go so far as to say brash."

"I agree," said Lady Stanley. "And it's certainly growing in popularity. People seem to love watching it almost as much as playing it."

"Yes, quite," added Arthur. "They're flocking to that new tin rink they've built in Lindsay. Perhaps, Father, some thought might be given to a championship trophy of some kind for all these men's hockey clubs that have sprung up. One bearing your name."

Lord Stanley looked up in surprise. "Why, that's a splendid idea, son. What do the rest of you think?"

"It's just what the game needs," said Algernon. "A challenge cup will be great incentive for hockey clubs, and make it more exciting for spectators if there's something tangible at the end of the chase."

"The rules will need to be standardized, of course," added Lord Kilcoursie. "Yes, it will help the new game immeasurably."

"But, Daddy," Isobel interjected, standing with her skates in hand, "why not a cup for the women, too?"

The men roared with laughter. The women did not. Lord Stanley thought for a moment, as was his habit. "I'm not convinced the gentle female nature is well suited to the rough and tumble of this game," he said, "although your ladies' exhibition matches are certainly evidence to the contrary. But perhaps, in good time, you members of the fairer sex will prove me wrong." He looked at his wife and winked. "It has happened once or twice before."

The governor-general stood then, amid the genial laughter, slung his skates through the blade of his stick and hoisted it over his shoulder. "At any rate, this cup idea has a lot of merit. I think we should discuss it over some hot chocolate by a roaring good fire. And perhaps over Christmas dinner with our guests, don't you agree?"

"Hear, hear!" they cried and rose to make their way back to Rideau Hall.

A Red River Christmas

Mon Dieu, I must speak to you of the things I have seen this day. I would not trouble you with my thoughts, but there is no priest for a thousand miles from where I sit here, hunched over on my pony. My feet are numb in these thin moccasins, my body cold and tired and sore from riding all day.

And I am one of the fortunate ones. You have given my family a humble home, where my beautiful wife, Marie-Anne, and our *petites enfants* await. I ask, *cher Dieu,* why did you pick me, Jean-Baptiste Lagimodière, a free Frenchman, to play *Père Noël* with nothing to give the poor souls assembled here on this Christmas Day, 1812?

Look at these miserable flapping tents, the meagre sod huts that huddle on these plains like clumps of buffalo dung, snow piled in drifts again them. The poor wretches inside arrived only in August of this year—settlers, perhaps a hundred men, a year-long nightmare of a journey behind them, even more ahead.

They'd come by ship last summer from Scotland, Orkney, and Ireland. On a diet of cold and scurvy at Fort York over the winter, many passed away. This summer brought no relief—a six-hundred-mile traverse inland, battling mosquitoes, blackflies, whitewater, and sucking muskeg before finally sloshing ashore half dead at Red River.

And what did they find? Lord Selkirk had prepared nothing for them. *Rien.* No food, no huts or tents, not even seeds for planting next year. Then, with the chill winds of October, the women and children arrived. *Comment?* This Lord in his Scottish castle, *il est un fou!* He must be mad, we said.

And yet their horrible journey was still not over. We Frenchmen and our Saulteaux friends took them to down to Pembina, a seventy-mile walk to the south. Winter would soon be here, and at Pembina, we told them, there would be buffalo. We helped them put up these tipis and build their rough, sod shacks. Governor Miles Macdonnell of Assiniboia gave me a job—organize the buffalo hunt for the settlers. I have fifteen French and *Métis* hunters, all crack shots. Fortunately, this winter has been mild so far. But *bon fortune* is a sword with two sharp edges. Because it's mild, the buffalo have stayed up north. The great herds did not come south to graze.

Since December, the hunger began. The people cook a little fish they buy from the *Métis* and Saulteaux. My friend, Chief Peguis, had taught them how to dig for breadroot. Some days, these dried roots are all they eat. They boil them, make a fish-head or marrow soup. Sometimes, my hunters are lucky, and we find a few buffalo, perhaps a deer or two. But not this week.

There is no *fête Noël* today. It is the hungry season. I go from tipi to tipi, from hut to hut to check on them. I stop to say *bonjour,* and their haggard faces stare up at me from their fires. Like Israelites in the wilderness, they hunger for their Promised Land even though they're sitting on it. *Mon Dieu,* it breaks my heart to hear those babies cry. If these Highlanders had not been raised so tough, many of them would have died or tumbled away like thistles in the wind. But there is something of granite in these people, a will so strong I will tell my wife about it when I go home. I almost feel ashamed to eat the tourtiere she is making. *Cher Dieu,* we cling to the promise that the birth of your Son offers us. I pray that you will feed these people so that they will learn to live with hope as we do, free in the beauty of this hard, magnificent land.

Three years later, Jean-Baptist Lagimodière made an urgent eighteen-hundred–mile journey, much of it on foot in winter, to Montréal to warn Lord Selkirk of the continuing plight of the Red River settlers. He is also known as the grandfather of Métis leader, Louis Riel.

TREE *of Lights*

"In your opinion, General Riedesel, will the Americans succeed in their revolution?"

Baron Frederick-Adolphus Riedesel looked up suddenly from his place at the end of the table. A spoon dropped on a china plate. Someone coughed into her linen serviette. General Riedesel eyed the British general who had posed the question and returned his steady, unblinking gaze.

Had the question, stated so publicly, come from anyone of a lesser rank, it would have been taken as insolent, a social and political gaffe of the highest order. Men had been horsewhipped for less. His wife, Frederika Luise Charlotte von Massow—radiant at the other end of the table—who had endured so much with him and his men, waited, too, her eyes glittering fiercely in the candlelight.

The pointed question was so unlike the British, who had raised nuance to a fine art. The general smiled to himself as he bought time to plan his answer. No, it was something one of his Prussian officers might have blurted out after a stein or two. Riedesel took a slow drink of beer, then leaned back and looked around the table at his friends and comrades in arms. There were eighteen guests in all, British and German army officers, their wives and lady friends, all costumed beautifully for this festive Christmas Eve dinner. Like the tree at the end of the room, they waited.

"My good friend, the general, has set the cat among the pigeons with his question, I think." He smiled, and there was a titter of nervous laughter along the table. Then his smile disappeared. "It was about six years ago that I left my beloved Braunschweig with almost four thousand foot soldiers and more than three hundred light cavalrymen and horses, under contract to our British allies here, *General.*" Riedesel's emphasis was subtle as he nodded to him.

"We campaigned with your General Burgoyne into northern New York, where at Saratoga, we met with excruciating defeat. How many British and German soldiers were captured in that disaster? Six thousand?" The British general's eyes were intent on his wine now as Riedesel continued. "You may recall that my own dear wife—and mother of our children—followed us into that awful encounter to attend our wounded and dying. By the time we surrendered, the Americans had fired eleven cannon balls through the house where she and the children were taking refuge."

Riedesel stopped and waited as the British general raised his face, now flushed and red, and nodded. "Yes, of course," he said.

"By the way, *mein liebe* Charlotte, you have directed this evening's meal like a general yourself," her husband said, smiling broadly down the table. "The roast pork was surely the best I have ever tasted."

He paused and nodded to his wife as cries of "Hear! Hear!" came from their British guests.

"Our young Auguste, who's now only ten, still has nightmares about it," General Riedesel continued, looking down the table at his guests, their eyes fixed on him, the women's powdered bosoms rising with each sympathetic breath.

"How very awful for you and the children," said one woman to Charlotte.

"I could never be so brave," confessed another.

"Who knows of what we are capable, except when faced with these dire circumstances ourselves," offered Baroness Riedesel. *"Liebling,* we have a special treat for our guests," she nodded towards the decorated tree behind her. "Please don't keep them waiting too long."

"Of course not, *mein Herz,"* her husband replied breezily. "War, perhaps, is the ultimate test of character," he resumed as if there had been no diversion. "But let us return to the question at hand. We surrendered after our ignominious defeat at Saratoga, buried our British and German dead, and became prisoners of war. For three years, Charlotte and I were held captive, first in Boston, then Virginia. Finally, we were released to that infernal heat of New York. How we welcomed the cool of Québec City! And now, finally, we have this new home here in Sorel, thanks to Governor Haldimand."

Riedesel looked around the room appreciatively, his smile turning again to a frown as he addressed the British officers. "God only knows that my German soldiers have fought fiercely and valiantly for you British, and paid dearly with their lives and their freedom. And that my own family—so far removed from our beloved Prussia and the comfort of my father's castle—has made great sacrifices for the cause of keeping the British Empire intact.

"However, in answer to your question, General—and you will forgive an old warhorse for being so long-winded—if I were to suggest that the Americans will win their independence from the Crown of England, then all this considerable sacrifice will have been made in vain. 'Full of sound and fury, signifying nothing'—to quote your own great English bard. My wife and children would never forgive me, sir. And if we were to go to into battle tomorrow to save Canada itself from the clutches of these fledgling republicans, how much would you trust our German resolve, General, if you knew we ourselves were predicting a British defeat?"

He stopped. Silence weighed heavily on the room, with only the sound of breathing, logs crackling on the fire, and the Riedesel children playing in the kitchen. With that, the general heaved his ample body to its feet and picked up his glass of beer. "Ladies and gentlemen, in a private military meeting, we might look at the numbers of cannons and foot soldiers and light infantry on this side, and that unmeasurable quality called morale and fighting spirit, and wish that we had more and the Americans had less. But I stand here as commander of the Duke of Braunschweig's army to tell you that this Prussian's only goal is victory."

"Bravo!" cried some of the British officers, rising quickly to their feet. Several applauded vigorously.

"Then please all rise and toast with me, friends." There was much scraping of chairs as the rest of the guests stood with their glasses. "To victory!" said the general, and he raised his glass, first to his British colleagues, then to a misty-eyed Charlotte. "A British victory!"

"To British victory!" they cried.

"Well said, Baron Riedesel," a British major offered. "I think our fighting men—"

"I'm sorry, Major," said General Riedesel, cutting him off with a wave of his hand. "Let's have no more talk of war and revolution this evening. I don't have the stomach for it. It is Christmas Eve, after all, and my dear Charlotte has prepared a special treat for you, our British guests—plum pudding!"

"Oh, my, you didn't!" exclaimed the major's wife as Charlotte stood at her end of the table. "However did you manage? First, this succulent roast and dumplings, and now pudding!"

Charlotte beamed in her velvet dress. "We have been very lucky to find good help among the local habitants. They really have worked very hard and efficiently." Then she turned to her husband. "But darling, before dessert, I think we should light the tree."

"Ah yes," said her husband, rising again.

"Light the tree?" someone asked, curiosity in his voice.

"Whatever do you mean?"

"Yes," Charlotte answered, laughing, as the tension drained from the room. "As you have seen, it is a custom in our country to bring an evergreen—a *tannenbaum,* in German—into the house and decorate it with candied fruits." She walked over to the fireplace, picked up a splinter of kindling, and held it in the flames. "Then at midnight—and it is almost that now—we light candles on the tree and turn down our lights."

Charlotte lit a second splinter for her husband. The two of them went to the tree. "You can bring the children in," she said in French to the young servant girl. In seconds, they entered from the kitchen: Auguste, at ten a serious dark-eyed girl; Friederike, at seven with green flashing eyes like her mother; and Caroline who at five already showed a jutting stubbornness inherited from her father. In her arms, the servant girl carried Amerika, born in New York not quite two years ago.

"Oh," exclaimed a woman, "they are darling."

"Come, children," called their mother, "help light the tree."

One by one, the Riedesel family lit the candles that had been placed in the tree.

"How splendid!" a guest cried as they gathered around.

"Utterly charming," said another.

When they were done and the tree was aglow, Charlotte whispered to the servant girl who snuffed out the candles in the wall sconces around the room. "The children will sing a German carol for you now," she said to the hushed room. "They've been practising all week."

O Tannenbaum, O Tannenbaum,
Wie treu sind deine Blätter.
Du grünst nicht nur zur Sommerzeit,
Nein, auch im Winter, wenn es schneit.
O Tannenbaum, O Tannenbaum,
Wie treu sind deine Blätter.

O Tannenbaum, O Tannenbaum,
du kannst mir sehr gefallen.
Wie oft hat nicht zur Weihnachtszeit
Ein Baum von dir mich hoch erfreut.
O Tannenbaum, O Tannenbaum,
du kannst mir sehr gefallen.

O Tannenbaum, O Tannenbaum,
dein Kleid will mich was lehren:
die Hoffnung und Beständigkeit

gibt Trost und Kraft zu aller Zeit.
O Tannenbaum, O Tannenbaum,
dein Kleid will mich was lehren.

"Well done!" the guests applauded when the children finished. Auguste and her sisters curtsied, and then they were all taken off to bed. The Riedesels and their guests had their plum pudding, which was pronounced exquisite by their delighted guests. It was followed by fine German schnapps and cigars for the men. Then the evening was over.

When the last of the visitors had left in horse-drawn sleighs, their harness bells fading into the night, Baron Riedesel closed the door and took his wife's hand. "Thank you, *mein Schatz. Danke schoen.* This was an excellent dinner, a wonderful evening." He kissed her.

"I thought your answer to the general's question was very restrained," she said.

"It was a stupid question," he scoffed. "Of course they're going to lose. Everyone knows that, including the British themselves. Saratoga was the turning point. You can't lose a quarter of your army and expect to win. The trick will be to hang onto this country and keep it out of those rapacious Yankees' hands—" Charlotte put her fingers gently against her husband's lips.

"Come," she whispered. She led him into the living room. They stood admiring the tree for a moment, enjoying the scent of fir, the wavering light of the candles, the ragged shadows on the walls and ceilings. Then they blew out the candles, one by one, and went up to bed.

The Riedesels' lighting of candles on their tree that Christmas Eve in Sorel, Québec, 1781, was the first time the German tradition had appeared in Canada. The 200th anniversary of the occasion was marked with a commemorative stamp by Canada Post in 1981.

O Christmas Tree

O Christmas tree, O Christmas tree!
How are thy leaves so verdant!
O Christmas tree, O Christmas tree,
How are thy leaves so verdant!
Not only in the summertime,
But even in winter is thy prime.

O Christmas tree, O Christmas tree,
How are thy leaves so verdant!
O Christmas tree, O Christmas tree,
Much pleasure doth thou bring me!

O Christmas tree, O Christmas tree,
Much pleasure doth thou bring me!
For every year the Christmas tree,
Brings to us all both joy and glee.

O Christmas tree, O Christmas tree,
Much pleasure doth thou bring me!
O Christmas tree, O Christmas tree,
Thy candles shine out brightly!

O Christmas tree, O Christmas tree,
Thy candles shine out brightly!
Each bough doth hold its tiny light,
That makes each toy to sparkle bright.
O Christmas tree, O Christmas tree,
Thy candles shine out brightly!

WRITING by Candlelight

The rough wooden door was open slightly. The priest stopped outside it. He could see firelight dancing lightly on the wooden walls inside, knots staring like dark, sightless eyes. The young man took a half step, careful to be quiet, his moccasins soundless on the cold floor, no rustle from his heavy French-spun robe. *I am not spying; I am merely concerned,* he said to himself. Leaning in farther, he saw a shadow on the wall and drew back, afraid of being seen. Tentatively, he put his hand to the door and pushed. It swung silently on iron hinges.

Father Jean de Brébeuf sat on a small bench, hunched over his writing desk, his back to the door, feet stretched towards the fire. A tallow candle wavered in front of him. Brébeuf seemed to be staring into the flames, deep in thought. His simple wood bed of feathers and furs was against one wall, a carved crucifix above it. A Bible sat on the battered trunk beside the bed. His outdoor robe hung from a wrought iron hook. A pair of snowshoes was propped in a corner. Then there was movement as Brébeuf's right arm reached out. He dipped his quill into the small inkwell. Nib scratched on paper, like a mouse, then stopped.

"Good evening, Father Buteux. You can come in if you want." Brébeuf's back stayed turned to the door.

"Excuse me, Father Brébeuf. I didn't mean to disturb—"

Brébeuf turned awkwardly, motioned him in with his good arm.

"How is your shoulder?" asked Jacques Buteux, glancing at the sling on Brébeuf's left arm, looped around his neck.

"It is healing well, thank you." Brébeuf motioned to the wooden trunk. "Come, sit. Tell me about life in Trois-Rivières."

"No, I am disturbing you. That wasn't my intention—"

"No, you're not disturbing me. I was thinking of our beloved Huron mission."

Buteux entered and perched himself on the trunk, stretching his legs towards the fire, too. "Ah, Saint Marie Among the Hurons. I think the Devil is among the Hurons now."

Brébeuf shook his head. "The Devil is among us always, here as well as among *les sauvages.*"

Buteux nodded. "I was thinking of the murderous Iroquois who ambushed our fall convoy and who hold Father Jogues in their torturous clutches now—may God protect him and give him strength." The priest crossed himself. "Have you heard any further news of Jogues and the others?"

Brébeuf frowned and turned to look at the fire. "Not since September." He paused. "They cut off his left thumb and crushed his right forefinger, you know. They burned him, too, and pulled out his beard and his fingernails. But I feel in my heart that he is still alive."

Buteux noted the dark circles under Brébeuf's eyes, the weariness that lingered there. The worry. "And what of the others?"

"One of our Frenchmen was tortured in the same way, then later killed. The others have been granted their lives, but these Iroquois are fickle and inconsistent. Nine Huron have also been massacred or tortured to death. Perhaps another fourteen or so still live. The five who escaped are wintering with me here at Sillery. They are very melancholy."

"And what then will happen to the mission?" Buteux looked Brébeuf in the eye. "Is God telling us to abandon Saint Marie to the evil that afflicts that country?"

Brébeuf returned his look, then shook his head. "The Lord gives, and the Lord takes away. May his name be blessed." The missionary paused and sighed deeply. "In spite of these unhappy afflictions, vice does not rule our Huron children. There are many now who show themselves to be virtuous and pious, and true sons of our Society, not just *les sauvages* who enroll their names in our faith, but others who do not yet profess their love of God. I am not yet ready to give them up to the Devil. In fact, I cannot wait to return and resume our work, Father Buteux."

Buteux nodded, smiling slightly in admiration at the priest's passion. "Perhaps the more lamentable the situation here, my friend, so much richer the heavenly gifts our Father has in store for us."

Brébeuf shook his head in disagreement. "I work not for my own reward, but for the salvation of *les sauvages.* I have come to love them. I miss them. I miss their singing and laughter, and their delight at the stories from the Holy Book. I wish I were there with them now in the snow to celebrate the Nativity." He paused for a moment, then picked up the parchment on which he'd been writing. "The Lord has moved me to write this," he said, passing the paper to Buteux. "You know the song, 'A Young Maid'?"

Buteux nodded. "Of course." He took the paper, started to read, stopped, and glanced up at Brébeuf, a puzzled look in his eyes.

"It's written in the Huron language," Brébeuf explained with a smile, "a carol for the *Noël,* so they can learn of the holy gift our Lord has given them."

"Sing it for me, Father," said Buteux, handing the paper back.

Brébeuf paused for a moment, then started singing, softly, hesitantly at first, then stronger as if the words themselves gave him courage.

Es-ten-nia-lon de tson-ou-e
Jesous a-ha-ton-hia,
On-naou-a-te-ou-a d'o-ki
N'on-ouan-da-skoua-en-tak;
En-non-chien skou-a-tri-ho-tat,
N'on-ou-an-di-lon-ra-cha-tha,
Jesous a-ha-ton-hia,
Jesous a-ha-ton-hi-a

Brébeuf finished. The two Jesuits sat, not speaking, as the fire snapped. Finally, Buteux looked at Brébeuf, his eyes sparkling. "This is indeed a gift from God," he said. "Only He could have inspired you to write with such beauty. You should sing it tonight for us at vespers."

Brébeuf lowered his head. "Perhaps I will teach it to our five Huron Christians, and we will sing it together," he said.

The original Huron Carol was written by St. Jean de Brébeuf in 1643 while he recuperated from a broken clavicle in Québec. It was written in the Huron/Wendat Language. The carol was translated into French and sung to the tune of a French folk song, "Une Jeune Pucelle" ("A Young Maid"). In 1926, Jesse Edgar Middleton wrote an English version of the carol loosely based on the flawed

French translation of Brébeuf's lyrics. This carol, "'Twas in the Moon of Winter Time," is the one we know and sing today. Father Brébeuf was captured, tortured, and killed by the Iroquois on March 16, 1649. On June 29, 1930, he was canonized—declared a saint—by Pope Pius XI.

'Twas in the Moon of Winter Time

'Twas in the moon of winter time,
When all the birds had fled,
That mighty Gitchi Manitou
Sent angel choirs instead;
Before their light the stars grew dim,
And wond'ring hunters heard the hymn:

Jesus your king is born!
Jesus is born: "In excelsis gloria!"

Within a lodge of broken bark
The tender babe was found,
A ragged robe of rabbit skin
Enwrapped his beauty 'round;
And as the hunter braves drew nigh,
The angel song rang loud and high:

Jesus your king is born!
Jesus is born: "In excelsis gloria!"

The earliest moon of winter time
Is not so round and fair
As was the ring of glory on
The helpless infant there.
The chiefs from far before him knelt
With gifts of fox and beaver pelt:

Jesus your king is born!
Jesus is born: "In excelsis gloria!"

O children of the forest free,
O sons of Manitou:
The holy child of earth and heaven
Is born today for you.
Come kneel before the radiant Boy,
Who brings you beauty, peace and joy:

Jesus your king is born!
Jesus is born: "In excelsis gloria!"

ORCA *Child*

Stephen took a deep breath and pulled. His kayak dropped off the grassy lip of the bank and scraped down across the driftwood and rocks. He gritted his teeth, hearing thin streaks of gelcoat peel off, then smiled ruefully, remembering how upset he used to get at the tiniest scratch. Stopping to rest again, he zipped up his anorak, pulled down his baseball cap. A shiver ran with cold feet up his spine and into his neck. It was impossible for him to stay warm these days. Even though the temperature was maybe ten degrees—a balmy December 24.

The moon was up, on the wane, definitely half empty. It loitered over the Coast Mountains like some gawking bystander not even pretending to look away. The snowy peaks were not so benign either, more like a great white shark's jagged smile gleaming in the dark, waiting. There was no wind, not even a breeze. The water in Camp Bay lay heavy and languid, the colour of mercury, rumpled and spent as an unmade bed. Tattered curtains of mist drifted here and there low over the surface and above, ancient light sprinkled down from a million stars. All was quiet, as if the world were holding its breath. No seagulls shrieked, no fur seals barked. No freighters or ferries rumbled by. No foghorns sounded. A silent night, an unholy night.

Stephen checked his watch. 11:15. *What difference does it make, really?* Forty-five minutes to go. His last Christmas Eve in paradise. Well, perhaps paradise lost. He smiled ruefully and wished Sean was there. But that would ruin everything.

Just three more metres. He bent over, grabbed the bow handle, and pulled. The kayak slid across the sandy beach, still wet from the receding tide. His rubber kayaking booties slipped on a rounded stone. His thin arms were almost useless. He leaned forward, using the weight of his body to pull the kayak. Although 120 pounds was hardly what you'd call weight. Where did that 80 pounds go? How quickly it had melted away, gone from stocky to skeletal in just a year. Stephen heard a sound and realized it was him. A laugh? A sob? Maybe both. He stopped at the water's edge, panting like a dog. After a moment, he stepped back, grabbed the cockpit coaming, and pushed until the bow nosed well into the water. Pausing again, he doubled over, eyes squeezed shut, pumping tears. The pain came from everywhere, cutting through the exhaustion and drugs like shards of glass.

Sean would be back from Vancouver tomorrow with the girls. They'd take the ferry to Sidney, then the Pender Island ferry home. Stephen had played this out in his mind a hundred times. He imagined Sean's daughters, Andrea and Sarah, chattering happily as they came up the stone path. Sean behind with his daughters' bags, enough clothes for a month, not the one week they usually had with him. They'd barge in the door, call out his name. And see the note on the table. His gift to them would be his absence.

Now the hard part. Stephen knelt beside his kayak on a flat rock, feeling the cold ocean water find the small tear in his nylon pants that he'd never got around to patching. Didn't matter much now if he got wet. He breathed slowly, trying to build his strength. How many times had he slipped into this favourite sea kayak, like a hand into an old glove, a foot into a well-worn slipper? It was such a natural, unthinking action, an unconscious part of his life on the water. Even as a kid in Richmond, he knew he had to be on the water. Marine biology had given him the perfect life. Marine mammal scientist is what they called him, out watching whales whenever he could. Hey man, his friends would say, call that a job?

He stood and straddled the cockpit, putting his paddle across and behind him. Leaning back, he lowered his weight onto the paddle and hovered unsteadily over the opening. First one leg, then the other, quickly lifted, bent, and shoved down into the dark shell. He dropped his bony bum into the seat and would have laughed at his awkwardness if the effort hadn't left him gasping for air.

When he could breathe normally again, Stephen leaned hard to his right, dug one curved blade of the paddle into the sand and pushed. Nothing. What if he keeled over right here and hit his head on that rock? How ironic! *Kayaker Dead After Wipe Out On Beach.* He laughed. *Why is this so funny? Am I going mad? Perhaps.*

He barked or yelped, made some guttural, mostly inhuman noise, sounding vaguely like a fur seal sliding into the water on his way to lunch. Wiggling his body sideways, he pushed hard with the paddle and squirmed until his kayak slipped into the water. *Free!* Just one more mountain to climb. And on the other side? Either the Promised Land or eternal, squid ink blackness.

Stephen sobbed, choked back more tears as he turned the kayak around and looked back at their house, a low log bungalow on the grassy meadow above the beach. Red Christmas lights traced the shallow slope of the roof that he and Sean had shingled with cedar shakes. White smoke rose lazily from the chimney into the night and made a delicious cocktail of the pungent air. He thought of the note lying there on the kitchen table, a time bomb ticking.

He dug the blades into the water, paddled south out of the bay, past the headland at Teece Point, then turned towards Saturna Island, following a silvery path laid down by the moon. It had been three weeks since he'd gone for a spin. It seemed like a lifetime ago. How could he have got so weak so fast? Lost so much muscle? He set the paddle down on the coaming in front of him, coasted for a bit to rest his arms. I am disappearing before my very eyes, he'd told Sean the other day. Sean had just turned away; Stephen knew he was weeping.

He paddled farther out, then turned south towards the tide-ripped, watery border separating Canada from the United States, the Canadian Gulf Islands from the American San Juan Islands. He inhaled the salt-fish perfume of sea air. Like the shuttle of a loom, his kayak pierced the warp and weft of misty threads dangling over the water. He counted five flashing beacons from lighthouses on the rocks and islands around him. If Sean had been there, if it had been the old days, they might have travelled across Plumper Sound to the southern end of Saturna to Murder Point or maybe Monarch Head. They would have stopped to admire the moon and mountains and the glowing lights of Bellingham, Washington. They'd have opened a Nalgene bottle half full of Oban, toasted, passed the peaty Scotch back and forth between them, their kayaks bumping against each other in the night. A ritual after a thousand moons, sun-speckled days, and misty, rainy weekend mornings. They would have kissed.

He pushed the kayak into the dark. Stroke, stroke, stroke. With effort, he managed some semblance of a rhythm, "lily-dipping," not really digging in the way he would have normally. But, hey, what's *normal* when you're queer anyway? He laughed out loud again, sure now that he was crazy. His *normal* had ended one night about eight years ago. He'd just broken up with Allen, went on a tear through too many bars, too many shooters, too many guys, one of them a penny stock swindler named Greg. Greg gave him some hot tips on a new diamond mine in Nunavut and a gold mine in Paraguay. He also gave him HIV.

Stephen felt the rumble before he heard it. To the north and east—well out in the strait—he spotted a green bow light at the end of a long, black shape low on the water. A freighter, loaded with logs maybe for Japan or prairie wheat for anywhere. If it had been daylight, he would have looked for the flag of convenience, probably Liberian, maybe a Filipino crew. He hated these rust buckets, the used oil and garbage they dumped in their wakes at sea, hated the companies that hired them and the governments that let them pollute the water, killing marine life at every level of the food chain. He watched as the high floodlit bridge of the ship appeared out of the mist, heard the faint woosh of the prop as the freighter chewed its way towards the Strait of Juan de Fuca and the Pacific. He was surprised to realize that he was still capable of being very, very angry.

Sean had not wanted to leave him alone. "Sure you'll be all right?"

"Of course."

"I can have Gloria stay with you." She was his home-care nurse.

"No, it's Christmas—let her be with her family. I'll call her if I need her. She can be here in ten minutes anyway."

Sean had carried in more firewood for the airtight stove, laid a fire in the fireplace, and then left. He'd called twice just to check on him, the last time as Stephen was writing the note.

It had always been an option, ever since his serious young doctor had confirmed what they both had known: that one clanging medical acronym had morphed into another that was even worse. He was her first AIDS patient, she told him, and felt as sorry as if she'd been responsible. He loved her for her compassion, gave her a teary hug, and went home in a fog to tell Sean. On the way back, he'd stared at the bow wave of the ferry and considered jumping right then, but it had seemed too public and ignoble. He needed time to think, to weigh his chances and to fight. He had also needed Sean. But, as too many of their friends had learned, love is no miracle drug.

And so, after three years of struggle, getting sicker and sicker, he'd made up his mind. He would not continue. It wasn't just the pain. He'd come to think his very existence had been a tiny cosmic mistake, and that explained why he was being slowly erased from the record of life on earth. "No," said the Great Biologist, "this experiment isn't working. Let's nip this evolutionary detour in the bud." He was sick of the pills, thirty a day, some with food, some without, some with fatty snacks, others with no fat, some a fixed number of hours apart. Tired of doctors and nurses, the endless tests, the probing needles, the bottomless vials of toxic blood; worn out by the sadistic torture of his mattress at night, the hopeless fog and nausea of drugged-up days. Life was now an ever-present lethargy, unmarked by enthusiasm or even joy. It had become a bone-wearying effort just to stay alive. Stephen had spent his whole life being a giver, someone always eager to help, wanting to make a contribution. He had discovered that he didn't know how to take, to receive, to accept Sean's and Gloria's care. What he had always wanted to do was save whales, especially orcas—*Orcinus orca*—his beautiful killer whales. They were out here, and they needed his help. He checked his watch again. Ten minutes to midnight.

They had become his family: three pods of Southern Residents, glistening, chattering black and white orcas. The scientists had named them J, K, and L pods. They roamed throughout the Strait of Georgia, around these southern Gulf and San Juan Islands. The Northern Residents, two hundred to three hundred whales, kept to themselves. They ranged from the north end of Vancouver Island to the British Columbia–Alaska border.

The southern resident pods left the area for up to four months every winter. Like a father, Stephen missed them when they left and worried about them until they returned. He loved the mystery, too, the fact that K and L pods went somewhere out into the Pacific to an unknown place. "We don't have all the answers," Stephen told his biology students. "They keep us humble." He thought they might go down along the coast, maybe as far as Monterey. J pod tended to stay closer to home, down in Puget Sound near Seattle. When they were back—from April to November—the orcas helped created a nice little industry of government scientists, university researchers, environmentalists, whale-watching tour operators, tourists, museums, photographers, and artists. In almost every home on these islands and coasts, powerful telescopes or binoculars were trained on the sea. Whale watching was a part of life that fuelled conversations on coffee row, in the post office and barbershop.

Yet he considered his work to be a failure. "*Endangered* has become an institutionalized word," he wrote in a published paper. "It's been stripped of meaning and any sense of urgency, no more shocking than the weekend highway death toll." There were only about eighty orcas left in the southern pods. The researchers watched over them, identifying them by the nicks and notches on their dorsal fins, the shape of their white saddle markings. They named them, photographed them, tracked their movements, and shared that information with each other through the Orca Network. When an old whale disappeared, hundreds of people held their collective breath until, after a few months, it was listed as dead. Then people mourned. The appearance of a new baby created almost as much joy as if it had been human. Telephones rang and emails flashed up and down the coast and around the world. Stephen had taken thousands of slide photographs of the orcas. Some were in published in books, in papers, some were posted on Web sites. One was a poster whose sale raised money for orca research. He hoped children in Norway and Japan would see the photos, fall in love with orcas, and grow up to end their countries' whaling industries. Yet, what the whalers didn't kill, what the fishing boats didn't trap in their nets—"trawler bycatch" was such an ugly euphemism—were slowly being poisoned by industrial chemicals and human sewage.

Stephen had been planning his exit for some time. He, who had lived so much of his life on the water with these noble, intelligent creatures, would die out here as well—at midnight on this Christmas morning. He was going to quietly roll his kayak over in the dark, slip away into the watery darkness of their world. He had no spray skirt to stop the water from pouring in, no life jacket to support his body. He would simply hold onto his beloved kayak under the stars and the moon and the mist until he was slowly lulled into a hypothermic sleep. He would drift down and be recycled into the marine food chain. Not ashes to ashes, but water to water.

One minute.

Guess it doesn't matter if I'm a little late. He reached inside the waterproof pocket on the front of his anorak. His fingers closed around a fat hand-rolled joint of Galiano Gold and his lighter. What had started years ago as an occasional recreational toke had become a daily medicinal one. Unprescribed, of course, by his doctor, but she knew and approved of its use for the pain, the nausea, and for the appetite she hoped it would give him. It was only fitting that this last smoke would be recreational again, simply for pleasure. His thumb flipped the lighter. The flash of light blinded him, killed his night vision, as he puffed fire into the marijuana. Leaning back, his head up, he drew smoke deep into his lungs. Even with his eyes closed, he could see the lighter's flame burned into his retina. Finally, he let go with a great exhalation into the night.

Whoosh.

Stephen's eyes opened. Wide. He sat up straight, blinked, trying to get his eyes adjusted to the dark again. *My mind, is it playing tricks on me?* That sound had not been him. *It sounded like—*

Whoosh.

Orcas!

Can it be? Stephen turned, fully alert, his heart pounding. Then he saw one, to the left and ahead, as a sprouting black dorsal fin cut across the moonlit water. A young male, he couldn't tell which one. Stephen smiled. His movements quickened as he quietly turned his boat and stopped again to peer into the night.

Then he heard them. A short series of sonar clicks. They were echolocating, talking back and forth, telling each other where they were. He sensed them more than saw them. He felt their benign intelligent presence around him. *They know I am here.* Stephen hoped that they recognized him. Then there was a long pulsing call.

Yes, it's J pod! He recognized their family dialect, different from all the other pods. They are travelling, he thought, not hunting. When they hunted, they were noisy, talking to each other as they identified and chased salmon—their favourite food. Tonight was a quiet little outing, back down to San Juan Island, maybe. Their black bodies sliding through black water. I am the only human being in the universe to be witnessing this, he thought.

There's another one. A large dorsal fin cut across in front of him, and beside it, a tiny perfect scimitar of a fin. "It's Oreo," Stephen said to himself. *She's got a new calf!* They passed slowly by and disappeared in the dark. Quickly, Stephen plunged his paddle in and turned in their direction. Oreo was eighteen. J-22 was her scientific name. He'd been watching her for his entire career. Five years ago, she'd shown up with her first calf, J-34, better known as DoubleStuf. She'd be close by, too. These maternal pods stayed together all their lives.

Where is she? Have they gone already? Stephen stopped to listen. Nothing but silence ringing in his ears. And a car door slamming far away on shore.

He didn't know why he turned left at that moment, but he did. In the moonlight, he saw the dorsal fin coming straight for him. And beside it, the small fin slicing clean as a knife. He held his breath. Five metres away, they dove in perfect unison. He watched as they continued towards him, blue-green phosphorescence streaming off the black outlines of their bodies. As they swam under his kayak, Stephen looked straight down at the black shapes of mother and child, living, breathing projectiles, running silently, sparks of mystical light streaming off them like nitrogen fuel off a rocket. The wake of underwater fireworks trailed after them off to his right and disappeared in the black void. Extinguished. Gone.

"Oh, my God."

It was a whisper. A prayer. Stephen sat there, stunned into silence. Into his mind, unbidden, came a line: "Unto us a child is born . . . and his name shall be called Wonderful." He thought for a moment that he should chase them, try to see it again, but instantly thought better of it. This was a gift. He couldn't ask for another. Instead, he bowed his head and wept.

The kayak rocked gently in the current, cradled in the restless, undulating tidal movement of ocean water. He stayed still for a long time, lost all track of time. It didn't matter anymore. It was Christmas morning now. His deadline had passed, and he knew one thing for certain: he would not die out here, not now, not like this. He thought of William Blake. He'd just seen the universe, not in a grain of sand, but in the shape of a baby orca and its contrail of microbial starlight. For Stephen, it was a cosmic message, felt more than words: there was still exquisite beauty in the world. There was love, and there was work to be done. If all he could do was sit propped up in bed by the window with his laptop and telescope, then that's what he would do. He would e-mail politicians. He would start petitions. He would write letters to the editor, to the International Whaling Commission, the United Nations, the prime minister, the premier, the minister of the environment. I will adopt that calf, he said to himself. I will use up whatever strength I have left to protect that baby and her family.

He thought of Sean then, and his girls. And he realized with horror how selfish he'd been. How he'd almost ruined their Christmas, and how every Christmas after would have haunted them. He shook his head in shame and vowed to accept their love—and return it.

He thought of Dean, one of their friends, whose funeral they'd recently attended. Dean had fought so hard to live, but when he went, he died with dignity and grace. And that in itself was a gift to those who loved him.

Stephen wiped his eyes with his gloved hands, then slowly began to paddle back to South Pender, to home. The first thing he would do is destroy the note. Burn it in the fireplace. Then he'd e-mail Ken at the Whale Research Station in Friday Harbor, send him a Christmas birth announcement. He'd e-mail Susan at Orca Network, too. And John at Fisheries. He'd call Sean and the girls this morning with the news.

In memory of Dean Shalden

Acknowledgements

The author thanks the following for their generous contributions in the writing of the stories.

When the Mummers Came

1. Carol Stanley, Toronto, Ontario
2. Enid Williams, Toronto, Ontario
3. Tina Novotny, Toronto, Ontario
4. Chris Brookes, co-founder of The Mummers' Troupe (now disbanded), St. John's, Newfoundland

Starry Night

5. John B. Nakogee, former Director of Education, Attawapiskat Education Authority, Attawapiskat, Ontario
6. Father RodrigueVézina, Saint Francis Xavier Church, Attawapiskat, Ontario
7. Stephanie Carver, Halifax, Nova Scotia, for the English translation of the carol, "Venez Pasteurs"

The Visitors

8. Tony Thompson, Nova Scotia Lighthouse Preservation Society, Halifax, Nova Scotia
9. Dan Conlin, Curator, Marine History, Maritime Museum of the Atlantic, Halifax, Nova Scotia
10. Chris Bailey, Curator, American Clock and Watch Museum, Bristol, Connecticut, USA

Chicken Noodle Soup

11. Gordon and Helen McInnis, Saskatoon, Saskatchewan
12. Renée Tratch, Toronto, Ontario
13. Kirk Nylen, Toronto, Ontario
14. Jutta van der Kuijp, Toronto, Ontario
15. Jan van der Kuijp, Oakville, Ontario

A Long String of Lights

16. Carl & Anna Tynes, Winnipeg, Manitoba
17. Doug Robbins, African Canadian Heritage Network, Chatham, Ontario
18. Wade Kojo Williams, Sr., President, Black History Month Celebration Committee, Winnipeg, Manitoba

The Legend of the Great White Pine

19. Judith Harbour, Kenora Ojibway Cultural Centre, Kenora, Ontario
20. Peter Boyle, Joe Winterburn, and Krista Graham, Old Fort William, Thunder Bay, Ontario

The Mitten Tree

21. Lorraine & Don Book, Outlook, Saskatchewan who put up a mitten tree in the Elbow Credit Union for 23 years.
22. Cheryl Book, Elbow, Saskatchewan
23. Mandana Goharnia, Toronto, Ontario
24. Glenda Hudson, owner of The Wool Emporium in Saskatoon, Saskatchewan, who loaned us 59 pairs of mittens made by Saskatoon knitters for inner city neighbours.

An Irish Boy's Christmas in Verdun

25. Hal Brown, Toronto, Ontario

Order of Good Cheer

26. Jo Marie Powers, Associate Professor, Hotel and Food Administration, University of Guelph (retired), Ontario
27. Wayne Melanson, Heritage Presentation Supervisor, Port Royal National Historic Site, Parks Canada, Nova Scotia

Mercy Flight

28. Pierre Verhelst, volunteer, Canadian Heritage Bushplane Museum, Sault Ste. Marie, Ontario
29. Tommy Cooke, Sault Ste. Marie, Ontario, pilot (retired), Ontario Air Service, Sault Ste. Marie, Ontario
30. Terry Wright, Canadian Heritage Bushplane Museum, Sault Ste. Marie, Ontario
31. Stan Johnson, aircraft engineer (retired), Ontario Air Service, Sault Ste. Marie, Ontario
32. Dr. Doug Sheltinga, M.D. (retired), Sault Ste. Marie, Ontario

Miracle at Forty Below

33. George & Philomene, Saskatoon, Saskatchewan
34. Bob & Betty Nylen, Saskatoon, Saskatchewan

The Monkey Doll

35. Karen Holsenback, North Bay, Ontario
36. Henni Niskanen, Welland, Ontario
37. Marnelle Tokio, Toronto, Ontario

The Lost Herd

41. Jack and Janey Nelson, Youngstown, Alberta
42. Dick Trew, Saskatoon, Saskatchewan

The One Who Became a Wolf

43. The story of Qisaruatsiaq, the one who became a wolf, is told by Saali Arngnaituq in the book, Inuit Stories, published by National Museums of Canada, 1988.
44. Korinne McDonald, English teacher, Kiilinik High School, Ikaluktutiak (Cambridge Bay), Northwest Territories
45. Julia Ogina, Language specialist, Kiilinik High School, Ikaluktutiak (Cambridge Bay), Northwest Territories

Incident at Gold Rush Creek

46. Mary Anne Nylen, Neepawa, Manitoba

Tim

47. Nancy Harvey, Toronto, Ontario
48. Doug Macfarlane, Toronto, Ontario
49. Gerry Cohen, professional dog walker and our photographic model, Toronto, Ontario
50. Jim and Shelley Glasspool, Toronto, Ontario, for the kind use of their front door

Rain on Gold Mountain

51. Janet Moorfield, Toronto, Ontario
52. Frank Yee, Toronto
53.. Dora Nipp, Ontario Human Rights Commission, Toronto
54. Huang Ke, translator, Shanghai, The Peoples' Republic of China

Lord Stanley's Cup

55. Sandy Allen, Research and Documentation Centre, Office of the Secretary to the Governor-General, Ottawa, Ontario

Tree of Lights

56. Verena von Stritzky, Toronto, Ontario
57. Olivier Mineau, Coordinator, Centre d'exposition des Gouverneurs, Sorel-Tracy, Québec
58. Marc Mineau, director, Centre d'interpretation du Patrimoine de Sorel, Sorel, Québec

Writing by Candlelight

59. Father Jacques Monet, Director, Canadian Institute of Jesuit Studies, Toronto

Orca Child

60. Dr. Astrid Maria von Gennekin, Whale Research Center, Friday Harbour, San Juan Islands, Washington, USA
61. Sheila Malcolmson, Gabriola Island Cycle & Kayak Ltd., Gabriola Island, British Columbia
62. Kelly Irvine, Pender Island, British Columbia
63. British Columbia Persons With AIDS, Vancouver, British Columbia
64. John Gaylord, AIDS Committee of Toronto, Toronto, Ontario
65. Sue Cronen, Kayak Pender Island, Pender Island, British Columbia

Readers

Carolyn Beck, Stephanie Beeley, Hadley Dyer, Marnelle Tokio, Betty Nylen, Bob Nylen, Abbey Neidik, Nancy Harvey, Doug Macfarlane, Tina Novotny, Irene Angelico, Beau Welter, Alison Book, David Langer, Anne Carter

To my agent, Hilary McMahon of Westwood Creative Artists, Toronto, for her cheerful support.

Peter Carver, who is not only editor, but also teacher, mentor, and friend.

Stephanie, thank you for your friendship and support.

To my children, Christopher and Alison, thank you for your love while I disappeared into this project.

Acknowledgments for Visual Materials

"When the Mummers Came"—"Expected Visitors" painting by Danielle Loranger, by permission of Danielle Loranger, Shediac, New Brunswick

"Starry Night"—Photo of dogteam courtesy Tessa Macintosh, photographer, Yellowknife, Northwest Territories

"The Visitors"—Abandonment of the Wreck and Departure from Cape Chatte Bay by George Russell Dartnell, courtesy of the National Archives of Canada; Engraving of Canso Lighthouse courtesy of The Maritime Museum of the Atlantic, Halifax, Nova Scotia M81.134.1B

"Chicken Noodle Soup"—Photo of liberation of The Netherlands courtesy of Fort Garry Horse Museum and Archives, Winnipeg, Manitoba.

"A Long String of Lights"—Photo of Carl Tynes courtesy of Carl Tynes, Winnipeg, Manitoba; photos of CN trains—images courtesy of the Canada Science and Technology Museum, Ottawa, Ontario

"The Legend of the Great White Pine"—Photo at Blackford Lake Lodge courtesy Tessa Macintosh, Yellowknife, Northwest Territories; photo of Old Fort William wintering house courtesy of Old Fort William, Thunder Bay, Ontario

"The Mitten Tree"—Photos courtesy Stephanie Beeley, photographer, Toronto, Ontario

"An Irish Boy's Christmas in Verdun"—Photos courtesy of Hal Brown, Toronto, Ontario

"The Order of Good Cheer"—Painting and pencil sketch of The Order of Good Cheer by Charles William Jefferys, courtesy of the National Archives of Canada

"Mercy Flight"—Photo of Buhl Airsedan courtesy of Canadian Heritage Bushplane Centre, Sault Ste. Marie, Ontario

"A Letter from New France"—Imaginary portrait of Jacques Cartier by Théophile Hamel, courtesy of the National Archives of Canada

"Miracle at Forty Below"—Aerial photo of Saskatoon courtesy of Prostock Images, Saskatoon, Saskatchewan

"The Monkey Doll"—painting of Frederick Schumacher by Ed Spehar, by permission of Ed Spehar, Timmins, Ontario; Photo of Eaton Beauty Doll © Canadian Museum of Civilization, photographer Merle Toole, catalogue no. 978.136.1, image no. D2003-8047

"The Lost Herd"—Photo reprinted with permission of the Calgary Herald, Calgary, Alberta

"The One Who Became A Wolf"—Photo of igloo at night by Richard Harrington, courtesy of National Archives of Canada; photo of dog team courtesy of Anglican Church of Canada.

"Incident at Gold Rush Creek"—Photo of Belgian Queen by E.A. Hegg, courtesy of The National Archives of Canada; photo of Gold Miners courtesy of Dawson City Museum, Dawson City, Yukon Territory

"Tim"—Photo of dogwalker and Misty courtesy Stephanie Beeley, photographer, Toronto, Ontario

"Rain on Gold Mountain"—Photo of Chinese at work on CPR in Mountains, by Ernest Brown, courtesy of The National Archives of Canada; Photo of Toronto city street courtesy of City of Toronto Archives, Series 372, Sub-Series 33, Item 251, Toronto, Ontario

"Les Habitants du Richelieu"—French Canadian habitants playing at cards by Cornelius Krieghoff, courtesy of National Archives of Canada

"Lord Stanley's Cup"—Photos of Lord Stanley and Lady Stanley by William James Topley, courtesy of the National Archives of Canada; Photo of Rideau Hall Skating Party courtesy of National Archives of Canada

"A Red River Christmas"—Buffalo Hunt on Snowshoes by George Catlin, courtesy of National Archives of Canada; Winter Travel Between St. Paul and Red River by William Armstrong, courtesy of National Archives of Canada.

"Tree of Lights"—Painting of General Riedesel and his wife courtesy Centre d'exposition des gouverneurs, Sorel, Québec

"Writing by Candlelight"—painting by Stanley Turner, courtesy of Mrs. C.D. Shadbolt, Toronto, Ontario

"Orca Child"—Photo by Stefan Jacobs courtesy of Centre for Whale Research, Friday Harbor, Washington, U.S.A.

"Acknowledgements"—Illustration courtesy Brooke Kerrigan, Toronto, Ontario

Rick Book is the award-winning author of *Necking With Louise,* a life-affirming collection of stories about coming of age on the prairies in the 1960s.

Book is also the author of three historical novellas, *Sacagawea, Blackships* and *Thanadelthur,* as well as a children's picture book.

He grew up in Saskatchewan and now lives in Toronto, where he is a voice actor and writer.